A
CONTEMPORARY
MYTHOS NOVEL

ARES

CARLY SPADE

ARES

A CONTEMPORARY MYTHOS NOVEL

Copyright © 2021 by Carly Spade

WWW.CARLYSPADE.COM

Published in the United States by World Tree Publishing, LLC

WORLD TREE
PUBLISHING, LLC

Cover and Interior Formatting by We Got You Covered Book Design

WWW.WEGOTYOUCOVEREDBOOKDESIGN.COM

It behooves a father to be blameless if he expects his child to be.

HOMER

ONE

𝕰𝕰𝕰𝕰𝕰𝕰𝕰𝕰𝕰𝕰𝕰𝕰𝕰𝕰𝕰

"TWO MORE REPS. COME on, you got this, Phil." I had an impressive clientele list for just starting at a new gym. Maybe winning the bantamweight MMA championship title helped.

Sweat poured down Phil's face as his arms shook, pushing the barbell away from his chest. The sun glinted through the surrounding windows, giving a three-hundred-sixty-degree view of the downtown Denver skyline. Plates clanked in rhythmic succession around us, men grunted, and the smell of sweat mixed with disinfectant permeated the air.

"I can't," he said through gritted teeth.

I hovered my hands over the bar, ready to grab it. "'Can't' shouldn't be in your vocabulary, Phil. Lift the bar. Yell, if you have to."

He let out a higher-pitched scream than I'd expected but succeeded in extending his arms the whole way. I took control of the bar and slammed it against the metal pegs with a loud *pang*.

Phil's arms fell slack at his sides. "You're a hardass, Makos."

"It's what you signed up for, right?" I pointed at the treadmills. "One mile, and you're good to go."

Phil sat up, dragging a hand through his sweat-soaked blonde hair. "Seriously?"

"You worked out your arms, not your legs. Cardio after weights will keep the fat burning." I removed the weight plates from the bar.

He took a deep breath, slapped his hands atop his knees, and stood. "You know best."

"Damn right, I do." I winked.

Once he situated himself at the treadmill, I slid on different weight plates and popped in my earbuds. After scrolling through several playlists on my phone, I settled for the new Unleash the Archers album. Brittney Slayes's metal screams were precisely what I needed to fuel my bench sets.

Tightening my ponytail, I lay down and wrapped my hands over the bar, performing fifteen reps before securing it on the rack and resting. My heel thumped against the floor in time with the music, and I readied myself for another set, closing my eyes. When I opened them, a man's face stared down at me, his hands on the bar. His spiky auburn hair paired well with his pale, freckled face. Green eyes squinted at me as his full lips smirked. I recognized him but couldn't put a name to the face.

"If it isn't Harmony Makos. The famous Amazon herself," the man said, his voice deep.

"I didn't ask for a spotter. And you must be new in town because nobody calls me by my full name." With a grunt, I sat up.

The name Harmony came with far too many memories. Memories I kept buried.

"Right." He held his palms out. "Harm is what you go by."

This guy wasn't going anywhere. I plucked my earbuds out and grabbed a bottle of disinfectant from the nearby storage bin. "If you're here about becoming one of my clients, I don't have any openings."

"No, no. Already have my own. I'm normally in the downstairs part of the gym, but I wanted the chance to meet you when I heard you worked here now." He extended his hand. "Name's Mitch Conway."

My eyes fell shut as I shook his hand. "Conway. Heavyweight champ."

"That's right." His eyes brightened.

"Sorry about that, I should've recognized you. Been a long day," I halfway lied. In truth, I barely paid attention to the men's side of MMA. It drove my publicist, Chelsea, crazy.

"Don't sweat it. I'm defending my title tonight in Denver."

"Oh? Against who?" I sprayed down the bench and wiped it with paper towels.

"Mars."

I froze, my pulse quickening. Mars was a name I *did* recognize. I'd never witnessed him fight in person, but in any clips I'd seen, he was a force to be reckoned with—toying with his opponents, giving them a false sense of security before dealing the TKO that'd be talked about for months.

"You have quite the challenge on your hands."

Mitch's gaze dropped to his shoes with a chuckle. "You're tellin' me. Anyway, I'll get out of your hair. I wanted to meet you, is all. Hope to catch one of your fights soon."

"Good luck tonight." It sounded more like a question.

I loathe small talk.

He stared at me for a moment as if hoping I'd say more. When I didn't, he nodded and walked off. I slid behind the front desk and plugged in the time spent with Phil onto my timesheet. Phil walked past with a towel around his neck and a gym bag on his shoulder.

"Looking forward to the continued training with you, Makos. See you Thursday." He gave a half-hearted salute before breezing through the door.

After ducking into the locker room to change into my dark skinny jeans, boots, and cropped leather jacket, I was all set to make a beeline straight for home until my phone buzzed in my back pocket. I hugged my full-face motorcycle helmet to my side, hitting my butt into the front door. The name Chelsea Stewart blazed in red on my phone screen. My publicist only ever called for two reasons. To bitch at me about something I'd forgotten to do or give me public relations assignments.

Wincing, I answered it. "Well, hey, Chelsea. How are you today?"

"Has your whole attempt at acting like a human being with me when I know you're just blowing smoke up my ass *ever* worked in your favor, Harm?"

I smirked as I walked through the parking lot. "No fooling you."

"You remember you're going to the heavyweight match tonight, correct?"

I groaned. "I was really hoping to curl up in a ball on my

couch and contemplate my life's choices."

"You'll have to reschedule. It's supposed to be one of the most iconic fights in years. The new women's bantamweight champion should be in attendance, don't you think?"

"I haven't been to any of the men's fights. Wouldn't it look a bit obvious?"

Chelsea held the phone away from her ear, yelling at someone in the background. "No. And if someone asks, say you wanted to see Mars in the flesh."

"Why would I say that?"

"He's the only fighter's dailies I've ever seen you watch. Obviously, he intrigues you."

My neck heated. "He fights like a boar. There's something to be said about it."

"All I'm asking is for you to show up, throw back a couple of beers, and watch Mars kick Conway's ass. Too much to ask?"

She was right. Conway didn't stand a chance, the poor guy.

"Fine. You should come with me, you know? I can only imagine what people will say if I show up alone."

"No can do, honeydew. I've other clients who need my attention. Gotta go. Have fun!" She hung up before I had the chance to say anything else.

I beat my phone against my forehead several times before heading for my parking space. My Harley Davidson Iron 883 beckoned me for a ride. A gift to myself after winning the championship. I dragged a finger over the matte black finish that matched the color of my hair and—of my soul.

Quickly braiding my hair and slipping on the helmet, I roared the beast to life. There was a calming sensation any time

I rode a motorcycle—the throaty thrum of the engine, the needed awareness to your surroundings, the feel of the clutch in my hand, and the warmth radiating from the tailpipe.

The gym being in Boulder gave me plenty of time to mentally prepare myself for chumming it up with the MMA crowd in downtown Denver. The popularity of the men's division wasn't surprising. Women's MMA made a rise, but at the end of the day, men have been beating the daylights out of each other since gladiatorial times of old.

The bass from the music blaring within the arena echoed off my chest as I pulled into a parking spot. After locking my helmet to one of the handlebars, I shoved my hands into my jacket pockets and made my way inside. Dipping my chin, I powerwalked past the never-ending line of attendees, heading straight for will call.

"Chelsea Stewart should've left a pass for me? Harm Makos?" I said through the small hole of the plexiglass window.

The man typed into his computer, clicked the mouse several times, and frowned. "I have a pass for a Harmony Makos?"

That little brat.

"Yes. That's me." I slapped my driver's license against the window.

He slid a ticket through the drawer. "Enjoy!"

I grabbed the pass with a grumble, shoving it in my pocket. As I slipped through the side door, the elevated cage came into view in the center of a vast space, nestled beneath a jumbotron currently scrolling through sponsor ads. Giant rounded lights hung from every corner, brightening the arena like a car dealership. Hundreds of people sat in stadium bleachers surrounding the cage, and rock music boomed over the speakers. I wasn't the one in a match tonight, but my pulse quickened all the same. When I wasn't fighting, I was just another product of a broken home, but inside the ring…I was royalty.

The fight wouldn't start for another fifteen minutes, so I turned for the beer stand. In Colorado, you could always rely on a refreshing Coors Light. A tall man with dirty blonde hair stood at the counter, leaning over it and pointing a finger in the cashier's face—a boy no older than early twenties who looked moments away from pissing his pants.

"What are you, some kind of moron? She asked for diet Coke, and you give her regular?" The man slammed a paper cup on the counter, knocking it over in the process. Sticky soda and ice cubes dripped over the edges.

"Sir. I'm sorry sir. I—" The boy stood rigid, pressing his back against the flimsy wall behind him.

"Figures you'd be incompetent with a job like this. I want two free Cokes now, or I go straight to your manager."

The boy stammered but couldn't hold a sentence together.

The skin between my eyes wrinkled as I dipped into a buried memory of high school. The back of my head slammed into a locker as two older kids called me stupid and poor. All because of my mother. If I were to ever run into them as an adult, I should thank them. They are the main reason I learned to fight.

"Some tough guy you are, taking advantage of a man half your age who can't talk back to you in fear of losing his job."

The man turned on his heel. "Who the hell do you—" His expression morphed from anger to shock.

"Hey there. I'm not sure if you get off on belittling those

you know won't defend themselves, but you wanna take another shot?" I made "come at me" gestures with my hands. "I'm more fair game."

"You've got some balls, Makos."

My blood pulsed, aching for him to take me up on the offer. An urge to fight—to explode has always itched my skin. Wayward punches filled most of my youth, and they never failed to get me in trouble. Becoming an MMA fighter was the only legitimate way I knew to let the beast out and keep it reined in when I wasn't in the ring.

"One of us has to have a pair." I pulled out my wallet.

The man glowered as he took a step forward.

"If it means all that much to you, I'll buy you *three* diet Cokes." Keeping his gaze, I slapped several bills on the counter. "Get your sugary drinks and go sit the hell down."

"If you were anyone else, I'd—" The man's fists shook at his sides.

The cashier slid three paper cups across the counter with trembling hands.

"Enjoy your free soda." My jaw twitched—the fury circling in my core, begging me to let him have it.

He scooped the cups with a grunt before brushing past me.

The boy's eyes were as wide as melons when I stepped to the counter.

"Holy. Hell. Harm Makos stood up for me. Me."

Heat flooded my cheeks. I was ecstatic I'd won the championship but already missed my anonymity. Fame didn't settle well with me, but being the champion meant more opportunities to fight.

"I know what it's like. Remember, there is no reason you should have to put up with that bullshit."

He nodded like he was taking mental notes. "And what can I get for the Amazon?" His smile brightened.

I curled my hair over my ears. "Coors Light."

"Coming right up." He flipped a plastic cup into his hand with a flourish.

Folding my arms, I looked at the cage behind me. How long would the fight last? On average, I'd seen Mars fight for no more than a few minutes. And usually, it was like even that amount of time was agonizing for him. As if he waited it out until he couldn't stand it anymore.

"Here you go." He scraped away the extra foam on top.

I took it with a half-smile. "Thanks."

"Mind if I ask why they call you Amazon?"

"Couldn't tell you. Aside from the fact I'm Greek by blood."

He leaned on the counter. "Mars is Greek, you know? Born and bred."

"Good for him." I shrugged. Considering Mars had an accent as thick as molasses, it was fairly obvious he was a legitimate Greek man.

Awkwardly, I raised my cup to him as another thank you before walking away.

"Nice meeting you," he yelled after me with a wave.

Maybe beer was a poor choice. It might be a whiskey kind of night.

The view of the fight was fine and dandy from this far back, but Chelsea wanted it to be known I was in attendance. It meant using my pass for the front row amidst other potential celebrities, but I'd wait until the last possible moment to sit. They'd still get their damn photos.

The lighting dimmed, spotlights blazing over the cage. With a sigh, I shuffled to my seat, holding the cup of beer above my head. A random woman bumped into me, causing a mouthful of liquid to splash on my shoes.

I ground my teeth together and partially crinkled the plastic cup. Sucking air through my nose, I glared at her. She was shorter than me by an entire foot and wore a skintight bright red dress. Her bleached-blonde hair flowed to her elbows, and the overhead lights glinted off her three-inch stilettos. The woman giggled from her plump lips.

"What the hell is wrong with you?" I asked, my chest heaving—pushing, coaxing the beast down.

When had humanity lost this much respect for each other? She had a clear three feet of clearance on the other side of me, and yet…

She slapped a hand over her cleavage and leaned back." Excuse me? There are like a ton of people in here. I didn't see you, for God's sake."

"Just watch where you're going."

She rolled her eyes. "Whatever, Giantess."

I pinched my eyes shut, grip tightening around my cup.

Walk away, Malibu Barbie. Walk away.

Getting into a fight *outside* of the cage wasn't the PR Chelsea had in mind. I opened one eye, noting the woman's blissful absence. Once I found my seat, I slumped into it, letting my neck rest on the back.

The lights went dark, and the colors blue and white spilled

over the crowd, followed by a steady, rhythmic drum blaring over the speakers, picking up pace. A deep bass drum vibrated in my chest, followed by bagpipes. The names *Mars vs. Conway* flashed across the jumbotron along with an animated Scottish flag. The crowd roared as Conway entered; Scotland's flag draped over his shoulders. Everyone stood, but I remained seated, sipping on my beer.

Several flashes went off from nearby cameras, and I groaned.

I could see the headline now: Women's Champion Lacking All Enthusiasm.

I pushed to my feet and slipped a hand in my pants pocket, tapping my feet to the beat of the drum. Conway handed off his flag and entered the cage, sashaying the perimeter to keep warm.

The Scottish music died down, and blood-red lights replaced the blue and white. My throat constricted as an ancient Greek song mixed with electric guitar and mind-pulsing drums thundered through the arena. A Spartan helmet with a flame flickering behind it displayed on the jumbotron, and my heart thumped against my chest.

The hulking form of Mars walked out. His arms tensed; hands balled into fists at his sides. The scowl overtaking his features could make lions cower away. His long, dark hair pulled into a tight bun at the base of his neck. He dragged a hand over his beard, blowing air through his nostrils in one quick huff. An ancient plated armor and chainmail tattoo started on his chest, spread over his shoulder, and led to his wrist.

I downed the rest of my drink and dragged my jacket sleeve over my mouth.

Definitely should've gone with whiskey.

He stepped into the cage, pacing back and forth, glaring at Conway like a bear ready to pounce.

"Gentlemen, this is for the heavyweight championship," the announcer said before the referee motioned for the two of them to approach the center.

They stood toe-to-toe, and the announcer held the microphone up for the ref.

"Mitch, Mars, you both received instructions in the locker room. Either of you have any questions?"

Conway feverishly shook his head, bouncing on the balls of his feet. Mars turned his head from one side to the other with calculated movements, standing motionless.

The ref nodded his head. "Fight clean. Fight hard."

The two men quickly touched gloves and retreated to their designated corners.

I folded one arm over my stomach and chewed on my thumbnail, sitting down only when the others around me did. Sliding the empty cup under the seat with my booted foot, I sat back.

The two fighters circled each other. Conway lifted his fists, immediately blocking his face. Good idea on his part. Mars's punches seemed like getting hit by a Mack Truck. Mars kept his fists at his sides, not attempting to block at all. Interesting. Conway threw a left jab, and Mars leaned away but didn't counter.

I sat up straighter.

They circled each other, and Conway threw another jab, testing the waters. Mars swatted it away like a fly.

"Come on," a man yelled next to me.

Mars's lip curled back.

Conway threw a punch, connecting to the side of Mars's jaw. Mars snarled as he slammed his head forward, stopping before it crashed into Conway's face. Mars turned away with a growl, clearly frustrated.

I scooted to the edge of my seat, hands gripping the armrests. Was Mars…holding back?

Conway grinned, circling Mars, but he stood still, cracking his neck from left to right. Conway launched forward. Mars leaped, bringing his rear leg forward, but snapped it back while throwing a cross—a Superman punch.

When Conway dropped to the floor, a mental flash hit me like a backdraft. The cheering audience drifted away. Ancient horns blared, followed by the sounds of a snorting wild boar. When Mars landed on his feet, he moved in slow motion. A Spartan helmet morphed over his head, and a red cape rolled down his back.

I gasped, snapping back to the present moment. My hands clung to the seat so tightly, my knuckles turned white. Did that over-enthusiastic arena employee make my beer a Boilermaker with a double shot of whiskey or something?

Mars loomed over Conway, throwing punch after punch even though he'd already knocked him out. The ref pulled at Mars, but he wouldn't stop. Finally, the ref and two others draped themselves over Conway, yelling at Mars to stop or forfeit his championship win.

Mars staggered backward, his chest pumping up and down, blood covering the knuckles of his gloves. He clenched and unclenched his fists with quickened breaths like it took every ounce of his remaining strength to calm down. His glare glued to the ground as the ref hesitantly walked over to him, reached for his arm, and lifted it, announcing him the new heavyweight champion.

He didn't move. Didn't speak. Didn't react. Until his gaze lifted to mine and a single eyebrow rose to the heavens.

TWO

🔲🔲🔲🔲🔲🔲🔲🔲🔲🔲🔲🔲🔲🔲

MY FISTS FLEW INTO the punching bag, the burn in my shoulders fueling my swings. Sweat rolled down my forehead, and I ran my forearm over it before switching to roundhouse kicks with the band Dead Posey blasting through my earbuds. Mars's steely gaze plagued my thoughts. How had he spotted me through hundreds of people? And why did he stare at me like that?

Kicking the bag three times, I gritted my teeth. With the final kick, I yelled.

A giant purse blocked the bag from swinging. I whirled around, yanking out one of my earbuds.

"Who do you imagine the bag is this time?" Chelsea, my publicist, cocked a thin auburn brow and put both hands on her hips. She wore her usual fancy designer pencil skirt, blouse, jacket, and a pair of tan heels.

I tugged at the Velcro straps on each glove. "Just the bag,

Chels."

"You don't want to talk about it. Shocker." Her heels clicked against the concrete floor as she made her way to a nearby table. She pulled a tablet from her bag and gave two quick swipes.

I slid my gloves under one arm and grabbed my water bottle, squirting some into my mouth.

"Have you seen this?" She held the tablet out.

I sputtered. It was me at the fight, puckering my lips with heavy-lidded eyes. It had to have been the weird mental image I had, but why did it have to make MMA Today's homepage? "You know they try to get the least flattering shots possible."

She tossed her wavy red hair over one shoulder. "Yeah? You look like you're having an orgasm."

I smirked. "Maybe I was."

Her bright blue eyes widened before dropping back to the tablet. "TMI, Harm." Swipe. Swipe. "TMI."

Halfway sitting on the table, I snorted.

"And then there's this." She flipped the tablet over again.

A big, bold headline read, "Mars Retires." I snatched the tablet from her pale fingers.

"Hey, you'll put sweaty fingerprints on it." She tried to grab it, but I turned away.

Dragging my knuckle over the screen, I narrowed my eyes. "Retired? He hasn't even been active for an entire year."

"It isn't uncommon. Maybe he wanted to go out on a high note. Won the championship and peaced out."

"Or maybe he didn't find it challenging," I mumbled.

Chelsea leaned forward. "Excuse me?"

"Nothing." I pursed my lips and held the tablet out to her. "How kind of him to step down and allow mere mortals a chance at the title."

Chelsea gave a wry grin. "What are you doing, anyway? Should you be overexerting yourself with the match tonight?"

"It's either the bag or sparring. Want to hop in the ring?" I nudged my head at the practice ring.

She held her hands up. "Oh, no. You don't wrinkle Dolce."

I smiled and tossed my gloves around in my palms.

"I'll meet you at the arena tonight." Chelsea hoisted her suitcase-sized purse on her shoulder and snapped her fingers. "That reminds me. I had them cue up different entrance music for you. A champion needs something better to walk to than *Another One Bites The Dust.*"

"What's wrong with Queen?"

"Absolutely nothing, but trust me, this song fits your persona better." She winked, squeezed my shoulder, and slipped her sunglasses onto her perky nose.

I stood in the locker room, bouncing back and forth on the balls of my feet and throwing jabs as my coach, Squirrely, made his motivational speech. The world went silent as the grave before a fight for me. Squirrely thought his speeches helped get me in the right frame of mind, and they may have if I listened. For most of my life, I had to rely on myself to get me anywhere. It was a habit that continued into adulthood and wouldn't stop just because I stepped into a ring.

"You ready, Harm?" Squirrely slapped me on the back.

Three magical words to snap me back into the moment.

After running my gloved hands over the French braids on each side of my head, I nodded once. "Time to defend my title."

My opponent, Fiona "Jaguar" Mills, was already in the ring after making her entrance. I bounced, throwing several jabs. The *Wonder Woman* movie theme music blasted through the arena, and the crowd went wild.

Cute, Chelsea. Real cute.

I wouldn't admit it to her, but she was right. The song ignited a fire in my belly. My jabs quickened, and I caught Fiona's gaze as soon as I slipped into the cage. Squirrely leaned past the exit railing, holding out my mouthpiece. Biting onto it, I held it at the corner of my lips while moving to the center of the ring. I spotted Chelsea lingering outside the cage, the buttons undone on her jacket.

"Defending her bantamweight title, Harm "Amazon" Makos vs. Fiona "Jaguar" Mills," the announcer's voice boomed.

The ref stepped beside us, making his usual obligatory remarks, and I held my hand out for her to shake.

Fiona reached but then snatched her hand away, sliding it over the side of her shaved head with a smirk. I narrowed my eyes, blood boiling.

So, it was going to be that kind of fight, was it?

Slipping the mouthguard over my teeth, I moved to my corner and waited for the starting signal. As soon as it went off, I sprinted and threw a jab at her left side. She deflected it with widened eyes.

Yeah. It *was* going to be that kind of a fight.

We circled each other, throwing jab after jab that didn't connect. I saw an opening and wrapped my arms around Fiona's torso, trying to take her to the ground. Every time I'd step over her foot to kick her leg from underneath her, she'd cross hers over mine. She dropped to her knees but sprung up. I threw my forearm into her chest, pinning her against the cage and kneeing her twice in the thigh.

Fiona curled her arms around my head, sticking us in a clench before pushing me away. Distanced, I front kicked her chest. She immediately countered with her own kick. I deflected it with my hand, and when she kicked again, I grabbed the back of her knee, pulling her to the ground. She held her feet up like a bug, and I wrapped my arm around her calves while getting the occasional punch on her face.

She wound her legs around my neck, clasping her feet, and I picked her up from the ground, working my hand underneath her calf to unwind her. She recoiled, dropping to her feet, and we circled each other again. She threw a right hook, and I blocked it, but she didn't close her fist all the way, and her thumb jabbed me in the eye. My vision went blurry. I rubbed it but couldn't see straight.

The ref called for a time out, and I trotted over to Squirrely, blinking tears.

"She fucking did that on purpose, didn't she?" I said as Squirrely peeled my eyelid back to survey the damage.

He glanced over my shoulder and pursed his lips. "She doesn't look mad about it."

A growl vibrated in the back of my throat, and I swatted his hand away. "Time to end this."

"Harm, there's no way you can fully see out of that eye yet." He grabbed my shoulder.

"The damage is already done. She thinks that's going to stop me?" I beat my fists together and pushed off the cage, nodding to the ref.

The ref cocked an eyebrow but held his hand up, and Fiona and I moved to the center. I blinked several times and charged forward as soon as his hand came down. I threw a right hook, connecting with her cheek. Throwing a left hook, I followed up with a knee to her stomach. She backpedaled away, continuously raising her arms to block my barrage of hits. Throwing my arms around her neck in a headlock, I continuously kneed her in the sides. She tried to wrap her arms around me but lost her footing and stumbled backward.

Fiona fell on her ass but did a quick back somersault and pushed to standing, falling on the cage behind her. Seizing the opportunity, I ran forward, and punched, and punched, and kneed. When my fist collided with her right temple, she fell to the floor like a sack of potatoes. Knockout. I bent forward to make sure she was down for the count, but the ref grabbed my waist and hoisted me away.

Title defended.

The crowd roared with thunderous applause. I knew the audience expected me to throw my fists in the air in triumph. To smile arrogantly and stride the perimeter of the cage with a victorious swagger. That wasn't me. I didn't train for fame and glory. Her cheap shot with her thumb still had me fuming. My victory lap was more like a stress-reducing pace. I wanted to keep punching her until both of her eyes swelled shut, but not only would they not let me, I'd get suspended or worse… kicked out. And I couldn't afford that. I *needed* this.

The adrenaline pumping through my veins, pulsing over my body, had me seeing stars. These fights were never enough, but they were all I had.

When she regained consciousness, they helped her to her feet. As she passed me, she slammed her shoulder into mine.

"You're going to *pay*, Amazon," Fiona snarled.

I yanked my mouthguard out and puffed out my chest. Sinking my face into hers, I pushed our foreheads together. "Is that a threat?"

Someone grabbed each of my arms from behind me and pulled me away. Squirrely. He knew I'd been three seconds away from headbutting her in the nose. I let him drag me to the cage exit, glaring at Fiona as she seethed at me.

"Harm," Chelsea said as I walked past her with my brow so furrowed it distorted my vision worse than it already was. I ignored her, heading for the locker room.

"Harmony," she yelled.

I stopped and tossed her a glare, my chest pumping up and down. Realizing I was staring Chelsea down like *she* was the one who pissed me off, I let my face soften.

"You just defended your title with a knockout. At least pretend to look somewhat thrilled about it." Chelsea didn't bat an eyelash.

"You know it's not why I do this."

"I know. But they don't." She pointed to the paparazzi flashing photos.

You'd think I'd have noticed hundreds of flashes going off

around me, but when the adrenaline-induced anger kicked in, it was like wearing blinders.

I shut my eyes for a brief second before opening them and hoisting a fist in the air. The rate of the flashes increased, and I did a slow circle, keeping my game face.

Once I made a full rotation, I dropped my hand and cocked an eyebrow at Chelsea. "Good enough?"

"That's my girl." Chelsea's grin sparkled.

"Harm, let the doc take a look at your eye," Squirrely said.

I shook my head. "I'm fine. I need to go home."

He sighed and put his hands on his hips, knowing it did no good to argue with me when I had my mind made up.

"Great job today, Harm."

I heard Chelsea say it but was already halfway into the locker room.

Shoving my gloves and fight attire into my bag, I slammed my hand into the door with the hood of my sweatshirt draped over my head. I slipped my leather jacket over it and hugged it around my chest once the brisk wind hit me outside. When I got to my bike, a white piece of paper stuck out from underneath the front tire.

I squatted down and plucked it, spying the words "Watch Your Back" written in all caps. With a squint, I did a full three-sixty turn, searching for signs of someone running off. A pit formed in my stomach as fear attempted to crawl up my spine. I gulped it down—buried it. Grimacing, I balled the paper up, shoved it in my pocket, and roared the metal horse to life.

As soon as I walked into my apartment and secured all three deadbolts, I tossed my helmet on the kitchen table. Heading for the bathroom, I left a clothes trail in my wake and took an extra steamy shower. After letting the hot water soothe the ache in my neck, I forced my jabbed eye open, rinsing it. Pressing my palms against the white tile, I sighed. The beast inside me finally started to settle.

After drying myself off, I crawled into bed naked and buried my face in the pillows. Sleep was my only savior, and it came sparingly.

"Get up, Harm. Now," Chelsea commanded.

I jolted awake, leaping to my feet, fists up and ready to strike.

Chelsea stood in my bedroom, her face fuming, despite my nudity.

I shifted my eyes and dragged a hand through the dark disarray of my hair. "I really regret giving you a key."

"The ref told me what Fiona said to you. And then you found this?" She held up the crumpled piece of paper. "Why the hell didn't you tell me she threatened you?"

I groaned and flopped back onto the bed, pulling the sheet over my head. "Because it's not a big deal. She felt humiliated. We all say stupid things when we're in the zone."

At least I hoped it wasn't a big deal. A small part of me believed Fiona, but only to keep from being blindsided in case she was serious.

Chelsea trailed both hands down her face. "You need to take this more seriously, Harm. For all you know, it wasn't an empty threat." She pulled the sheet away.

"Lighten up, would you, Chels?" I rubbed my jabbed eye.

"Tell that to Nancy Kerrigan." She crossed her arms in a huff.

"If someone comes after me with a tire iron, I'll shove it straight up their ass."

She tapped her high heel against the wooden floor. "I made a few calls after I left the arena. You're getting a bodyguard until all of this blows over."

I shot up like a rocket. "A bodyguard? Are you out of your mind?"

"No, Harm. I'm not. You are, though, if you think I'm going to let some second-rate fighter hire goons to whack you because they lost a goddamned fight." Her pale cheeks flushed.

"Whack me?" I bit back a smile and interlaced my fingers behind my head before dropping them with a sigh. "I appreciate your concern, but it isn't necessary. I can take care of myself if the threats are real."

"This isn't up for debate. Bodyguarding starts tonight."

I glared at her. "What?"

Knock. Knock. Knock.

My shoulders tightened.

Chelsea gave a snarky grin before turning on her heel. "That'd be him now. You may want to get dressed."

After slipping on the first tank top and underwear I could find, I stayed in my bedroom, shifting my bare feet across the floor and hovering near the doorway.

"Sorry I'm late," a deep male voice said, thick with a Greek accent—a voice that sounded far too familiar.

"She's in here. She's just hiding," Chelsea said.

I walked out, and my eyes narrowed into slits. His dark gaze lifted to mine and a stare challenge ensued. He wore a black military-style jacket with the buttons undone. A white t-shirt hugged his broad chest, and several chains hung around his neck. His dark hair pulled back into a small bun at the base of his skull.

Mars.

You've got to be shitting me.

THREE

"YOU HIRED AN MMA fighter to bodyguard an MMA fighter?" I asked Chelsea, trying to ignore Mars's looming presence in the middle of my living room.

Somehow, he matched well standing near my black leather couch, his boots complimenting the deep red colors of my boho paisley area rug.

"Retired MMA fighter. Considering his track record, I couldn't think of anyone more suited to the task. Lucky for us, he's been moonlighting as a bodyguard." Chelsea grabbed her purse with a wide smile.

Mars remained silent, raising a brow and studying me. A younger me might've been attracted to someone like him. The long hair. The beard. The full-sleeve tattoo I knew lurked beneath his jacket. I clucked my tongue against my teeth.

"You know me, Chelsea. Think throwing a stranger at me to play sleepover with is going to go well?" I clenched my hands into fists.

"He's not some stranger off the street. He's a bodyguard through a legitimate company, has signed privacy agreements and liability contracts. You're not head locking your way out of this. No tap outs." She pointed at me. "Play nice Harm. I'll see you tomorrow."

And with that, Chelsea abandoned me.

My jaw tightened. "This isn't necessary. Why don't you go back to your company and let them know I turned it down? I'm a lone wolf. I can take care of myself."

"I'm going to be the bigger man here." He extended his hand. "I'm Mars."

My gaze dropped to his hand—his large, masculine, olive-toned hand. "I know who you are."

"And I know who you are. That doesn't mean we've met."

My shoulders tensed, and I wiped my palm against my thigh before shaking his hand. "Nice to meet you. Need me to show you where the door is?" The calluses of his palm scraped against my skin, making my stomach flutter.

He dropped my hand with a quirk of his lip. "Funny how you think you have a say in this." He brushed past, towering over me like a skyscraper.

Squaring off my shoulders, I pushed a hand against his chest—his extremely *firm* chest. At five foot ten, I wasn't used to looking *up* at people. It only added to the list of items that irritated me about him.

"I'm serious." I dropped my voice an octave.

His nostrils flared, and his eyes narrowed at my hand on him before raising back to my face. "As am I. I didn't even want to take this job, but your publicist can be very convincing."

I slid my hand from his chest. At least we had one thing in common: neither of us wanted to be here. There was no getting out of this. "I'm going back to sleep. You can take the couch, the bathtub. Frankly, I don't care." I flicked my wrist, turned for my bedroom, and slammed the door shut.

Instead of the satisfying sound of wood slapping against wood, flesh hit the door, followed by a masculine growl.

"Vlákas, you're more stubborn than I am," he said through a grunt.

"I never sleep with my bedroom door open."

He shoved it back with a stiff arm. "You do now. I think you misunderstand the whole point of bodyguarding." His chocolate-colored eyes dropped to my underwear for a beat before panning up, pausing on my Greek-inspired tattoo that started on my right shoulder and continued over my bicep.

I snapped his fingers to draw his attention back to my face. "The minute you start snoring, the door shuts. I'm a light sleeper."

He rubbed the full beard on his chin before narrowing his eyes. "So am I."

Our gazes locked, the intensity in his stare reminding me of the way he'd zeroed in on me from the ring. His dark eyes were mystery and mayhem wrapped in a chocolate swirl.

Fuming, I crawled back under the sheets and pulled the comforter over my head. Hearing his feet shuffle, I peeked out to make sure he'd left. He walked past the doorway once, twice, three times. The doorknob jiggled, and his palm hit the window locks until finally, the lights dimmed, and darkness swept across the apartment. He laid down on the couch near my bedroom doorway, propping his hand on the armrest and nestling his head on it.

I flipped to my other side with a sigh. Sleep was never easy for me, and now, with this brute in my personal space, I'd probably go sleepless for nights on end.

Beep. Beep. Beep.

I jolted awake in dazed confusion. My hair was all over my face, and I slid it to one side.

When had I fallen asleep?

My headboard was at my feet.

And why did I feel the need to sleep at the *foot* of my bed?

I groaned and slid out from under the covers. Rustling sounds echoed from my kitchen, and my body stiffened. I rushed for the door, stubbing my toe on the weight set in the corner—the only other object in my room beside my bed and nightstand. Cursing under my breath, I grabbed the baseball bat I kept behind my door. My heart rate sped into a sprint. If the threats were real, someone could be waiting to kill me right around the corner. I held it above my head and walked to the living room.

Mars stood in my kitchen, casually leaning against the counter with a steaming cup of coffee. *My* coffee. He wore a shirt with the sleeves cut off, creating gaping holes on each side, showing a good portion of skin. He wrapped both hands around the cup as he blew on the hot liquid. My tiny kitchen made him look like a giant.

"Kaliméra," he said, not looking up from his cup.

I lowered the bat. "What the hell are you doing?"

He shifted his stance, revealing a plate of egg whites resting on the counter behind him. "Pretty sure it's called 'breakfast.'" He shoveled food into his mouth.

Tightening my grip on the bat's handle, I clenched my jaw.

After swallowing, he said, "Didn't expect me to start the day with no caffeine or sustenance, did you?" Finally, he looked at me, cocking his eyebrow.

My blood boiled, and I stormed forward with the bat in hand. "No. Paying for your *sustenance* has nothing to do with babysitting me."

I reached for the plate, but he scooped it in his hand and held it above his head with a scowl.

"Who said you paid for this?"

I eyed the freshly brewed pot of coffee like a succulent steak and bit my lip. "That's still *my* coffee maker."

He leaned forward, sticking his thumb in his mouth to rid it of egg remnants. "There's plenty for you too, yiachní."

His speaking Greek at random times would get old very quickly.

I shoved past him to grab a cup from the cabinet, slipping the bat between my knees to free both hands.

He continued to eat his eggs, sliding away from me. "Is there a reason you have five gallons of cookie dough ice cream in your freezer?"

I had the coffee pot in my grasp and paused mid-pour. "First ground rule. Do not snoop through my stuff."

"No promises. And you didn't answer my question."

After slamming the pot back on the burner, I yanked the bat into my hand and sipped my coffee with the other. "And I'm not going to. I need to take a shower before work."

He wiped a napkin over his full lips, taking an extra swipe over the beard surrounding his mouth. "Don't close the door."

I shoved the bat under my arm and held my cup with two hands. "I don't think so. I'll be naked." Scoffing, I moved past him.

"Like I've never seen a naked woman before."

My insides did a curious twist.

I rested the bat on my shoulder and glared at him as I backpedaled. "You won't see this one."

He shook his head.

After slipping into the bathroom, I shut the door with no hesitation, tossed my clothes in a corner, and hopped in.

It was the longest shower I'd taken in my adult life. Turning off the faucet meant facing reality—a reality who hulked in my kitchen and scoped my weakness for flavored cream. After beating my forehead against the tiled wall, I turned off the water and peeled back the curtain. The bathroom door was halfway open. Grabbing a towel, I wrapped it around myself and, still soaking wet, yanked the door open.

He sat on the armrest of the couch, his legs spread wide and his forearms resting on his knees.

I opened my mouth to start an argument.

"It's called a compromise," he said, interrupting me. He stalked toward me. His eyes dropped to the towel, and I clutched it against my chest.

I'd never been the shy type, but the intensity hidden in his gaze made me wish the towel fell to my ankles.

"You're going to ruin the wood." He cocked an eyebrow and pointed at the puddles forming at my feet.

I growled under my breath and stormed into my bedroom. Always leaving doors open or even somewhat ajar would eventually drive me insane. It was easier for me to hear someone sneaking in if they had to turn the knob. I'd taken care of myself since I was a kid. Relying on someone else felt about as foreign to me as him speaking Greek.

After throwing on my gym attire and pulling my hair into a high ponytail, I grabbed an apple from the basket on the kitchen table and moved straight for the door.

"I'll ride with you."

I bit back a smile. "Of course, by all means."

He narrowed his eyes, and I whistled a random ditty as we made our way down the two flights of stairs that led to the apartment complex parking lot.

With my head held high, I strolled to my Harley, plucking the lock off for the helmet.

He folded his arms. "I knew you were too quick to agree."

"I'm sorry, did you think I drove a car?"

He jutted behind him with his thumb. "Move. I'll drive."

"Excuse me? There's absolutely no way you're driving *my* bike and making me ride bitch." I straddled it, further clarifying my point.

His lip twitched, and he balled his hand into a fist. "I'm not riding on the back. I'd barely fit."

"Fine. Walk, call an Uber, whatever form of transportation

you want to get yourself to the gym, but the only way you're getting on this bike is behind me." I slipped the helmet on and secured the strap.

He snarled as he took two hesitant steps forward and squinted. "Tell me, if you're such a lone wolf, why did you get a passenger seat installed? I know this model doesn't come standard with it."

I flipped the visor up, glared at him, and roared the bike to life. "You have five seconds before I peel out of here."

"Me spáseis ta nérva mou," he mumbled, mounting the bike behind me.

"It's extremely frustrating when I can't tell what you're saying."

"Tough." He scooted forward, and I felt his hips pressing against my backside.

My stomach flipped.

Maybe I should've called us *both* an Uber. I didn't think he'd actually go through with it.

"I don't have an extra helmet."

He grimaced. I'm sure the fact he was on the back of a bike, behind a woman no less, infuriated him. *Good.*

"I can deal." He wrapped his arms around my waist.

My body stiffened, and I threw my hands up as if his arms were venomous snakes. "What the hell are you doing?"

He eyed me as if I asked him to summon rainclouds. "Do you want me to fall off?"

"Do you want me to answer honestly?" I cocked a brow.

His face fell. "Just drive, Makos." He pulled me tighter against him.

Blowing air through my nostrils, I flipped the visor down and tried to ignore the hardness nestled against my ass. Hopefully, it was a cell phone.

We made it to the gym in record time. Mostly because I didn't want to deal with the way my ovaries betrayed me from the feel of his arms around me. Sure, I was a woman, but I refused to think about sex with a man like Mars. He threw up far too many red flags to count. Not to mention, he had the alpha mentality. The moment he sensed a pack, he'd want to piss all over it. I was my pack—alpha, beta, delta…all of them. It could get exhausting, though. The idea of sharing my burdens—dividing them, always itched at me, but it was far too fragile to rest in anyone else's hands.

He hopped off the bike before it came to a complete stop and rolled his shoulders with a grunt. After slipping the helmet off and securing it, I grabbed my items from the saddlebag.

"There's a perimeter of windows. You can stay in the lobby. No need to come into the gym," I said, not bothering to wait for him as I made my way inside.

He stood still, eyes shifting as I walked past him. His boots scraped against the asphalt, hovering near me, but giving distance. I whisked in like he was an invisible shadow, going about my normal routine. The receptionist, Lilly, peeked up from the computer, eyeing Mars over the rim of her glasses.

"Bring a friend, Harm?" Lilly asked with a sparkling grin. She twirled her finger around the strings of her lanyard.

Mostly ignoring her, I logged into the computer. "Ignore him, Lilly."

Mars slid his aviator sunglasses on top of his head and did

several circles on the area rug in the lobby before sitting on one of the four leather couches. He leaned back, stretching his arms along the length of it, their span covering the width of the sofa.

"Do you see the size of that man? You say ignore? I can't take my eyes off him," Lilly muttered, clutching her lanyard so tightly around her neck it dug into her skin.

I cocked an eyebrow. "Just…don't talk to him. He might bite your finger off."

Her eyes widened. "Not him."

"Lilly." I leaned my forearms on the desk, so we were face-to-face. "That's Mars. Former heavyweight champion. He's knocked men out for clipping him on the shoulder."

Her eyes shifted at him and then snapped back to me.

"Stay away," I reiterated.

Once I was convinced I had her terrified enough to keep her virginal paws off him, I entered the gym.

Phil stood there like an eager beaver, waving his water bottle at me. "You look great today, Miss Makos."

I raised my brow, didn't pause for small talk, and walked straight to the hamstring curl machine. "Thanks, Phil. You warmed up?"

"These calves are apple pie." He laid down on his stomach.

I looked skyward and bit down on my lip. It wouldn't be the first time a male client flirted with me, but Phil hadn't shown any signs he'd be the type at our first session.

After adjusting the weight, I tapped Phil on the knee, letting him know he could start curling. He grunted through three reps.

"Okay, stop. Too much." I lessened the weight. "Alright, try that. Twelve reps."

I focused on his legs, watching for signs of strain, but they stayed motionless.

"Holy shit. Is that who I think it is?" Phil raised to his elbows, staring in awe across the room.

Instinct told me who it was before my eyes lifted. Mars lay on a bench, pressing a barbell with what looked like nearly six hundred pounds on it. He didn't grunt, nor did his face twitch.

Phil hopped from the machine and started to walk over.

"Phil, you have another six sets," I ordered, but it did no good. He walked over to Mars like a sheep to its shepherd.

One of our regular muscle heads, Antonio, walked over to Mars with his burly arms crossed. Antonio was five foot six with arms wider than his head and legs about as thin as mine. He spent so much time working on his arms with little to no cardio that he had a rounded belly. He ran a hand over his slick black hair styled with so much gel it glinted the overhead lights more than the gold chain around his neck.

"Heard you retired after winning the championship, Mars. You afraid of losing it to the first person who challenges you, huh?" Antonio grinned wide as several men around him snickered.

Kanéna distagmós.

The words whispered across my ears like a gust of wind. I furrowed my brow, snapping my attention to Mars's face. He sat up with the scowl of a raging lion, his eyes glowing red.

Was he on steroids?

Another feeling twisted in my stomach, propelling my feet forward.

Mars stood up, swung his leg over the bench, and grabbed a fifty-pound plate from the rack, holding it in one hand like a bag of flour. He loomed over Antonio, gripping the plate in his hand. Antonio looked like he was ten seconds away from pissing his pants. As Mars raised the plate above his head, I sprang forward and grabbed it, seething up at him.

With me between the two men, Antonio suddenly found the courage to clear his throat. "You're fucking crazy, bro." He pointed at Mars before power-walking away.

"Smack talking is legal. Bashing a guy's face in with a weight plate? Is not," I said to him through gritted teeth.

He growled, yanking the plate from me and sliding it back on the rack. "I was only going to give him a love tap."

"I've seen your love taps in the cage." I crossed my arms. "He would've left on a stretcher or a body bag. Neither of which I care to explain."

His nostrils flared, and he paced back and forth like he was in a confined space.

"Are you juicing?" I lowered my voice.

He stopped and glared at me. "That's for cowards. Do I look like a coward?"

His eyes were back to their usual dark color, not a hint of red.

"Why did your eyes look red a second ago?"

"How the hell should I know?"

I recognized that look, the way he paced, the rise in decibel of his voice. He was moments away from flipping a bench.

"Real professional of you. One quick call to Chelsea and I could have you packing faster than you could say 'leather chaps.'"

He ignored me, his chest pumping up and down. "So many of them talk as if what they say has no consequence anymore. It's infuriating."

Them?

"Mars—," I started. "What's your real name? I'm tired of calling you a damn planet."

He leaned in. The smell of leather, metal, and wood chips permeated the air despite him wearing a tank top and gym shorts. "Mars is all you're getting."

Now it was my turn to get angry. I squared off my shoulders and lifted my chin. "Why don't you go check out the ellipticals?"

He took another step forward, his face so close now I could feel his breath on my lips. His scent sent an endless wave of mixed emotions through my head—my body. He smelled like carnage. Like…war.

"Do I look like the type to use an elliptical?"

I clenched my hands so tightly, they shook. "Then just go over there if you insist on being in here. You're distracting my clients and causing a scene. I *need* this job."

He scanned my face before grunting and brushing my shoulder as he passed. Antonio laid on the bench press with his entourage surrounding him to spot. Mars stood across the room, legs wide, arms folded over his chest. The scowl creasing his brow deepened until he looked downright sinister.

Antonio grunted as the bar fell on his chest. He pushed up

but only managed to make his face redder than a strawberry. I ran over, grabbing onto one end and motioning to any of the three men standing there doing nothing.

"Will you all stop staring and help me?"

One man grabbed the other end, and we pulled, but the bar didn't budge. The other two men grabbed hold, and with all of us lifting, it remained plastered on Antonio's chest.

"Move," Mars said from behind us.

The three men shuffled away, but I remained, narrowing my eyes at Mars.

He wrapped one hand around the bar and sunk his face to Antonio's. "Maybe you should stick to a spin class, *maláka*." He lifted the bar, and it hit against the metal posts with an echoing *pang*.

Mars breezed past me without so much as a glance, heat radiating from his skin. Antonio groaned, clutching his chest and rolling back and forth on the bench. Antonio's friends turned to help him, but I couldn't take my eyes off Mars. How did he manage to lift with one hand what four of us couldn't? And there he sat, on the leg press machine, pushing the max amount of weight possible with the speed of a jackhammer.

I don't think Chelsea knew what she was doing putting the two of us together. What did you get when you combine one hurricane with another? Cataclysmic destruction.

FOUR

THE NEXT DAY, I opted for an Uber to take us to the practice arena, an open-space gym with punching bags in every corner and a sparring ring in the center. It seemed particularly needed after discovering the weirdo known as Mars didn't carry a cell phone. My fists flew into the bag with more zeal than usual. Who could blame me? One day I was celebrating my championship. The next, I'm getting death threats and forced to have Big Foot as my shadow for the unforeseeable future.

It didn't help matters that the aforementioned hairy oaf moved to the side of the ring and watched me during my session. I could see him in my peripheral vision, brow furrowed, and arms folded like he judged every muscle in my body.

"You could get more power in your swings if you leaned into it more," he said.

Heat shot up my neck, and I grabbed the swinging bag. "Are you seriously trying to tell me how to throw a punch?"

"No." His jaw tightened. "How to throw a better one."

I dropped my hands at my sides and stepped away from the bag with narrowed eyes. "You win one championship, and suddenly you think you're the god of the MMA?"

His scowl deepened, and he took a step forward, brushing our toes together.

"Well, glad to see you two are getting along so swimmingly." Chelsea breezed into the room with the grace of a ballerina.

Mars and I glared at each other. No telling what would've happened if Chelsea hadn't interrupted.

"That was a joke, by the way. You could cut the tension in here with a butcher knife," Chelsea unbuttoned the one button on her suit jacket and put her hands on her hips.

Yanking off my gloves, I kept watching Mars from the corner of my eye as I crawled out of the ring. "To what do I owe this visit, Chelsea?"

"You're going on tour."

I cocked an eyebrow. "I'm what?"

"A tour through the US. The Amazon defends her title." She motioned her hands like a billboard.

Mars sliced his hand in front of him. "No. Following her ass all over the damn country was *not* part of the deal."

Chelsea sighed, reached into her purse, and threw a stack of papers on the table. "You signed a contract to guard *her*." She pointed at me. "We never specified a location. Therefore, you go where she goes."

"Yia tin agápi tou día," Mars rattled off as he interlaced his fingers behind his head.

I pinched my eyes shut. "Is this really the best time? You

were the one worried about the threat."

"Harm, you got a dozen requests for matches yesterday alone. This will be a huge opportunity for you." She frowned. "And *if* that note were real, it'd be better for you to get out of town anyway, right?"

My stomach twisted into knots. "If you're so worried about it, why not get the cops involved?"

"We don't know if the letter was from Fiona. It's all speculation right now, but it doesn't mean we can't be cautious."

Mars escaped to a corner of the room, mumbling incoherently to himself.

I fixed my gaze on his calf muscles tightening as he paced, occasionally pausing to punch the bag hanging from the ceiling. "We've barely survived these past couple of days. You think traveling and hotel rooms together are going to help matters?"

Chelsea stepped in front of me, blocking my view of Mars. "Why did you hire me?"

"Uh." I shifted my eyes. "Because I have no idea what I'm doing?"

"Yes, but the biggest part of my job is protecting your interests as both a public figure *and* person." She nudged my shoulder. "This will be a good thing. Trust me."

I looked past her at Mars punching the mat-covered walls. "Sometimes I think you're crazier than I am."

"The first match is in Colorado Springs. I e-mailed you an itinerary of locations and hotels where you'll be staying. I mapped it out so you can drive to each and avoid flying."

Chelsea knew I hated planes. When the only close family member you've ever had died in a crash, one tends to develop a dislike for them. I pulled my cell from my gym bag and opened her e-mail with a sigh.

"What are the ones with an asterisk by them?" My stomach churned as I gazed at the endless list of locations.

"The matches I'll be able to attend. Harm, listen." Chelsea placed a gentle hand on my forearm. "Why don't you and I go grab a cup of coffee? Talk about this some more?"

"Coffee? You know I only drink that stuff as a pick-me-up."

"Okay, whiskey?"

I shrugged.

She tossed her hair. "Let's drink liquid somewhere and chat."

"What about the Hulk over there?" I motioned at Mars with my head.

"I'm sure he won't mind staying at a reasonable distance to give us some girl time. Right, Mars?"

He grunted—a deep caveman-like grunt.

Chelsea beamed.

"Fine. Finnigan's?"

"Perfect. We can take my car since I didn't see your bike out front. What's going on there?"

"Don't ask."

Finnigan's was your typical Irish pub fare. A dozen high-top tables in the center, green booths lined the perimeter, a jukebox, the bar, neon signs of popular beer. Simple. Just the way I liked it.

Curling my hands around a tumbler of scotch, I kept an eye on Mars playing a game of pool by himself while waiting for Chelsea. The anger that consumed his face at the gym still baffled me. He was like a lit fuse waiting to explode.

Chelsea walked up to our high-top table, a Manhattan in hand. I'd never seen her drink anything else in the few times I'd witnessed her indulging in alcohol. After setting the glass down, she tousled her fiery hair and put her hands on her hips.

"I'm taking off the publicist hat for this evening and speaking to you as a friend." Chelsea slipped her jacket off, folded it, and draped it over the back of her chair with perfect creases.

"Woah, there." I held my palms up. "Watch out. Gloves are coming off and everything."

She tossed an exasperated glare before hopping on her stool. "Harm, I'm serious. This tour is the best for you professionally, personally, everything-ly."

"I don't doubt you, but when have I ever agreed to something with ease?" As I sipped my scotch, I stole a glance at Mars over her shoulder.

She squinted at me and twisted her torso to look behind her.

Mars held the pool stick in his hand as if readying to throw a spear, stalking the corners of the table like a warrior preparing to strike. The pool balls were enemy soldiers, unaware of his presence.

"Is he always this intense?" Chelsea asked before facing me again.

"Yes." I snorted into my glass. "I told you."

"Good." She plucked the maraschino cherry from its stick and held it between her teeth. "His eyes won't leave your ass then."

I held my glass between two fingers lazily, letting it dangle. "I'd much rather his eyes be elsewhere."

She laughed. "Please. That guy is your type a million times over."

"I don't have a type." I made half-hearted quote gestures with my fingers.

"Right. Right. You have flings, no dates, but flings with betas to guarantee control." A sinister grin flashed over her mouth.

My lip twitched. The words stung—mostly because they were right.

"I can count on one finger the times we've talked about my love life." I held up my middle finger.

She slapped my hand. "Because you don't have one. It's part of my job as a friend and publicist to be aware of what's going on."

"Why?"

She twirled the sword-shaped toothpick between her fingers. "In case something leaks into the media, and I need to cover it up for you."

"I'll be sure to let you know the next time I go to an orgy." My face turned to stone, staring at her.

Mars's head lifted, his gaze falling on me, a wicked glint in his eye. I crossed my legs and rubbed the back of my neck, turning my focus on Chelsea.

A thin red eyebrow slowly rose as she studied me, more than likely gauging if I was full of shit or not.

"I'm kidding, Chelsea. Come on."

She took a long swig of her drink. "I wouldn't put it past you. I never thought I'd have to explain your sudden green thumb, but the jungle growing on your terrace out of two hundred planters proved me wrong."

I finished my drink and traced my finger around the rim.

Chelsea watched my finger before lifting her gaze back to my face. "How are you doing? Truly."

The question jarred me. "Can't complain, I guess?"

"Have you given therapy any more thought?"

My jaw clenched. "No, Chelsea. We've talked about this a dozen times. My therapy is getting to beat the shit out of people without consequence."

She tapped her fingernail against her glass. "It's been over twenty years, Harm. Do you really feel any better?"

"Does anyone ever feel better after a childhood like mine?" I cracked my neck. "Does it ever go away?"

Mars slipped the rubber band holding his hair between his lips and combed his hands through his long dark locks several times before securing it back in a bun. I uncrossed my legs and bit the inside of my cheek.

She sighed and took a tiny sip of her drink. "I don't know what it's like to go through what you have, and I'm not trying to pretend I do. I just worry about you."

I slid my tumbler across the table from one hand to the other. "You know there's no need for your concern. Besides, I have Godzilla watching over me now, right?"

"Godzilla?" She bit down on her lip, trying to hold back a laugh. "You know what they say about big feet…"

"Big ego?"

Mars bent over the pool table, his back facing me, and my eyes fell straight to his ass.

Chelsea laughed, and I snapped my gaze back to her.

The dreaded small talk again. It was probably the reason Chelsea didn't often ask for these drink and conversation moments. "So, uh—how are you and—" I pinched my eyes shut. Name. Name. Remember his name. I snapped my fingers. "Tim."

"You know his name. I'm impressed. We're good. Caught him scoping out my Sparkly Things Pinterest board."

"Oh? Think he's gonna pop the question?"

"Who knows." She shrugged. "Could be looking for ideas for an anniversary gift. I'm not in any hurry to get hitched."

"Amen to that, sister." Holding a finger up, I flagged the bartender, wiggling my empty tumbler. "I assume you've already talked to my work about this, haven't you?"

She grinned. "Yes. They have another trainer filling in for you with your clients. Some guy named Phil didn't seem very happy about it."

"Phil's new. He's one of the overenthusiastic varieties. Pretty sure he's got a crush on me too."

"You *think* he does?"

"Do you want to say that again, but not like a maláka, hm?"

Mars stood toe-to-toe with a man only a few inches shorter than him. Both men's arms bulged with veins.

"Shit." I jumped off my stool.

"You heard me, asshole. That girl of yours over there is a grade-A bitch. Thinking she owns the ring," the man said.

I shimmied my way in between them, facing Mars. "Mars, care to introduce me to your new friend?"

"Speak of the devil," the man grumbled.

Mars widened his stance. "This maláka called you a bitch."

"I've been called way worse. Trust me. And considering I hold the title right now, it's not going to get any better."

"Yeah. Listen to your little pet here," the man said, chuckling.

Mars locked eyes with me. My hands tightened on his shoulders, and I could feel the fury burning through my core. He gave a subtle nod, his left brow raising. The fury built to a pulsating boil, and my head flew back, straight into the man's nose.

Chelsea leaped off her stool, threw money on the table, and grabbed her jacket. She held her hands in the air toward the bartender and plastered her widest fake smile. "We're leaving! We're leaving."

Mars cocked his head to the side, gazing at me like the world's most mysterious Rubik's Cube.

"She broke my goddamned nose," the man behind me whined.

Mars lifted his arm behind me. His left eyebrow twitched.

"You know, I've always hated that you don't like football. Who doesn't like football?" Mr. Broken Nose said to one of his friends before sucker-punching him in the face.

My jaw dropped, and Mars wrapped a hand around my bicep, turned me, and led us toward the exit.

"Oh yeah? You couldn't hit a golf ball if your own balls were on the line," another man said before half of the bar erupted in a fisted frenzy.

What started as a slip-up on my part became a distant memory thanks to their commotion, breaking beer bottles and throwing each other onto tables.

It didn't make any sense.

The evening mountain breeze whipped over my face as we walked outside. Chelsea's heels clicked against the concrete, and she pointed a finger in my face. "What the hell was that, Harm? We don't need any unwanted attention right now."

Chelsea was back in publicist mode.

The back of my head still ached, but it'd soon fade away. The memory of Mars's expression as I'd slammed into the asshole…*that* was etched into my brain.

"You can only poke the bear so many times," I told Chelsea, squinting at Mars over my shoulder.

"We took care of it. No harm, no foul," Mars added, keeping his gaze forward.

Chelsea rubbed her temples and dug into her purse. She held a paper out to Mars. "It may not be part of your job description, but it's in Harm's best interests that what happened in there doesn't happen on this tour."

The skin under Mars's eyes bounced as he looked at the paper, not answering her one way or the other.

"I'm not a kid, Chels. I've had it in check. One slip-up doesn't mean I'm going to go ape-shit on some innocent bystander."

She ignored me and re-emphasized the paper in her hand to Mars. "Please."

Mars's dark gaze fell on me, his tongue subtly licking along his bottom lip before he looked back at Chelsea. "I can attempt to dissuade her." He plucked the paper with two fingers. "But you should know I'm not exactly the best person to douse someone's inner fire." A sharp glint sparked in his eyes.

The two of them stared at each other for what seemed an eternity. Chelsea slipped her hand in the top part of her blouse, dragging her fingers over her collarbone. Her cheeks flushed with pink, and her eyes widened, unblinking. It was like she was in a trance.

"I'll have to be happy with an attempt then, I guess," she said, monotone and still not closing her damn eyes.

What in the ever-loving hell?

Mars held up the paper. "What is this?"

As if being snapped back to reality, she shifted her stance and cleared her throat. "Right. That's the uh—the rental car confirmation. Scheduled to pick up tomorrow morning at 0900 sharp."

He slipped the paper into the front pocket of his jacket. "We should head back so Harm can get some rest."

"Only I need rest? What about you, tough guy?"

He played with the ring on his finger. "Figured you could use the beauty sleep." He brushed past, making his way to the car.

I narrowed my eyes, still thinking about the way he looked at me in the bar. I'd caught his gaze, and it was as if he willed me to hit the guy behind me—encouraged it. The moment he nodded, I'd felt an uncontrollable urge and did it without a passing thought. It wasn't the headbutt that terrified me, no. It was the sinking realization that in the brief moment…I *let* him encourage me.

FIVE

MARS AND I STOOD in the rental car parking lot, staring at the white Honda Accord.

"Not going to argue to drive this one?" Mars asked with a smirk.

"Nope. All you, big guy." I whipped open the back passenger side door.

Mars grabbed it. "You're not sitting up front?"

"Sitting in front would imply lengthy conversation. Let's be real. Neither one of us is a talker. I'll do us both a favor and seclude myself in the backseat." I plopped down and pulled the door shut, not bothering to wait for his hand to move.

He pulled his fingers away and clucked his tongue against the roof of his mouth before slipping on a pair of Aviator sunglasses. His hair was down today, hanging in wavy tendrils of chocolate brown past his collarbone. When he reached the driver's side, he bent forward, looking at his reflection, and pulled his hair back into a bun. He dragged a hand over his beard, took a quick glance around, and then slipped into the car.

He grunted as his knees hit the steering wheel and fumbled with the controls on the side of the seat. The motor carried the seat back until it almost hit the bench seat next to me. He rolled his shoulders, pushed the button to start the car, and we were off.

Traffic backed up I-25 from the intersection to the on-ramp. No surprise there. It was one of *the* most headache-inducing highways, and I lived in D.C. for several years. I sighed and pressed my forehead against the window, internally screaming at the slow crawl.

Snagging my phone from my pocket, I made myself look busy by mindlessly scrolling through random screens. Try as I might concentrate on cat memes and click-bait ads, there was far too much bullshit fogging my brain. I'd never let fear show on the surface. But it was there—always there. Could I keep my championship title? Was the threat to my life real? Would someone try to kill me? Would they succeed? I glared at Mars's reflection in the rearview mirror. With his focus on the road, he didn't look at me. His face irritated me as attractive as it was. His face represented a painful zit on my ass. One put there by the one woman I trusted and considered a friend—a sister. And *why* was he so damn mysterious?

Fuck silence.

"Why did you retire so early?"

He peeked at me in the mirror over the rim of his sunglasses. "I thought we weren't talking?"

"Considering this traffic, I'd say we have several hours until we get there." I crossed my arms and slouched.

He propped one elbow on the window sill and draped a finger on the bottom rung of the steering wheel. "It wasn't challenging enough. Got tired of pulling punches."

"Challenging enough? And bodyguarding is?"

His gaze turned devious. "I never had to kill anyone in the ring."

My throat dried. "You're saying what I've seen in the ring, wasn't to your full capability?"

"Not even close." His jaw tightened.

My stomach clenched, and I pressed my thighs together, sinking back into the comfort of my leather backseat.

"Why do you do it?" He rubbed his chin.

"Do what? Fight?"

He shook his head. "No. Make wicker baskets."

The story of my life was far too personal. I didn't go that deep with anyone. I'd barely gone there with Chelsea. "I'm good at it."

"You also enjoy it." Despite his sunglasses, I could feel his stare singeing me through the mirror. "The feel of your blood boiling."

I clenched the edge of my seat with both hands. "Yes."

"The look in your opponent's eye right before you deliver that last devastating punch."

Min kathysteríseis.

The words fluttered over my brain, making my head fuzzy. I was a dissected frog on display, pinned to a board. "Yes."

"And there are times you wish you could've finished the job. If the ref—if the world—didn't hold you back."

How did he know? I'd never told a soul. I parted my lips to stumble through an answer.

A car cut in front of us, almost clipping the front bumper, but Mars swerved in time to avoid it. He laid on the horn and threw both hands in the air.

"Maláka!" He punched the steering wheel, making the horn toot again. "Mou éprikse ta nérva!"

The same ancient horn sound I'd heard in the gym blasted through my ears, followed by hooves scraping the ground.

"Where did you go?" His voice jolted me back to the present.

I rubbed the skin between my brows. "What?"

He tore the sunglasses from his face. "You stared off into space with your eyes as wide as grapefruits for a solid thirty seconds."

Had it been thirty seconds? Felt more like a millisecond.

"A daydream."

He stared at me through the mirror far too long for comfort.

"How did you lift that barbell?" I glared.

He snorted through his nostrils like a bull. "What?"

"The bar. At the gym. You lifted it like it was a damn pillow."

He mumbled in Greek, clearly still pissed at the guy who cut us off, before wiping the back of his hand over his mouth. "I'm strong."

"Three dudes and I weren't able to handle it. You lifted it with one hand, Mars. One."

His hand tightened around the top of the steering wheel. "Magic."

"Magic," I repeated, pursing my lips. "Is that what they're

calling muscle enhancement drugs nowadays?"

His left nostril bounced in a snarl. "Know what? I'm going to let you think what you want to think. That head of yours is so thick. Once you're mind's settled, there's no convincing you."

"You don't know me." I seethed, the familiar fury pulling at my spine.

His eyebrow twitched at me in the mirror.

I ground my teeth together before kicking the back of the seat in front of me.

"Don't I?"

I wanted to kick the seat with such force it'd tear a hole in the upholstery. "Would you flip the radio on?"

He slipped the Aviators back on. "With pleasure." He slammed his palm against the dashboard, pushing the power button.

The song *This Means War* by Avenged Sevenfold echoed through the car interior. I focused on the traffic creeping by us out the window, forcing my thoughts elsewhere.

The car lurched forward as Mars slammed on the brakes. My seatbelt tightened, forcing me back.

"Malákas traffic!" He held his hand out toward the car, who'd slammed its brakes in front of us. "Why do mortals feel the need to slam on the gas at every opportunity knowing they'll only get a few meters, hm? Can you explain it to me?" Veins sprouted on his neck, and he gripped the steering wheel with both hands.

That's the second time he referenced "mortals." This guy *had* to be high on something.

I undid my seatbelt and slid forward, delicately resting my

hand on his shoulder. "Hey, big guy, it's going to be okay."

He nudged my hand away. "Don't patronize me."

"I want to get to the hotel, you know, alive." I narrowed my eyes. "You don't always have to be ready to rip someone's head off."

His chest pumped up and down. "Put your seatbelt back on," he said before turning the volume up on the radio.

I rolled my eyes and threw the back of my skull against the headrest with a sigh. Since Chelsea and I started working together, she'd come up with a lot of harebrained ideas. This one was undoubtedly the worst. I decided to let her know. After taking a quick shot of my view from the backseat, I attached it to the following text to my darling public relations agent:

Me: See this guy? He's yelled Greek obscenities for the past hour over every single car that's cut us off. I'm pretty sure if I weren't here, he'd have climbed out of the car and pulled someone through their window by now. Seriously. WHERE DID YOU FIND THIS GUY?

Send.

It took us three and a half hours to make it to the hotel. While Mars managed to wrangle his temper, there were several times I thought one of his eyeballs would pop out of its socket. When we got out of the car, he slammed the door shut and turned his back to me, interlacing his fingers behind his neck.

I popped the trunk and cocked an eyebrow, watching him. "Ever consider anger management classes?"

He turned with a snarl, snatching my suitcase before I had a chance to grab it.

"Not now, Harm. You say I don't know you? You definitely don't know me." He threw his duffel and garment bag over his shoulder and flung the trunk shut.

I leaned against the car as he stormed across the parking lot by himself. It didn't take him long to realize I wasn't beside him.

He turned on his heel and glowered at me over his shoulder. "What are you doing?"

I pushed off the car with my elbow and lazily made my way over. "Seeing how long it took you to notice." Slipping my hand over the handle of my suitcase, I tried to yank it from his grasp. "I'm perfectly capable of wheeling my own suitcase."

He lowered his face. "Are you always such a hard ass?"

"Yes." I pulled again with more force, and he let go. It happened so suddenly, I fumbled with it before setting it upright.

He started to walk away but stopped abruptly, unzipping his bag. He pulled out a baseball cap and slipped it over my head. It sunk over my eyebrows, given the strap was adjusted for his oversized melon.

"What is this about?" I glared up at him.

"The fewer people recognize you, the better."

"I'm flattered, I really am. But I'm not *that* well known."

He removed a pair of sunglasses and slid them over my nose. The tips of his fingers brushed against my cheekbones, sending tingles down my neck. The skin above his nose wrinkled, and he dropped his hands as though they burned.

"Can't be too careful." He turned away.

Deciding to bury the brief awkward moment we'd had, I

pointed at the hat. "Are you going to at least tell me what's on it?"

"My Zodiac symbol." He kept his head held low as he rummaged through his bag.

"Which is?"

"Aries."

An invisible force pushed on my chest. "Mine…too."

His eyes gleamed. "Your zodiac sign," he started, turning to face me. "Is Aries?"

"Yes," I whispered.

A single strand of his dark hair fell from the bun at the back of his head, and he secured it over his ear. "Small world."

He took three strides and made it halfway to the door before I hitch-stepped to catch up with him.

"Wait a minute." I grabbed the strap of his bag.

He stopped and glowered at my hand.

"You're worried about someone recognizing me, but not you? As much as it pains me to admit, you're far more popular than me."

He pulled out his sunglasses from an inside jacket pocket. "I haven't gotten any death threats." He slipped the glasses on and leaned forward, flashing a villainous grin. "Do these make you feel better?"

I ground my teeth together, trying to ignore the scent of leather wafting from his neck, despite the fact, there wasn't one strip of leather on him. Adjusting the hat on my head, I followed him into the lobby. It was an average hotel that wasn't as fancy as the Ritz but not as questionable as a Motel 8. They didn't charge for rooms by the hour, so that was a good sign. The lobby's white marbled floor was extra glossy like they waxed it this morning. There were enough fake plants in every corner of the entry we could've filmed the *Jungle Book*.

"Should be a room booked under a Chelsea Stewart," Mars said to the front desk attendant after removing his glasses.

The woman's chest visibly flushed when her eyes lifted from the computer monitor and roamed over Mars.

"Absolutely. Let me get that pulled right up for you." Her grin widened, displaying her pearly whites. "And may I say, I love your accent. Where are you from?"

Mars leaned on the wooden counter with one arm, circling his beard with a hand. "Greece."

"Greece?" Her smile spread. "I've always wanted to go there. See all the temples and columns."

"Who's your favorite Greek god?" Mars asked.

She giggled and tapped her finger against her lips. "If I had to choose, probably Apollo."

Mars rolled his eyes, and his body stiffened.

"Is Miss Stewart, your…wife?" The attendant curled a finger into the collar of her maroon jacket.

"No. My client's publicist."

"Oh? A client of?" She raised a thin blonde eyebrow and bit her lip.

I'd had just about enough of it and shoved past him. "Me. I'm the client. Could you pull up the reservation? I'm tired."

The attendant cleared her throat and worked her manicured nails across the keyboard. "Of course. My apologies."

Mars's hand wrapped around my shoulder, and he coaxed me back. "You'll have to excuse her." He peeked at her nametag. "Cynthia. She tends to get cranky when she hasn't been laid in a while."

My jaw dropped, and I whipped the sunglasses off so he could see my stare of death.

Cynthia's cheeks turned pink. She did quick work with mouse clicks and typing before slapping two room keys and an invoice on the counter.

"Room 111. First floor. Down the hallway to the left." She pointed and pulled at the collar of her blouse, fanning herself.

Mars gave a two-fingered salute, grabbed the room keys, and turned for the hallway.

"Was that necessary?" I clipped at his boot heel.

He'd put his sunglasses back on and raised a brow over them.

"Oh, please. You know exactly what I'm talking about," I added.

"She was getting too familiar for my taste."

My mouth formed an "o" shape, ready to rattle off another dozen questions.

"Well, well. Fancy seeing you here," a man said.

Mars whipped around and tore the Aviators away with a sneer. "You."

The man sat on a cranberry-colored lobby couch with his legs crossed. The pin-striped gray suit shifted as he stood up, clutching his pale white hands on the lapels.

"It's been so long. Is that any way to greet an old friend?" His hair was white as snow and fell in unruly shambles over his face. A pair of glacial blue eyes gleamed through the strands.

"You say friend, I say nuisance," Mars replied with a snarl.

"Are you going to introduce me?" I asked.

The man gasped and pressed a hand over his chest. "My counterpart here can be dreadfully rude most of the time. My name is Morpheus." He extended his hand with a wicked smile.

I lifted my hand. Mars blocked it with his forearm, and I frowned. Morpheus' eyes sparkled in Mars's direction.

I elbowed Mars in the side, making him grunt. "Morpheus? Like from The Matrix?"

"Yes, precisely. My parents thought we both looked so much alike," he chuckled and displayed his hands over himself.

I snorted and extended my hand again. "I'm Harm."

"Harm. Short for something I'd imagine?" He moved his hand toward mine, but Mars blocked it again with his arm.

I tossed Mars an exasperated look before returning to Morpheus. "It is, but I don't go by it anymore."

Morpheus wiggled his fingers. "How curious." He looked at Mars with a toothy grin.

Mars's nostrils flared.

"Oookay. I think we should head to our room. It was a pleasure meeting you, Morpheus," I said, shoving past Mars to grab Morpheus's hand so we could finally shake.

Morpheus's grin turned downright sinister, and his grip tightened. A tingle traveled down my arm, my neck and settled over the back of my skull.

He hovered his lips near my ear and whispered, "Sweet dreams, Harm."

I shook my head and blew out a breath once he let go of my hand.

He waved at Mars with his fingers. "Tootles."

"I was trying to avoid your shaking hands for a reason." Mar blocked my path.

"Why?"

His eyes shifted. "Because. He's—you know. He's—weird."

"I've met weirder."

"Remember that I tried to stop you," he snapped before moving for the hallway.

The truly peculiar one here was Mars. Morpheus was, at most—quirky. After catching up to him in front of our room, I caught his gaze. "Stop me from what?"

He slid the card into the reader and pressed his shoulder into the door, staring down at me. "You'll see."

And now he was cryptic.

It was a modest room with two queen-sized beds, a desk, a TV, and a mini-fridge—the usual.

"I half expected her to screw with me and book only one bed," I said with a snort.

Mars tossed the keys onto the nightstand and slid his jacket off, tossing it over the desk chair. "I can push the beds together if it'd make you more comfortable?" He bumped his knee against one bed with a wicked quirk of his brow.

"I'm good, thanks." Tossing my suitcase onto the single lounge chair near the window, I unzipped it, immediately grabbing my nightly attire.

The bathroom door shut with a click, and my shoulders sank. The sound of the shower turning on sounded through the thin door.

Great. He didn't even *ask* if I wanted to go first. I sulked on the edge of one bed, grimacing at the ugly pattern of the comforter—green, orange, and purple paisley. Grabbing the remote, I started channel surfing. Re-runs of *Friends*. Local news. An interview recap of some surf competition in California with a guy named Simon something. Dozens of channels and nothing to watch. Go figure.

I flopped on the bed, spreading my arms wide and staring at the white popcorn ceiling. There were questionable brown stains here and there and circular cork-sized marks every few feet. The bathroom door creaked open, steam creeping out.

"It's about—" My words caught in my throat.

Mars walked out in nothing but a hotel room towel wrapped around his waist. Hotel room towels were never big enough, especially for a man his size. It stopped at his upper thighs. I'd seen him half-naked plenty of times in the ring, but this was entirely different. His deeply tanned skin glistened with water beads. His chest peppered with just the right amount of hair to scream masculine without turning into a forest. The water made his dark hair slick back, cascading down in wavy tendrils. He brushed his teeth with the full-sleeve tattoo arm, and his muscles tightened with each stroke.

He cocked an eyebrow and pointed at the bathroom with the toothbrush. "You want to use it?" he asked, holding back a mouthful of toothpaste.

My stomach twisted into never-ending knots, and I clutched my pajamas to my chest before springing off the bed.

"Yes. Yes, I do." I zoomed into the bathroom and slammed the door behind me.

"Can I at least spit this out first?" he asked through the door.

If I saw that chest again, I wasn't sure what I'd do. Be tempted to lick it? Or worse.

"Use the trashcan. I'm already undressed," I lied, pressing my ear to the door to listen for him walking away.

He growled and the sound of his feet brushing across the carpet made me exhale.

When I came back out, I was relieved to find Mars under the sheets, his body fully covered with his back turned. I crawled under the comforter, sighed, and nestled into the pillows for a good night's sleep. Or so I thought.

SIX

IT WAS A TYPICAL day on the battlefield. The sun blazed over my bronzed skin as scents of blood, metal, and sweat wafted through the air. Athens and Sparta still at each other's throats. Particularly today, after Athens launched a surprise attack, leaving an entire village decimated. And I remained on the Spartan side, as I always had. Moments ago, my shield cracked from repeated blows of an Athenian Warhammer. I threw it to the sandy dirt and adjusted the Corinthian-style helmet, glaring through the narrowed openings. Several soldiers advanced toward me. I growled, tossing my dark braid behind me and pulling my xiphos sword from its sheath.

A man with a javelin through his chest flew past, landing on his back with a gurgle. Mars stormed ahead, clad in his matching Spartan armor, no helmet, and a fully intact shield clutched to his left forearm. The leather pteruges flaps swung with the tunic draped over his legs as he launched himself to the fallen man, grabbed the javelin, and yanked it out in one swift motion.

Mars turned to me, a wicked grin playing over his lips. His beard was longer than I remembered, braided at the tip. A braided headband circled his head, continuing down his back to the middle of his shoulder blades.

"Where's your shield?" He asked.

"I had to beat an Athenian hammer with it. And your helmet?" I swung the sword once, biting my lip at the mere sight of him.

He side-stepped across the sand to my side. "I see better without it."

As the Athenian soldiers trudged forward, flying their blue banners high, Mars slammed his shield into the face of one man and jabbed his javelin into the chest of another. He ducked as a sword flew over his head, jumped, and struck downward, stabbing the soldier in the neck. He yanked the xiphos from the fallen man's sheath and tossed it to me.

"Are you going to join me?" Mars asked with a smirk.

I caught the sword and twirled them both in my hands before slicing one man across the face—once upward, once downward. As he stumbled, I spun around and dragged both blades across his abdomen. Another soldier with a shield ran up to me, and I sliced at the bronze covered metal several times until his grip weakened, his shield flying to the ground. I slashed both blades across his chest, carving them away from each other. Planting a single kick into his chest, I sent him flying into Mars's awaiting javelin point.

We grinned at each other before his smile faded into a

frown, glaring over my shoulder. I crouched, ready to strike, but Mars lunged, stabbing him in the chest. Another ran up behind Mars, and I used his shield to propel me, slashing one sword across the man's sternum. I spun behind him and stabbed the other sword through his neck. We removed our blades from our kills in unison as another soldier with a shield saddled between us.

Mars stuck him in the chest with his javelin as I ducked under Mars's arm and slashed the man across the stomach. Mars threw his shield into the man's face, knocking him to the ground.

"They're retreating," a Spartan soldier yelled.

A sea of blue plumes scattered away from us on the battlefield. I slid my helmet off, dragging a palm over my sweat-soaked forehead.

Mars peered at me through tendrils of smoke from burning arrows embedded in the ground. Embers floated past our faces, and we both knew what the other was thinking. We'd save the celebration with our fellow soldiers for later. Running to our tent, no sooner had the flap dropped, we were a fury of flying metal greaves, bracers, sandals, and tunics.

Both devoid of confinements, his mouth crashed against mine. The rate of my heartbeat rivaled that of the battle we'd just fought. My fingers dug into his hair as I pressed my chest against his, swirling my tongue into his mouth.

More. I needed more.

Dirt, blood, and sweat caked our faces, but we didn't care. It only added to the ferocity of the fight—the passion of war. I pushed my palms against his chest, backing him to the nearest table. Pulling away from the kiss, he let his bottom lip drag through my teeth. I stared up at him with carnal need.

I didn't need to say the word "more" out loud. He knew. He always knew.

He snarled, grabbed my hips, and hoisted me onto the table. I wrapped my legs around his waist, waiting for him to fill me. He kissed my neck, giving it a tender bite before plowing into me. My head flew back…

…and my eyes burst open. I sat up straight in my hotel bed, panting, sweaty, and confused.

A dream? But it all felt *so* real. I clutched the sheets, needing something physical to ground myself. Through the darkness, a pair of dark eyes stared at me. Mars sat on the edge of his bed, elbows on his knees, leaning forward.

I jumped. "What the hell is wrong with you? Why are you staring at me in the dark like a complete creep?"

"Well, I *would* be sleeping if someone hadn't been battling in her sleep."

My throat dried. "What do you mean?"

"Judging from the way you twirled your arms around, I'd say you were fighting with a sword. Two, maybe?"

I hugged my knees to my chest. "I was fighting you. And winning, might I add."

"Uh, huh." He smirked. "Your battle cry was so loud I'm certain the rooms on either side of us are awake too."

"You're telling me you never move in your sleep?"

He interlaced his fingers, letting them hang between his knees. "You also kept repeating the word 'more.'"

My chest tightened. "Right. I wanted to kill more of you.

One wasn't enough."

"Oh, really?" A corner of his lip lifted. "Because you were moaning it."

My lips parted. He stared at me—challenging me to come up with an excuse for *that* one.

"I'm going back to sleep." I turned my back to him and flopped my head on the pillow.

"Óneira glyká," he whispered.

"I hate you too."

He let out a deep, raspy chuckle. I pinched my eyes shut, praying once I fell asleep, the dream didn't pick up right where it left off.

MMA weigh-ins. One of the most awkward yet necessary events in any fight. They couldn't allow someone over the weight for their division. They put fighters on display like a piece of meat—scale and all, in front of hundreds of people. It was one of the rare moments I let my hair down and did my make-up, on Chelsea's insistence, of course. No fighting. Simply undressing to my skivvies, getting weighed, and having a ten-second stare down with my opponent.

I sat in the locker room with my hoodie zipped up to my neck, staring at the tiled floor. Mars had stepped into one of the stalls to change. What could he possibly need to change into for a simple weigh-in?

The stall's door creaked open, and he walked out in a crisp black suit, thin black necktie, and a white shirt. He moved past me to the mirror, adjusting his tie and smoothing back his hair, ensuring the bun secured it at the back of his head.

I sat up straighter, ignoring the flip my stomach did. "It's just a weigh-in."

"I'm a professional." He cocked an eyebrow at my reflection in the mirror. "What do you think I should be wearing? Jeans and a polo?"

For some reason, I couldn't picture him in such an outfit. It didn't suit him. I shrugged and glanced at the clock hanging on the back wall. "Where the hell is Squirrely? I need to be out there in five minutes."

"I dismissed him." Mars adjusted his wristwatch, not looking at me.

Heat shot up my neck, and I stood. "What's that supposed to mean?"

"I dismissed him," he repeated, lifting his eyes to meet mine. "Sent him home."

"Only for the weigh-in, right?"

Strong fingers worked the buttons of his jacket. "For as long as I'm your bodyguard."

"What?" I slid in front of him. "You don't have the right. He's my coach."

He puckered his lips before standing up straight, towering over me. "I inherited the right as soon as I signed the contract to guard you. The fewer people in your space, the easier it is for me to do my job." He clasped his hands in front of him. "You never needed him, and you know that."

He was right. How could he possibly be right so much of the time and not know me?

"Regardless, he's still my coach. Every fighter needs one."

"I'll be there. Do you want to keep up appearances in the ring? Ask advice? Ask me." There was a glint in his eyes as he stared down at me, waiting for a response.

I clenched my fist until my knuckles cracked. "Unbelievable," I said under my breath, turning away. "Let's get this over with."

After exiting the locker room, I waited in the wings as my opponent did her weigh-in. Priscila Andrade. Brazilian. Five-foot eight and said to be a jiu-jitsu master. *We'll see about that.* Mars loomed behind me, and I risked a peek over my shoulder. He slid his Aviators on and cocked his head to the side, cracking his neck.

"And now for the bantamweight champion of the world," the announcer started.

I shook my hands as I walked toward the stage with Mars close behind me.

"Harm 'The Amazon' Makos." The announcer's voice said through the loudspeakers.

My brow furrowed, not making eye contact with my opponent yet. The generic black scale beckoned me as I slipped off my shoes. I unzipped my hoodie and slid it off, turning to Mars.

"If you insist on being the only member of Team Makos, that makes you the clothes rack." I tossed him the jacket.

His lips thinned as he threw it over his shoulder.

The sweatpants came off next, inside out, and I didn't bother fixing them.

"Take it off," a man yelled from the crowd.

Mars's hand clutched my pants once I handed them to him,

a growl vibrating in the back of his throat as he peered at the audience from behind his sunglasses.

I stood on display in only a sports bra and booty shorts to have my weight announced to the world. It may have been mortifying in any other profession, but it didn't faze me anymore. Climbing onto the scale, I brushed my hair over my shoulder and stuck my chest out, staring at the fluctuating red numbers of the digital display.

Catcalls and whistles poured from a group of men in the audience. Mars tossed my clothes at his feet and stormed into the crowd. My chest tightened, unable to move or speak until they announced my weight.

"This isn't a burlesque show," Mars said to the group of men, pointing at them.

One laughed and slapped a hand over his chest. "Oh, come on, man. Lighten up. We're just having fun."

"134.4 for the champion," the announcer said.

I forced a fake smile, raising a fist in the air as the audience cheered. Squinting against the bright lights beaming on the stage, I watched Mars, hoping he wasn't stupid enough to start a fight here, of all places.

Mars ripped the sunglasses from his face, nostrils flaring, and leaned forward. One man crawled over the back of his seat while the others held their forearms up.

"Sorry, man, sorry," the leader stammered.

Mars narrowed his eyes before slipping the glasses back on and making his way to the stage.

I licked my lips as I approached my opponent for our eternal stare down. Moving into a fighting stance, I clenched my jaw.

She mirrored my position but stood straight and held up her middle finger inches from my face.

Keep cool, Harm. She *wants* you to lose it.

I could hear Chelsea's pleas from wherever she watched.

I fought every compulsion not to bite her finger off. Once the stare down was complete, I smacked her hand away. She gave me her best shit-eating grin before sauntering over to the announcer.

"Priscila, I sense a bit of contention here. What was that all about?" The announcer said into the microphone before holding it out to her.

"Makos has won *two* fights. She's not ready for me." She leaned past the announcer, pointing her forefinger and thumb at me like a sideways pistol. "Have you fought enough people to beat the sting of a crackhead trailer trash mama away yet?"

The crowd gasped, and I saw red. The fury festered, boiled, and clawed at my chest, begging me to set it free. Guilt soon followed. They were merely petty words spoken by an idiot. And yet, I still let them eat at me. The sound of Mars's feet sliding behind me kept me at bay as the announcer walked over. He frowned, not saying a word, and simply held out the microphone.

"You watch this piece of trailer trash humiliate you in the cage tomorrow," I snapped and shoved my fist in the air, facing the crowd.

Not bothering to collect my clothes, I stormed off the stage. If I caught sight of her smug face, I knew it would all be over.

"Harm," Mars called after me, but I kept moving, plowing through the locker room and out to the parking lot.

The sunbaked asphalt stung against my bare feet, but it helped soothe the screaming beast. The door swung open. Mars threw his arms out at his sides with my clothes draped over them. He threw my shoes at the ground near my feet, and I stumbled into them. He opened his mouth, and I held a hand up.

"Let's just get back to the room." I pulled on the car door handle—locked. My shoulders drooped in defeat, and I stared at my reflection in the window.

Mars stepped beside me, the sleeve of his jacket brushing against my bare arm. He pressed a button on the passenger side door, unlocking it before opening it for me with slow and calculated movements. He held my clothes out, and I grabbed them, flopping onto the seat.

The entire car ride to the hotel, we were silent as the grave. On occasion, I'd catch him staring at me in the rearview only to shift his eyes back to the road unabashedly. It was like he didn't care I saw him.

Once back in the room, I tried to slam the door behind me, forgetting my living shadow. His palm slammed into the wood with a snarl.

"That's going to be the last time you slam a door in my face," he said, locking it behind him.

"Or what?"

He turned around with narrowed eyes, sliding the jacket off and tossing it to one bed. "Is that why you *really* do it?" He loosened the tie, slipping it off, and pulled the white shirt from his pants, working his fingers down the buttons.

"We're not talking about this." I threw my hands in the air

and marched past him to the bathroom.

"You've been fighting for yourself a long time, haven't you?"

"Are you deaf?" With my hand on the doorknob, I swung the door. But instead of it closing or his hand hitting it, the door flew open and slammed against the tub behind it as a gust of wind rushed through the room. Mars seethed from the opposite side of the doorway, yanking his shirt off and tossing it aside.

"Don't make the mistake of thinking you're the only one with family issues." His bare arms bulged from his tank top—the chainmail armor tattoo flexing with every twitch of his muscle.

"Daddy cut you off?"

He cracked his knuckles against his palm. "Disowned."

"Why?"

"My…temper." One side of his lip twitched as his gaze fell to his feet.

"I never even knew my dad." The words flew out of my mouth before I had a chance to stop them. I pinched my eyes closed. "Fuck. I don't know why I told you that."

We fell silent and stared at each other through the doorway. I wanted to tell him more about me—about my past. The thought terrified me, but what was more frightening…was I wanted to know more about *him*.

My eyesight went black, and a wave washed over me. The ancient horns were so loud this time that I had to clamp my hands over my ears. I staggered backward, unable to see where I was going. My calves knocked against the tub, and I started to fall. A large, rough hand caught my wrist, and the world snapped back to normal.

His eyes roamed over my face, making my chest flush. "What just happened, Harm? What aren't you telling me?"

His mouth was so close to mine, his beard brushed against my chin. I shook my head and stood up, pulling my arm from his grasp. "Nothing. I got dizzy. Didn't exactly sleep well last night."

Mars rolled his shoulders, staring me down like he knew I was lying straight through my teeth.

"Shower and rest up, then. You got an ass to kick tomorrow." He left the bathroom, leaving the door ajar.

I wrapped my arms around myself and ran a hand down my face. I'd kicked Priscila's ass, sure, but I'd also been doing a fine enough job beating up my own.

SEVEN

I BOUNCED ON THE balls of my feet, staring at the grooves of the concrete wall. A new location. A new gym. This one wasn't much different from the others—a ring in the center, punching bags in each corner, mats scattered every few feet, and any upper body weight system you could imagine. In minutes, I'd be in the cage defending my title for the second time. It felt good to bear the championship title, but at the same time, it added unavoidable stress. The moment defeat came for a champion, the fight offers would dwindle. I didn't need to be on top, but I did need women still pining to fight me.

"Punching the air will do nothing to condition you. Here. Come on." Mars held his palms out in front of him.

"What?" I stared at his hands like they were two octopuses.

"You think you're going to hurt me?" He punched a fist against his opposite palm. "Come on."

I furrowed my brow, watching his fixed gaze beckoning

me—luring me. I threw a punch at half-speed, raising my left hand to shield my face. I'd sought every opportunity to punch him, but now that I had the chance, I wussed out? Huh.

He dropped his hands. "Vlákas, Harm. I've swatted mosquitoes with more force. Hit me. Come. On." He growled his last words, beating his knuckles before opening his palms. He glowered down at me, his hands framing his head.

Priscila's face shimmered across my brain as she called me out on live television. My jaw shook, and I slammed my fist into his hand with a grunt.

"Good. Again. Harder."

My chest pumped, and I sent two more punches into his hands with a yell.

"Again. Don't hold back, Makos."

I let out a battle cry and slammed my fist into his with such force it hurt *my* hand, despite wearing gloves. Yet, he barely staggered backward.

"What the hell are you doing, Mars?" I shook my hand with a grimace.

"What you need."

"What I need?" I guffawed. "And you know what I need?"

"Yes." He stalked toward me.

I backed up until my ass hit the matted wall.

"I know about the fire inside you. The eternal flame you can never seem to squelch no matter how often you fool yourself into thinking otherwise."

I dug my nails into the mat behind me. His face dipped, and my eyes dropped to the plumpness of his lips peeking out from his beard.

"You need to recognize the opportunity to let it explode, or it will consume you. I know it. And you know it."

I concentrated on the bumpy texture pressed against my fingertips, distracting myself from his proximity as his scent twisted my insides. The announcer's voice echoed over the speakers, calling me to the wings. I let out a haggard breath as Mars stepped away, slipping on his Aviators.

"You ready, Amazon?"

Ready? I wasn't even sure I could stand upright. Gulping, I secured the French braids on each side of my head and threw on the hood of my sweatshirt. The knuckles of my gloves creaked as I pressed them together. The *Wonder Woman* theme blared through the arena.

The music. The crowd. Through my tunneled vision, I saw none of it—heard none of it. My focus glued on Priscila's smug grin as she leaned against the cage with her arms folded, staring me down. I threw jabs as I walked, echoes of swords clanging against shields pounding in my ears—the same sounds of war I'd dreamt the night before. Mars stayed on my heels; his arms stretched to either side. He didn't hesitate to push anyone back who stepped too close, giving extra oomph to the paparazzi.

After slipping a mouthguard over my teeth, I held my arms behind me to let Mars remove my jacket. His fingers grazed my arms, dragging the sleeves down, littering my skin with goosebumps. I shook my head, refocusing my brain on my opponent and shoving aside the continued mixed feelings I'd been experiencing for my bodyguard.

I climbed into the ring, seething at Priscila, who paced

back and forth, pointing at me. The sounds of the cheering audience in the surrounding stadium seating faded away. The blazing lights glaring from all directions further boosted the adrenaline in my veins.

"Harm," Mars beckoned outside the cage.

I turned to face him.

"She pissed you off. She insulted you." He lowered his sunglasses, resting them on the tip of his nose, staring at me with a glint in his eye. "Out there—" He gestured behind him. "You're judged. In here, you're the executioner. Battles aren't won at half strength." His gaze reddened like that time in the gym. "*Use* it." He used his forefinger to slide the glasses back over his eyes.

An inferno raged up my spine, and I turned on my heel, glaring daggers into my opponent's very essence. The ref called us forward, and Priscila and I stood toe-to-toe. The smirk creasing the corner of her lips fed gasoline to my fire.

"If you want to touch gloves, touch gloves now," the ref said.

Fuck that. I beat my knuckles together as I backed away. She had no idea the beatdown she was about to endure.

We both shuffled forward. No sooner was she in arm's reach, I threw a right hook, clipping her ear. Her eyes widened, and I curled my arm over her neck, trying to take her down, but she stayed. We circled each other several times, and I backed down for nothing. Every moment she slid into my reach zone, I threw another hook. Prepared for her retaliation, I grabbed her arm when she threw a hook, wrapped mine around it, and secured my hand behind her shoulder. My free hand became a fury of uppercuts and jabs, landing in her gut or face.

She slipped her hand around the back of my head. I ducked and shoved my forearm into her chest, sending her toppling backward on her ass. She scrambled to her feet, and I launched forward. My vision turned crimson, and she held her arms up, preparing for the hits she knew were coming. I threw left hook after right hook repeatedly, clipping the side of her head and chin with each swing. A left punch landed square against her cheek, and I switched to kneeing her in the side. As her defense faltered, concentrating on my lower half, I went in for the devastating blow. A right hook straight across her face, sending spit, blood, and her mouthguard flying.

She fell to her knees in a slump, head falling to the ground. The inferno still boiled, and I moved over her, pulling my hand back. The ref hugged me from behind. Despite my protests, clawing at his hands, he forced me away. I yanked my mouthpiece and blew out a harsh breath, sucking air through my nose. Adrenaline pumped through my system, making my vision blur.

"Amazon," Mars yelled.

I ran to him, trying to tame the beast with each step. He latched onto my arm, leading me through the sea of people flanking the walkway. The repeated flashes from surrounding cameras irritated me more than usual. Once we reached the locker room, Mars locked the door behind us.

Controlled breathing wasn't working. There was an itch far from being scratched, and it drove me crazy. I bit my nails, walking back and forth between the rows of lockers.

"How did it feel?" Mars slipped off his glasses, hanging

them from the front pocket of his suit jacket.

"Are you kidding? It had to be a record knock-out for me. But it—it wasn't enough."

"Because you pulled several of your punches, gatáki." He twirled the large silver ring on his middle finger with his thumb.

"It's the MMA, Mars. A thirty-second takedown is bad enough. They want a show." My legs kept moving, propelling me from one side of the small room to the other. The muscles in my biceps twitched as if begging me for more.

"Who gives a shit what they want. You do this for you."

The raging boil inside turned downright aggressive. The AC in the overhead vents kicked on, sending a waft of leather, oil, and burnt wood. I closed my eyes before bursting them open and leaping across the room, curling my arms around Mars's neck. His back slammed into a nearby locker, denting it. My mouth crashed against his, the taste of smoke and whiskey coating my tongue. He hesitated at first but slid his lips over mine and snaked his arms around my waist, pulling me against him.

A flash of my dream with him between my legs in the battlefield tent jarred me. I peeled away, shoving my palms into his chest, and pushing away. He threw his hands out at each side as if to show me there was no foul play. The tip of his tongue dragged over his lower lip, his chest heaving. He peered at me from across the room.

"Are we chalking this up to the adrenaline?" He let one arm relax and dabbed the corner of his mouth with a thumb.

My chest tightened. "Yes. Yes, we are."

A strand of dark hair fell over his eyes. I wanted to reach forward and slip it over his ear. Instead, I put my hands on my hips.

"Thought so," he said with a smirk.

I rapped my fingers against my hip bones, counting the tiles on the floor.

"Food?" Mars brushed past.

Grazing right over it. Alright. I sniffed, letting it roll off my shoulders. But it didn't roll—it didn't even crawl.

Giving a curt nod, I threw my hoodie back on. "Absolutely."

He slipped his sunglasses from his jacket and motioned for me to go ahead of him. I flipped the hood up, took a deep breath, and threw open the door. Dozens of paparazzi crowded the exit. Mars appeared at my side, shoving his forearm into one man who'd gotten so close I could feel his breath on my cheek. The man tripped backward, falling into several of the others.

"What the hell, man? I'm just doing my job," the fallen man said, still pressing the shutter repeatedly.

Mars bent forward. "Stay out of her face, and I won't have to do it again, *man*."

The color drained from the man's cheeks. He took one last shot, a close up of Mars's face, and pushed through the crowd of people and cameras to escape. Mars took the lead, and I grabbed the back of his jacket so I could keep my head down. Once we reached the room, I face-planted onto the nearest bed.

Mars went through his ritualistic "de-bodyguarding" routine, tossing his sunglasses and watch on the desk, followed by slipping the tie and jacket off.

"Greek good with you?"

I lifted my head long enough to answer. "Sure. I could go for a gyro."

Pronunciation: JIE-row.

Mars sat on the opposite bed, grabbing a list of restaurants from the nightstand. "It's pronounced gyros."

Pronunciation: YEE-ros.

Ignoring the flip my stomach made at his accent, I buried my face back into the comforter. "Same thing."

"You know there are better Greek dishes than gyros. I could order you something else."

I sighed and pushed up on my elbows. "I haven't had anything else. I wouldn't know what I like. Gyro is fine. I'll live."

He'd lifted the phone receiver but paused mid-way to his ear. "You're full-blooded Greek, and you've never had anything but gyros?"

I never told him I was full-blooded.

"You heard about my mom. Think she paused between coke binges to make Greek cuisine for me?"

He frowned. "Grandmother?"

"Nope." I flopped on my back, staring at the ceiling. "Only thing my mom ever told me was she died when I was a kid in Greece."

Mars cleared his throat, not asking any more questions. He pressed the phone to his ear and dialed.

"Kalispéra," he said to whoever answered. He continued talking in Greek. The only word I picked up on was "gyros."

Once he hung up, I slid off the bed. "I'm going to take a shower."

"Good." He rested his elbows atop his thighs. "You stink."

I tossed him a glare, biting back a smile before slipping into the bathroom. The door handle was in my hand. All I had to do was shut it again in defiance. So why did I stop it a few inches from closing? I rolled my eyes, turned the shower on as hot as it'd let me, and waited for the steam to fog up the mirror. Satisfied the room looked like walking through a cloud, I undressed and slipped in, wincing as the scalding water hit my back.

When I stepped out, I wrapped my body and hair in towels. Damn it all to hell. I forgot to bring in fresh clothes. Did my fight attire smell *that* bad? I scrunched my nose, scooped them up, and snuck into the room.

Mars stood in the middle of the open space between the beds and TV, holding an imaginary sword, performing striking patterns. Each move made his forearms bulge. When he heard me, he stood straight and dropped his hand at his sides like I'd caught him jacking off or something.

"What uh—what were you doing?" I made a circle in the air with a single finger.

His face softened, those dark eyes dropping to my chest. "Combinations I don't want to forget." His eyes lingered on the towel like he had x-ray vision.

After tossing my clothes into my suitcase, I pressed my forearms over my boobs.

A knock sounded at the door. We both stiffened.

He pointed. "I'm going to get that."

"Right." I scampered to my suitcase to grab new clothes before whisking into the bathroom.

When I came back out, he'd displayed our food on the table

and tossed a plastic utensils package by my gyro. A glorious smell filled the air, and I closed my eyes, inhaling it.

"What is that smell?"

He peeled the foil on his food. "Not your gyros."

"What is that?" I stared at his delicious-looking meal as I took a seat—a lamb shank, potatoes, and rosemary sprigs.

"Kleftiko."

I mouthed the word to myself, shifting my eyes between my plain gyro and his food. His eyes dropped to my lips before cutting the lamb into several chunks. Saliva collected between my bottom lip and teeth, and I tried to suck it back discreetly.

"Would you—" He hesitated. "—like to try some?"

I bit my lip. "Yes. Before you get your spit all over it." Ripping the plastic, I yanked my fork out and stabbed it into a piece of potato, followed by a bite of lamb.

"Pretty sure if you were going to catch something from my spit, it happened about thirty minutes ago." His gaze turned wicked, a corner of his lip lifting.

I paused with my mouth open. Nope. I still planned to graze over it. Garlic, olive oil, onion, lamb, and feta cheese flavors burst across my tongue. I pinched my eyes shut, stifling a moan.

"So many complex flavors and so very, very good." I groaned.

He chuckled, slipping a bite into his mouth. "Glad you approve."

I opened my gyro with a sigh. It wasn't as if gyros tasted terrible. They simply paled in comparison to what I'd just experienced.

We ate in silence for the next few minutes with only the idle sounds of chewing, paper rustling, and swallowing as ambient noise.

"So, do you have any siblings?" My knee bounced underneath the table.

"A few." His eyes shifted. "You?"

"Nope."

We both nodded.

Silence.

Mars coughed. "Nice weather today, huh?"

"Little chilly." I tore pieces from my aluminum wrapper.

Mars dragged a napkin over his mouth and beard before leaning back.

"We suck at this whole small talk thing, don't we?"

He half-smiled. "Completely."

"Why do your eyes turn red?" I snapped my gaze to his.

"Hm?"

"Your eyes. They flash red. I've seen it several times."

He waved his hand in the air. "My eyes get dry. Bloodshot more than likely."

"I know what bloodshot eyes look like. Yours turn *completely* red, Mars."

He gritted his teeth, making his jaw pop at the corners. "I'm tired." He leaped up, his chair toppling over.

"Wha—"

Did I say something wrong?

He balled up his garbage, reached across the table for mine, and tossed them in the can across the room.

"Mars, what the hell?" I slapped my hand on the table,

standing up.

"I'm going to sleep," he growled, yanking off his pants. He crawled into bed in only his boxers and tank top, pulling the comforter over his head.

Moving to my bed, I clucked my tongue against my teeth. "Vlákas," I said under my breath.

His head shot up with a glare.

"What? You deserved it." I slipped under the covers.

He grunted and shoved his head back under the comforter.

I curled the blankets under my chin. My question irritated him. It was as if he couldn't answer or didn't know how to respond. Little did he know, answering me would've been far easier on him. Now, I was a hound with a fox.

EIGHT

╟╢╟╢╟╢╟╢╟╢╟╢╟╢╟╢╟╢╟╢╟╢╟╢

WE'D BEEN IN THE car for the past half hour, making our way to Santa Fe, New Mexico, and Mars barely moved a muscle. Not so much as a cheek twitch. I wanted to catch his red eyes again. Mostly because I wanted to prove to myself and him, I wasn't crazy.

"Is this why you wanted to sit up front?" He eyed me sidelong. "To stare at me?"

I turned in my seat, prying the seatbelt away from my chest with a thumb and staring at him with narrowed eyes. "You said you retired because you didn't feel challenged. What *would* be a challenge for you?"

He leaned toward the window, looking at me like I was a crazed stalker. "Avoiding this conversation seems to be challenging enough."

"I mean, what would it take? Multiple opponents? A ring of fire?"

My attempt at convincing myself I wasn't crazy spiraled rapidly.

He peered at me over the rim of his sunglasses. "Those both sound more…difficult. So, sure."

"You said you had several siblings. How many specifically?"

He sighed and raised one finger at a time, his lips mouthing numbers. "I don't know. Ten? Twelve?"

"Wait, you don't know how many brothers and sisters you have?"

"After ten, I lost count."

"But they're your family." The words made the skin between my eyes crinkle.

He rolled his shoulder. "Barely. Most are products of my dad's fondness for women. Half-siblings. Hardly see any of them."

Okay, now we're getting somewhere.

"I see. So, your dad's a manwhore?"

He made a tsking sound. "If that's what you want to call it."

"What's your dad do?"

He scrunched his face. "What do you mean?"

"His job? What he does to make a living?"

"Oh uh…lawyer."

I caught that. He hesitated. "Wow. And he had nothing to say about his son beating men's faces in as a career?"

"We don't *say* much of anything to each other anymore." His right nostril twitched in a subdued snarl.

"Right. The whole disowned thing. I'd imagine that would put some stress on things."

He grunted.

Silence fell again, and I tapped my fingertips against my knees.

"Why don't you fly?" He asked without turning his head.

"Airplanes?"

He cocked an eyebrow. "Unless you're hiding a set of wings under that jacket."

"Because the only father figure I ever had died in a plane crash. My uncle." I clenched my hand into a fist on the seat, digging my nails into my palm.

"I was closer to my uncle, too, growing up."

"Yeah?" I sulked in my seat. "I was ten. I'd just started hanging out with him more. He'd take me places when his sister, my mom, would forget to pick me up at school."

I could feel him looking at me, studying my face.

"And then just like that…gone."

A deep sigh escaped his lungs, and we both went quiet. I concentrated on the sounds of tires rolling against the asphalt. I'd told a handful of people about my uncle. Mars was the first not to say he was sorry or something about a tragedy. It was refreshing because, really, why would a stranger apologize for an event out of their control?

After several minutes of compartmentalizing my thoughts, I turned toward him. "Are you on drugs? Seriously, no judgment here."

He ripped his sunglasses off, his grip on the steering wheel tightening. "I've already told you no."

"I should know if my bodyguard isn't in top form. That's all." My heart thumped against my chest.

"Believe me. I'm in top form." He shoved the glasses back

on.

"Okay. You're right. We're in way too close of quarters for this conversation."

He flicked the radio on and sat back in a huff, dragging his fingers through his beard.

We spent the rest of the two-hour drive in silence. Every time I'd try to sneak a peek at him from the corner of my eye, he'd be looking at me. Didn't they say something about being able to share silence with someone? Was there anything to say about *us* sharing the silence, considering we weren't very talkative people? If what they said were true, it'd mean we were becoming more comfortable with each other. It would mean another dent in my armor.

"We're here," he said, already stepping out.

The hotel looked a hell of a lot fancier than the one in the Springs. Tall spires reached to the sky, resembling medieval castle structures, and the main building's size compared to a university campus.

I bumped the car door closed with my hip and whistled. "Well, hello, Santa Fe."

Mars grabbed the bags without so much as glancing at the building.

"How are you not impressed with this?"

He slung my duffel over his shoulder, shoved his bag on top of my suitcase, and walked to the entrance, wheeling it behind him. "My architectural likes go back a bit further than medieval times, gatáki."

I trailed behind him. "The heavyweight champ is so cultured. Who knew?"

He tossed me a sarcastic grin over his shoulder before stepping through the automatic doors. Chelsea stood in the lobby with her face plastered to her phone. An ecstatic grin spread over her lips when she spotted me, and with the phone still in hand, she ran over. Her heels clicked against the marbled tile, and she hugged me.

I stiffened with my arms pinned at my sides. "Why are we hugging? We never hug."

"Can't I be happy to see you?" She peeled back, gripping my shoulders.

I cocked a single eyebrow.

"I saw the weigh-in. So very glad you wiped the floor with that bitch. I've never seen you fight like that." Her large blue eyes blinked with the speed of a hummingbird.

Mars brushed past us, lowering his sunglasses enough to look at me. I held back a smile.

Chelsea shifted her gaze from Mars, who'd moved several feet away, back to me. "You two seem to be getting along better."

"Don't let it fool you. We've reached an impasse and, therefore, a tolerable understanding."

"Somebody's been using the word-a-day calendar they got for Christmas." She half-smiled as she dug her tablet from her purse. "That fight has gotten you some amazing press. Your opponent tomorrow, Kelly Fitz, already released a statement."

I took the tablet and glared at Kelly Fitz's Twitter page. "She's trying to threaten me through a tweet? I need to kick her teeth in on basic principle now."

"Agreed, but read what she said."

"When someone feels on top of the world, all it takes is one push," I read aloud before handing the device back. "And she thinks she's a poet. Rich."

"It should be an interesting weigh-in later. I checked you both in. Figured you'd be exhausted after a four-hour drive."

"Thanks, Chels. I am. I also need to piss like a racehorse." I looked for the lobby bathrooms.

Chelsea jutted her thumb behind her with her eyes planted on her phone screen. "I'm inviting my sister, by the way."

Chelsea's little sister Elani. Every fight, Chelsea would invite her. Not once had Elani taken her up on the offer.

"Why do you do that to yourself, Chels? You know she hates the fights."

Chelsea let out a deep sigh, her eyes beaming with hope. "I don't care. I barely see her since she moved to Canada, and there *will* be two passes waiting for her at will call every time."

I lightly nudged her shoulder with my knuckle before heading for the bathrooms. As I was about to enter, Mars slid his arm past me, holding the door open. "What are you doing?"

"You truly don't get what the job of a bodyguard is, do you?"

"I have to use the restroom."

He cocked his head to one side. "You think you won't get attacked in a bathroom?"

"What if I have to do more than pee?"

He pressed his forearm on the doorframe above my head. "I guess we'll both have to get over it."

I growled, storming into the nearest stall and locking it behind me before he had a chance to crawl in the damn thing with me. I could hear him securing the main bathroom door.

Visible under the stall frame, his booted feet scuffed the floor. I sat with my pants around my knees. For the first time in my adult life, I had pissing anxiety.

"I can't do this with you in here, Mars." I slapped a hand over my face.

"Do you need me to hold your hand?"

I ground my teeth. "No. It's too quiet."

The sound of water flowing from every faucet of every sink echoed off the stall walls.

"Better, princess?"

I didn't answer and simply let the water flow. Once finished, I kicked the stall door open with enough force to make it bounce. He leaned against the counter with his burly arms crossed, a shit-eating grin stretching his lips.

"Not a word." I pointed at him and washed my hands.

He gave me a full smile, which made my stomach flip. I averted my gaze, busying myself with the blow dryer on my wet palms.

When we walked out, Chelsea stood in the same spot, with her phone covering her face. She glanced up only long enough to make sure it was us.

"If you take a nap, remember to set the alarm." She handed Mars, not me, room keys. "Weigh-in is at eight." Pressing the phone to her ear, she turned away. "Hello? Drew, hi."

"Yes, mother," I mumbled to myself.

The room was twice the size of the last one. Two king-sized beds nestled side by side with ornate red and gold comforters, each with equally decorated headboards. On one wall hung a painting of a knight in glistening armor. On the other, replica medieval swords crossed at the blades, secured to a shield.

"The middle ages," Mars grumbled. "Not the best period, but at least they still had the decency to fight with swords." He tossed my bag on the bed near the swords.

"What the hell are you talking about, weirdo?" I ran my finger down the hilt of one sword.

A bright light flashed over my eyes, and I was running in a forest. Glancing behind me, a horde of Greek soldiers neared. I took a knee, yanking an arrow from my quiver. Pulling the string back on my bow, I took one out with a blow to the head. The remaining three stormed after me, blades raised. I drew my sword, holding it with both hands, waiting for the opportune moment.

The same light flashed, and I stood in the hotel room. A sword was in my hand; the blade pointed at Mars's throat. His forearm pressed against mine, blocking my blow. My arms trembled, and I stepped back, dropping the weapon.

Mars caught it by the hilt with ease before it hit the carpet. "Is there something you want to tell me?"

I grabbed my head with both hands and backed up until I hit the nearest wall. "No."

With cautious movements, he rested the sword on the table, not moving his gaze away from me. "A dream was one thing. This is something else entirely."

"You'll think I'm insane."

He half-way sat on the table and interlaced his fingers on his lap. "Talk to me, gatáki."

"I—I get these weird flashes." I pinched the bridge of my nose.

"Of light? Or actual images?"

I pressed my fingertips against the wall behind me and met his gaze. "Not just images. Scenes. Moments. As if—as if I was there."

"And what do you see?" He stood; the intrigue evident on his face from the intensity in his stare.

I rolled my bottom lip past my teeth, trying to sort out my thoughts. "It started as quick glimpses or sounds. But it's always battles. Fighting."

"Battles with firearms? Grenades?" He rubbed his chin.

"No. Swords. Bow and arrows."

His face softened. "And this time, right now. Was it different?"

"It lasted longer." I stared at the sword. "And I *felt* like I was there. It wasn't me watching myself in a movie. I *was* me." Shaking my head, I flicked my hand. "I know this doesn't make any sense I—"

"You're not crazy, Harm," he interrupted. "How much do you know about your family's history?"

"I think you know the answer."

He nodded, his eyes drifting to stare at his boots. "Well, you're not crazy."

"I need to take a nap. I feel like shit." I toed off my shoes and fell onto the bed. "Ugh, I need to set the alarm." Pushing to my elbows, I sighed. Even the thought of getting up to grab my phone tired me out.

"I'll wake you up," Mars mumbled.

I peeked at him through the strands of my dark hair falling over my eyes. He concentrated on the floor, repeatedly running the tip of his thumb over his bottom lip. I sank to the bed and, within seconds, fell asleep.

"Harm," Mars's distant voice said.

I grumbled and turned on my side.

"Makos, get up. You're going to be late." He shook my shoulder.

I sat up, batting his arm away and striking my palm at his throat. He deflected my hand and forced it down. My eyes widened.

"That's the thanks I get for waking you up?" He let go.

His moves were lightning fast. I rubbed my wrist, expecting to see scorch marks on it or something. After palming the sleepiness from my eyes, I slid from the bed and begrudgingly got dressed, put on make-up, and made my hair presentable. When we left the room, Chelsea stood in the hallway, tapping her foot.

"Cutting it a little close, aren't we?" She looked between Mars and me.

Mars pointed at himself. "Don't look at me. She almost sucker-punched me in the neck."

Chelsea threw me an exasperated glare.

"Hey. He touched me while I was sleeping. I can't help it if he doesn't know the rules."

Mars shook his head before slipping his glasses on.

Chelsea eyeballed my face. "My God, Harm. Did you even *try* to cover up those bags under your eyes?" She dug into her purse, producing a compact. Dipping her finger into the powder, she dabbed my skin.

"This isn't necessary." I looked up to avoid her accidentally poking me in the eye.

"You always say that, and like always, I'm ignoring you." She fluffed my hair and took a step back. "There. Much better."

The same routine at yet another weigh-in—strip down, hop on the scale, and stand with your opponent. Unlike before, however, Mars managed to stay on stage and not intimidate every man who whistled.

Putting on my best mean mug, I held my fists up, posing with Kelly Fitz. Once the news crews took enough photos, we dropped our hands. I turned to walk away, but she grabbed my forearm.

"Your kind should've been eradicated," she said, a fire in her eyes.

I yanked my arm away, clenching my fists. "What did you just say?"

"What the hell are you talking about?" Kelly leaned back. "I didn't say anything."

Glancing around at the perplexed expressions on everyone else, I had no choice but to believe her. I pinched my eyes shut and shook my head.

Mars's hands slipped over my shoulders, coaxing me to the end of the stage.

"Harm, are you okay?" Chelsea asked as we passed her.

"I'm fine."

I rubbed my temples as we made our way out of the hotel ballroom and into the hallway. My thoughts were so jumbled I couldn't keep them straight. I made a beeline for the bathrooms, pausing at the door. Mars stopped right behind me.

"I don't need you in here. Seriously, there aren't even any windows."

He squared his shoulders. "We've talked about this."

"I need some fucking space, Mars." My head ached, and I fought back a wince.

Backing away, he threw his palms up. "Know what? Fine. But if something happens, don't cry to me about it." He turned away, mumbling in Greek.

Moving to the first stall, I plopped on the toilet seat. All I needed was a minute or two of peace—a moment to clear my head and let the dizziness fizzle away.

Holding my head in my hands, I concentrated on the buzzing from one of the overhead fluorescent lights. With each passing second, my brain calmed, and the world stopped spinning. I opened the stall door, expecting to see Mars standing there. When he wasn't, I frowned. Leaning on the sink, I turned on cold water, waiting for it to get icy. Splashing it on my face, I let the cold sting send a wave of calm down my spine. With eyes closed, I reached for a paper towel.

The sound of a foot shifting alerted me. My eyes flew open. A fist aimed at the back of my head, and I spun around, grabbing the arm and deflecting it into the mirror. Shattered glass fell across the counter and into the sinks. The attacker wore gloves, a bulky jacket, ski mask—judging from their gait and wide frame, I guessed it was a man.

He growled, and I dashed for the exit, but he slid in front of me. He threw a right hook, followed by a left, and moved forward. He threw the punches at such speed, I couldn't find a moment to go on the offense and just kept blocking his shots. My back hit the wall. He leaped at me, shoving his forearm into my throat. I kneed him in the sides but couldn't push him away.

The bathroom door swung open, bending the hinges. Mars. He snarled before closing the space between us in two strides. He grabbed the attacker, lifting him by the collar of his jacket. The attacker whimpered, punching at Mars's arm, his feet kicking, trying to find the floor. Mars's upper lip twitched, his eyes turned blood red, and he slammed the man into the tiled floor, cracking it.

The attacker shrieked. Mars pulled his fist back and hit him square in the face. His chest heaved, and he hit him again and again and again. I pushed off the wall, holding my hands out like I approached a lion tearing flesh from his meal. The attacker's face looked like cherry pie through the holes of the ski mask, and I knew one more punch…would be it.

"Mars." I kept my tone calm and even.

He whipped his head over his shoulder, glaring at me with his fist in mid-air, covered in the attacker's blood. Harsh breaths escaped his mouth, causing his cheeks to flap. I slid a hand on his forearm and slowly pushed it down. At first, he resisted, but then his snarl turned into a frown, and he let me pull him away.

"You don't need a life on your hands because of me," I whispered.

He stared at me, blinking, before letting go of the man's jacket and standing. It should've pissed me off he lost his cool. But something in my gut told me what just happened was part of a much bigger picture—a pain we both shared but didn't voice.

Now that he was calm…

I loomed over the attacker. "Who sent you?"

The man groaned, tilting his head left to right.

With a growl coiling from my gut, I dropped to my knees, grabbing the man's jacket and bringing his bloodied face to mine. "Who sent you?"

The man sputtered, sending red spackle against my cheek. A rage thundered inside, making my arms shake. Right as I went in for a head butt, Mars's arms circled my waist, and he dragged me away. I punched at his arms with a growl.

"What did you just say to me, Harm? Hm? We *both* need to get out of here."

I pulled at his arm one last time and went limp in his grasp.

His fingers curled under my chin, turning it to look at him. "We'll figure this out. But not now."

I nodded, the muscles in my arms still twitching.

He plucked a paper towel from the dispenser and dragged it over my cheek.

I turned for the exit. "Let's get out of here before someone walks in."

He reached a hand for the door handle, his knuckles caked with blood.

"Wait." I dropped my gaze to his stained skin.

He clenched his jaw and wrapped the same paper towel over his knuckles. We walked into the bathroom as two hardheads, forced together due to unforeseen circumstances. We left as two people with a shared secret and even *more* unshared ones.

NINE

~~~
[decorative Greek key border]
~~~

THE NEXT MORNING, I sat in one of the hotel room lounge chairs, not thinking about the fight hours away. A flash of the man's ski-mask kept torturing my thoughts. I hugged a knee to my chest, staring off into oblivion.

"He was a professional fighter," I muttered.

Mars set a Styrofoam cup of steaming coffee on the table before taking the seat opposite me. He took the lid off his coffee and blew on it. "How could you tell?"

"The way he moved." I cupped my hands around the warm cup, flicking my thumbnail against the groove at the top. "He was quick with calculated swings."

"It would make sense she'd hire another fighter to attack you. Anyone else wouldn't stand a chance."

I brightened. "Was that another compliment?"

"You said it yourself. You're good at what you do." His lip twitched like he wanted to smile but held back.

I creased my brow. "He could've killed me. He had me, Mars."

"Don't do that to yourself. You're alive."

"Because you were there. What if—" Tremors laced my voice, making it crack.

"Harm."

I dragged a shaky hand across my forehead.

He cocked his head to one side, face softening. "Is this more about him trying to kill you, or because you weren't the one to stop him?"

I opened my mouth and snapped it shut.

His glance dropped to the floor before returning to me. "There's no shame in fear. It's a driving force."

"I don't need a lecture."

"And I'm not a damn professor. You conquer fear by *doing* something about it. Your actions mold you. And I know you're a doer, Harm." He pierced me with his heated gaze.

I slid my pinky across my lips. "It pisses me off that I don't even know who tried to kill me."

Our dark eyes met, making my chest tighten.

"These things tend to have a way of working themselves out." He rested his cup on the table. "The whole ordeal started as an act of passionate revenge. They were bound to fuck up from the beginning."

"How would you know?"

He played with his ring, gaze falling to his palms. "I've seen it happen enough."

I took a swig of my coffee and looked at his knuckles—no cuts, no bruises. "You almost killed him."

"He pissed me off." He held up two fingers as I readied to retort. "I know it's no excuse, gatáki, but he got what he deserved."

I peeled away the mouthpiece of the coffee lid. "And if I pissed you off?"

His palm slid over my hand, making my breath hitch in my throat. "I'm not sure where you're going with that question, Makos, but I'd never hurt you."

I gave an absent nod, focusing on our fingers touching. It felt normal—like home. His eyes shot to his hand before he cleared his throat and pulled away.

"Chelsea can't know about it," I mumbled, sitting back and holding my cup with both hands.

"Care to tell me why?"

"If she knew someone tried to kill me, that the threat was real—" I sighed. "Christ, she might pull me from the tour. I *need* this, Mars." We stared at each other, welcoming the brief silence.

"Alright."

We went quiet, sipping our coffees and peering at each other.

I tapped my finger on the table, moving my gaze to his hand. "How's your hand?"

"Eh, it's fine." He showed me his palm and closed it into a fist. "I heal pretty quickly."

I snatched his hand, staring at his perfectly unharmed knuckles. He yanked it back with a growl.

"Are you *growling* at me?"

"Why'd you do that?"

I slapped the table. "Because there's stuff about you that doesn't add up. Every time I ask you certain things, you avoid answering."

He glared at me over the rim of his cup as he took a long swig. "You don't need to know everything, Harm. If it personally affects you, I'll tell you."

I huffed. "Convenient."

The conversation came to a screeching halt, and we sat still, slurping our coffees and looking anywhere else but at each other.

We'd been far too comfortable with quiet lately. I shot to my feet. "I need to swim. You want to swim?"

"Like I have a choice?"

"Good point. Lemme grab my suit."

After grabbing my red bikini from my suitcase, I slipped into the bathroom to change. I didn't always have access to a pool before a fight, but it helped warm up my muscles and relax them simultaneously. And it'd been way too long.

When I walked back out, Mars had his back turned as he slipped a pair of red and black board shorts over his hips. I was given a brief peek at the top of his muscular ass cheeks and had to grip the doorframe.

He cocked an eyebrow over his shoulder, his expression softening once his eyes roamed over my bikini-clad body. He turned around, tying up his shorts, and my gaze lingered on his chest. It was the second time he'd been half-naked, standing right in front of me, but now my feminine desires desperately tried to betray me.

I cleared my throat, wrapping one of the bath towels around myself, before tossing one at him. He caught it with one hand, watching me tighten my towel.

"You could at least cover your nipples for our walk over there." I slipped into my flip-flops and moved for the door.

He wrapped the towel around the back of his neck, holding it out to the sides as he strutted over to me. "My nipples, gatáki?"

My eyes drifted down, and his pecs bounced.

"What does gatáki mean anyway? Pissant or something?"

He gave a wry grin and let the towel fall over his chest, reaching past me to open the door. "Guess you'll never know."

I glared at him as he passed and walked into the hallway. Chelsea whisked by, paused, and backpedaled.

"Do you listen for the sound of my door opening? How the hell are you always here?" I asked.

She looked at my towel. "Pure coincidence. Are you going to the spa or something?"

I snort laughed. "Me? At the spa? Please. I'm going to do laps in the pool."

Mars stepped from behind me, and Chelsea's face reddened before she let out an obnoxious cackle. I slowly turned my head in her direction with a raised brow.

"Kaliméra, Chelsea," Mars said with a twinkle in his eye.

The cackle turned into a nervous giggle, and she played with the golden chain around her neck. "Well, you two have fun. I'm going to uh—call Tim and check in on him." She waved, turned on her heel, and jogged away.

"Chelsea can be weird, but that was downright odd," I muttered, watching her until she dove in after fumbling with her room key.

"She can't help it."

"She can't help get flustered around you?"

"Maybe it's my nipples."

"You're impossible." I bit back a smile.

When we got to the pool, every pair of female eyes stared at him—the two senior citizens sipping mimosas at a nearby table, a group of college-aged women, and a couple of mothers fumbling with arm floaties on their kids. I glared, not approving of the mysterious possessiveness boiling in my stomach.

Whipping off the towel, I jumped into the water, sputtering when I breached the surface. A shadow passed by me, splashing water at my face. Mars's head poked out, and he dragged a hand over his beard.

"You want to race?" I asked.

His gaze darkened. "Are you sure you can handle me?"

"Well, when you put it that way." I glared at him. "I have to beat you now."

He swished his arms under the water, the top part of his lip quirking. "You're on, Makos. But I don't want to hear any whining when you lose."

"First to the end and back."

"Just say when." His eyes flashed.

"When." I pushed my arms through the water.

It wasn't long before I saw him swimming beside me, matching stroke for stroke. It only fueled my speed. I fluttered my feet behind me until I felt the concrete at the other end of the pool against my fingers. Doing a flip, I pushed off the wall with my feet and started in the other direction. The opposite wall was soon an arm's length away.

So. Close.

A gust charged through the water, sending me in a spiral. Bubbles impeded my vision, and when I could finally see, Mars leaned on the far wall with a smirk on his face.

I smoothed my hair back. "Did you feel that?"

"Feel what?"

"There was an underwater tornado. How could you not feel it?"

"I've heard a lot of excuses for losing, but that's a bit extreme, don't you think?"

I rushed for the stairs. Each passing day became more confusing than the last—hearing things I shouldn't be hearing, dreaming stuff I shouldn't be dreaming, and now feeling unexplained motions underwater? I wrung my hair once I was out of the pool.

"Dear god. Who *is* that?" A woman sitting at a nearby table said. She ran her finger under the strap of her swimsuit.

Mars ran his hands over his head as he ascended the stairs. He pulled the rubber band from his hair, letting it fall in wavy, wet tendrils. The boardshorts clung to his lower half, droplets of water rolling over each piece of carved muscle. He had this sensual squint to his eyes as he shook his hair out.

"Do you do that on purpose?" I arched my back.

"Do what?" He slipped the rubber band over his wrist.

I stared at the piece of hair falling over his right eye and clenched my fist behind my back. "Nothing. Nothing. I need to get ready for the fight. My mind is one big jumble right now." Grabbing my towel, I headed for the exit.

The sound of Mars's heavy footsteps slapping against the

wet concrete followed me.

"It's getting old having to chase after you," Mars grunted.

I turned around with narrowed eyes. "You're a bodyguard. Don't tell me I'm the first unwilling participant."

He rolled his shoulders in silence.

"That's what I thought." I slammed my palm into the door.

He reached past me and pulled it shut. "You need to get your head clear. I know a lot has happened, but you go into the fight like this, you're going to lose."

"This isn't my first rodeo, slick." I glanced at his hand blocking my way before shooting an exasperated glare.

He let go, mumbling in Greek.

He followed me back to the room but kept a reasonable distance, not on my heels like normal. I resorted to drinking green tea while watching re-runs of *Friends* to ease the tension. If Chelsea had seen me, she would've lost her mind. Only in dire straits would you see me drinking tea. Mars brooded in a corner the entire time, not talking to me. Occasionally, I'd glance over to see if he smiled at Rachel or Joey's antics, but the same neutral expression would be there along with a furrowed brow.

I waited for the *Wonder Woman* music to play while bouncing on the balls of my feet in the wings. Chelsea attempted a pep talk and rubbed my shoulders several times before disappearing to her spot outside the cage. When the electric cello blared through the arena, I trounced forward, ready to defend my title for the third time. As I slipped into the ring, Mars caught my elbow.

"Clear. Your. Head. All it takes is one second—one moment of distraction. Forget about the attack yesterday, gatáki. Focus on *now*." Mars seethed at me over the rim of his glasses.

"I got it. I got it." I yanked my arm away.

He shook his head, backed up, and folded his arms.

I stared at my opponent as we came to the center to bump gloves. No sooner had they told us to fight, I threw a punch. I wanted it done—quick and to the point. She dodged it with ease and side shuffled away. I advanced, attempting to clip her when given the opportunity. Flashes of Mars beating the attacker's face washed over my brain, overlapping us in ancient Greece standing side by side on the battlefield.

Her fist clipped my chin, warping me back to the present moment. I shook my head. The taste of iron coated my lips. I held my fists up, but not as high as before.

Why did running through that forest feel *so* real? I could smell the pine and my own sweat. *Feel* the adrenaline as a band of soldiers chased me.

She clipped me again straight in the nose. I tripped onto one knee but pushed myself up with a sniffle, falling back on the cage behind me. She continued to shimmy around the ring, only stopping long enough to hit me.

I snarled under my breath, staggering forward. The two hits made my vision blur. As I chased her, desperation fueled my swings. With every throw, I knew they'd only meet dead air.

How was his hand unharmed? Even wearing gloves, I'd gotten bruises during a fight.

She threw a hook. I caught it but lost my footing. Her shoulder nudged me, and I fell to a knee, stumbling back to standing. When I turned around to face her, her foot slammed into my face. Starbursts exploded across my eyes, and I fell to the ground in a slump. Cheers and boos echoed through the arena, muffling in my ears. I lay on my back, unable to sit up.

Mars's face dipped into mine, and he patted my cheek. "Makos. Sit up."

He wore a Spartan helmet with a red plume. I touched the side of his head. "Why are you wearing a helmet?"

He squinted. "Come on, Amazon. Get up." His words were a command, and he hoisted me to sit up.

At first, I didn't keep steady until I felt the warmth of his palm on my back.

"I lost, didn't I?" I needed to hear it from him.

"You can get it back." He stood, bringing me with him. Wrapping his hands around each of my hips to stabilize me, he waited until I stopped wavering to let go.

I moved next to the woman who defeated me and forced my chin to lift. My sinuses stung as I watched the belt wrapping around her waist. She hugged me, the salt from her happy tears burning the cut on my cheek. I patted her back before turning away and storming for the exit.

"Harm." Chelsea fluttered after me. Her loose auburn curls bounced with each step. "You can win it back."

I froze and pointed at her. "I shouldn't have lost it in the first place." Spying Mars prowling after me from the corner of my eye, I turned away.

I'd lost because my head wasn't in the right space. Mars was right. But he was the reason for my mind being anywhere but the here and now.

TEN

I STORMED TO THE locker room with Chelsea and Mars trailing behind me. My palms slammed into the door, and Chelsea glided in, but I stopped Mars.

"If a guy tries to attack me right now, I'd rip off his testicles. I'll be fine for five minutes." A growl surrounded my words.

Mars scratched the back of his head. "Yeah, I'll uh—I'll be right outside."

Letting the door shut, I swooped to the locker and tore off my fighting attire, throwing them straight into the garbage— clothes I'd lost in.

"Harm," Chelsea squeaked.

"You know what I need to do right now, Chels. I haven't lost in years. *Years.*" I yanked my jeans, shirt, and jacket from their hangers. "I had the championship. And I blew it."

Chelsea clasped her hands under her chin. "I do know what you need to do right now, and I'm not trying to stop you. But, with the threat, is it best to be in public like that?"

I finished buttoning my jeans and threw the leather jacket over my shoulders. "If they somehow survive my right hook, I have a brooding flesh wall as a shadow. Remember?"

"Right." The skin between her eyes creased.

Flicking my hair from the jacket's collar, I whipped the door open. As promised, Mars stood right behind it, leaning on a wall. He pushed off as I passed, but I wasn't stopping for anyone.

"Go with her, please. She's going to wherever the nearest bar is." The concern in Chelsea's tone was evident.

"Is that the best idea?" Mars's voice gruff.

"No. But I wouldn't recommend trying to dissuade her." Her heels quickened until the sound lingered behind me.

"Harm, there's going to be dozens of cell phones. Phones mean photos. Just promise to keep your shirt on." Chelsea stopped following at the door.

"Can't promise anything."

"She'll keep it on," Mars grunted as he passed her.

I clenched my fists as I walked to the bar across the hotel parking lot.

"Going to drown your fears, Makos?"

I whipped around to face Mars. He stood with his arms crossed, squinting at me.

"Fear? You think this is fear? I'm furious." I could feel the veins bulging from my neck and forehead.

The squint turned into a glare, and he dropped his hands at his sides. "You know nothing of true fury, Amazon. The sooner you can face the fact that you're afraid your loss will ruin your career, the sooner you can *do* something about it. Remember what I said earlier?"

I ground my teeth together, not willing to admit he was spot on. "Whatever the case may be, a revelation isn't happening tonight."

"I can train you." He didn't follow me as I power walked across the parking lot.

"Excuse me?"

"You're good. Very good. But I can make you the best."

I clucked my tongue against the inside of my cheek. "And you think you're qualified?"

"Beyond qualified." His stare burned into my skin, reeling me in.

I looked away with a flick of my wrist. "I don't have time for this."

Turning on my heel, I walked into the bar. The familiar smells of beer, stale corn nuts, and varying body fragrances hit me like a slap to the face. Music made ambient noise amidst the dozens of conversations, laughter, and shouts at a TV in the corner playing a basketball game.

Several pairs of eyes turned to us as I headed for the bar. Whether they were looking at me or Hulk behind me, I could care less.

The bartender raised his brows. It was clear he recognized me. If he knew what was best for him, tonight of all nights, he'd pretend I was someone else.

"What can I get you?" The bartender tossed a towel over his shoulder.

Good man.

"Jack. Neat. Make it a double. And keep them coming."

Mars sighed as he leaned his forearms on the bar top next to me.

"Are you going to drink with me or be the wet blanket I assume you are?" I tapped my fingernails against the wood.

He grumbled. "I'll have one, maybe two."

"Make that two," I said to the bartender.

"Well, well, well," a man's voice purred behind us.

Mars's gaze flicked upward. "Vlákas."

A man with wavy dark hair sprigged with blonde streaks leaned back in a chair, legs spread wide. He held a bottle of beer by its neck between two fingers. The deepened smirk on his face made his eyes squint.

"Mars, do you know him?"

Mars motioned at the bartender to hurry our order. "Technically, he's my brother. *Half*-brother."

"Mars?" The man laughed, folding his free arm over his bearded mouth. He wore a linen shirt with the buttons undone far enough to peek at his terra-cotta-colored chest. "That's what you're going by nowadays?"

Mars's finger tapped harshly against the bar.

The bartender set our tumblers in front of us, and I snatched one, downing it and circling my hand for another before the tender could walk away.

"Allow me to introduce myself," the man said with a devious glint in his eye. "The name's Dion." He extended his hand.

I peeked at Mars. He didn't look like he wanted to kill him. It had to be a decent sign, so I quickly shook his hand. "Harm."

Dion grinned, making his light brown eyes narrow. "Harm. Nickname?"

"Something like that."

His eyebrows rose when I turned back to the bar, looking for the tender.

"Not going to elaborate?" Dion chuckled.

I held my hand out for the tumbler as he came back. "None of your business."

"Oh, Mars, my brother, I like her." Dion shook Mars's shoulder. Mars shrugged him off with a grunt.

I downed the whiskey again and slid it across the bar top, signaling for another.

"I *really* like her," Dion added, slapping Mars on the back.

Mars spun around, and chest bumped Dion. They stood the same height, but Mars's body looked wider. At least what I could tell with both of them wearing so many clothes. Shame.

"Don't even think about it." Mars pointed a finger in his face.

Dion fake gasped. "Whatever do you mean? Your girl here looks as if she likes to have a good time. Something I *know* you're horrible at. So—" He reached past me and held a hand up to the bartender.

The bartender tried to mask his obvious annoyance as he walked back over for the fourth time in thirty minutes. "Yes?"

Dion slapped a gold credit card and slid it to him. "Bring over the bottle and a couple of glasses. Her drinks are on me all night."

My jaw dropped. "I can't let you do that."

"Why don't you beat it, Dion? She already came in here to

get drunk. The last thing she needs is your…influence," Mars snapped.

There he went assuming he knew what I needed again.

"I'm perfectly capable of making my own decisions."

Mars let out an exasperated sigh, eyes lifting to the ceiling.

"I'll take you up on your offer, Dino." I poured him a glass.

Dino…that was his name, right?

Dino opened his mouth like he was about to say something but snapped it shut with a grin. He tilted his head back and finished the bottle of beer before slamming it down on the bar, taking the whiskey I offered him.

"Cheers," I said.

Dino's eyes shifted toward the jukebox just as the song *War* by Edwin Starr played.

"Yámas." Dino clanked his glass against mine.

Mars fumed.

Five drinks later…

"Okay, okay, okay, let me get this straight, Dino." I raised a finger.

Dino rested his elbow on the bar top and his cheek against his hand. "Mm?" He grinned at Mars over my shoulder.

"The woman was trapped in a locked closet by her own son? Why?"

"Let's just say she wasn't very nice to Heph. Now, this is where the story gets extra interesting."

"I think you've told enough," Mars growled.

I reached a hand behind me and pushed a finger against Mars's lips. His coarse beard brushing my fingertips made my toes curl inside my shoes. Dino's smile widened.

"Dozens of people tried to get the door open, but nothing worked. Her son, the one who trapped her, refused to help," Dino continued.

My hand slid from Mars's mouth, catching on his bottom lip, a bit of saliva coating my finger. "But that's so mean."

"He had his reasons. Anyway, so Mars here, this was his mother too, tried to talk Heph into opening the door."

"Wait a minute. Hold the phone." I waved my arms back and forth. "You two are brothers, but you weren't a brother to this other brother?"

Dino looked skyward, pointing his finger in several directions as if replaying my words. "Precisely. Mars and I share the same dad."

"Ah, the manwhore. Got it. Continue."

Mars sighed. "Can I get another whiskey?" He flagged the bartender.

"Now, keep in mind Mars's mother hated me. I was, after all, yet another product of her husband's infidelity. And Mars couldn't convince his own brother to free their mom." Dino bit back a laugh.

I wasn't finding the story to be as amusing as Dino let on. Judging by the scowl on Mars's face, neither did he. Mars shoved his nose into his glass, sipping, his hand tightening around it with each passing word from Dino.

"But I did," Dino concluded.

I cocked a brow. "You convinced his brother to free her? How?"

He poked a finger against my whiskey with a devious smile.

"You got him drunk?"

"Yup. He had the key on him the whole time."

I did one slow blink. "Well, shit."

"The real kicker? The 'ol stepmom and my dad invited me to live in their uh…mansion." He wiggled his eyebrows, peering at Mars behind me.

"You're an asshole," Mars grumbled into his glass.

They disowned Mars…

I turned in my stool, raising my hand near Mars's arm, but Dino shoved another whiskey glass in it instead.

"Let's get back to a lighter note, shall we?" Dino asked with a shimmy of his hips. "You drink. I'll be right back." He patted my back and walked past us, thrusting his arms out to his sides while walking toward a group of women.

"Chelsea is my only friend. My only friend is my goddamned publicist," I blurted, snorting into my glass.

Mars leaned his elbows on the bar next to me. "Do you think I have many friends?"

"I mean—" I bit back a smile. "I didn't want to assume or anything."

He chuckled and slid an inch closer. "Tell me why you're a loner."

"Seems a little one-sided. Quid pro quo?"

He gave a single nod.

"I don't trust people. Plain and simple." My words started to slur.

"That's hardly an answer, gatáki. You want me to answer something? You're gonna have to give me more."

I swirled the liquid in my glass. "Anyone I ever loved let me down. To let someone in equals hurt in my eyes. It's easier mentally, emotionally to go it alone."

He canted his head to one side and said nothing.

"I'm going to ask you one question, and then we're taking this serious party in another direction. Deal?" I swigged back more whiskey.

"I'm on the edge of my seat," he replied monotone.

I slammed the glass down. "You said you have a lot on your shoulders. 'Splain."

"Family. Life. Work. You name it. I tend to keep things bottled in." He knocked his knuckles on the bar.

"You don't say," I mocked, slapping him on the shoulder with a goofy grin.

He half-smiled, glancing at his shoulder before meeting my eyes.

I slid off my stool. His hand shot out, gripping my hip to steady me.

"My knight in shining armor," I cooed before snickering.

He pushed me back to the comfort of my seat. "You know what I want to say, right?"

I waved the empty bottle at the bartender. "That I should think about not drinking anymore for the night. But you won't say it because you don't want to step on my toes."

"Pretty insightful for a drunk woman."

The bartender set the bottle down with a knowing smile. I poured some in my glass, watching the liquid slosh around. "I think I get smarter with alcohol in my system."

"Uh-huh." Mars shook his head.

Dino appeared behind us, hanging his arms over our shoulders. "You two need to bone and get it over with.

Watching you is making my neck tense."

"Get tired of your hen house?" I took another sippy sip.

He let out a deep, raspy chuckle. "Why are you hanging out with this stick in the mud, hm?" Dino pointed at Mars with his beer-holding hand.

"He's not half bad. I'm pretty sure he's not even human." I burped.

Both of their faces went blank.

I snorted, almost shooting whiskey out of my nose. "Holy balls, you two, I'm kidding."

"You know what the hilarious thing is?" Dino's lips took a devious upturn.

Mars stood straight and glared at him.

Dino leaned in, looking at Mars, moving his lips near my ear. "He's not."

I stared at Mars.

Dino and I burst into a fit of laughter.

"Fége apo ethó." Mars's nostrils flared.

Dino flashed his palms and ran a hand through his wild mane of waves. "You two kids have fun."

As soon as Dino left, I reached forward, hooking Mars's chains with my finger. "How does a girl go about getting these beads?"

His brows shot up, and he panned his eyes to my roaming hand. "Those are chains."

"Potato. Tomato."

He continued to stare at me like I was a cyclops.

I sighed and dropped the chain. "You *are* no fun."

"I can be." He flagged the bartender. "When the situation

allows it."

"When you're not babysitting me, you mean?" I stuck my bottom lip out.

He tapped the tip of my nose with his finger. "Cheese sticks, please," he said to the bartender.

"Cheese sticks?"

"What's wrong with them?"

"Nothing. I expected you to order mini burgers or something. I don't know." I reached for the rubber band in his hair.

He leaned back, blocking my hand like I'd been about to slap him. "What are you doing?"

"I wanted to see you with your hair down."

"Really?" He raised a brow.

I bit down on my bottom lip and nodded.

He reached his hands behind him and paused. "You're not going to pull it, are you?"

I made a crisscross gesture over my heart. "Promise. Or my name's not Harmony Makos."

His eyes brightened as he pulled the band away, letting his dark hair fall in a perfect frame around his face. "Your name is Harmony?"

My breath hitched as I reached forward to run my fingers through the wavy tendrils. "Did I say that out loud?"

He peered down at my fingers, his face softening. "Yes."

"Whoops." I beamed.

"One steaming plate of cheese sticks," the tender said, resting it between us.

I focused on Mars's disgustingly gorgeous hair. A man

shouldn't be allowed to have hair like that, but it suited him so damn well. Mars reached for a cheese stick, keeping his gaze on me as he bit half of it, resting the other half back on the plate.

Reaching for my own cheese stick, I grabbed the half Mars put back, and popped it in my mouth.

"You realize you ate the one I ate?" He half-smiled.

I paused and shrugged. "You said it yourself. We've already swapped spit."

"How could I forget." He leaned forward, dragging his non-greasy hand through his hair. Grabbing another stick, he popped the whole thing in his mouth.

Once we finished the entire plate, I gasped at its familiar shape. I yanked it off the table and held it vertically. "Oh my god, it looks like a chakram."

"You're not going to thr—"

I swung my arm back. "Ayiyiyi!"

Mars caught the plate mid-swing and set it back on the bar. "Calm down there, Xena, or you'll take someone's eye out with this thing."

"My aim's not that bad." I shifted my eyes. "Sober."

"Uh-huh."

"Fine." I threw my hand up.

"Fine…what?"

"You can train me, I guess."

He pointed at the plate, then back at me. "Because of the plate?"

"Because you're like the best MMA fighter ever or something." I halfway stuck my tongue out.

"You're like a cat with a shiny bauble when you're drunk," he said through a deep chuckle.

I gasped. "Have you ever seen the movie *Coyote Ugly*? No. Probably not. But I've always wanted to do it!"

"Do—"

I climbed onto the bar.

"—what. Harm, what are you doing?"

Standing on top of the bar, I ignored the bartender's protests and threw my hands in the air. "Dancing."

Dino sat in the corner, his grin spread wide and gave me a thumbs up. *Shape of You* by Ed Sheeran played in the background. It wasn't exactly my type of song, but anything with a melody would suit me right now just fine.

Mars gazed up at me with the sternest face I'd seen on him yet. His hands kept flying up with each of my wobbles, ready to keep me from falling on my ass. I called him many things, but honestly, he was a nice guy when you stripped him down. *It* down?

After a couple of hip sways, I slipped my hands under my shirt, lifting it. Mars reached up and yanked it back down.

"Alright, Amazon, I'm cutting you off. Come on, let's go." He motioned with his hand for me to jump down.

"But Mars," I whined.

"Yeah, Mars, let her do what she wants," a random man sitting at the bar said.

Mars pointed at him with a snarl. "You're lucky she's my number one concern right now."

Before I had a chance to say "Bob's Your Uncle," Mars had me over his shoulder, fireman style. From this angle, I had a fabulous view of the rounded hunks of flesh that made up his ass. Dino waved at me as we neared the door, and my stomach gurgled.

Oh, boy.

Don't puke. Whatever you do. Don't. Puke.

He set me down in the parking lot, and I clamped my hands over my mouth.

His eyes bulged out of his skull. "Are you going to—"

I shook my head frantically with my hands still on my face and took a deep breath. "I'm fine. I'm fine."

Walking was another matter entirely. I took a step forward and stumbled, tripping over my own feet with a giggle. He scooped me up and threw one of my arms over the back of his neck. His one hand was inches from my boob, while the other cradled my legs.

"Thank you, my Sparkly Snicker-doo." I buried my face in his hair.

"Sparkly?" His voice sounded deeper through his chest.

I snickered. "I don't even know what I'm saying anymore."

In the short walk from the parking lot to our hotel room, I fell asleep, only waking up when I felt the softness of a pillow against my cheek. Mars turned off the light and moved about as if trying to keep quiet as a mouse.

I grabbed his arm. "Stay with me."

"Stay with you?"

"Mmhmm. Right here." I pointed to my back.

He cleared his throat, and I felt the bed dip. "Alright."

His warmth pressed to my back, hips resting against my butt. He curled one leg between mine and wrapped his burly arms around me. I never realized how safe one man's touch could feel. He rested his head behind mine on the pillow, and his nose brushed my neck.

"Thanks, Mars," I cooed.

His breath shuddered over my ear. "My real name…is Ares."

"Like the zodiac sign?" I yawned.

"No." His whiskers tickled the skin behind my ear. "The God of War."

I smiled. "If you were the God of War, it'd make a lot of sense." Sleep pulled at my brain.

"I am," he whispered.

ELEVEN

SUNLIGHT BURST THROUGH THE singular crack in the curtains, stinging my eyes. I buried my face in the pillow with a groan. Memories of last night poured through my mind like water let loose from a dam. Mars's brother Dino. Whiskey. The song *Shape of You*, for some reason? Wait. Did I call Mars a Sparkly Snicker-doo? The familiar scent of leather and burnt wood plagued the sheets. I slowly lifted my head, peering at the empty spot beside me.

What a relief.

A rounded imprint in the shape of a shoulder embedded in the mattress stared back at me—a *big* shoulder.

Oh, dear God.

The door creaked open, and I grabbed a pillow, clutching it to my chest like I'd been caught naked. My heart thumped against my ribcage as I took one last glance at the bed.

"You're up." Mars walked in holding two coffees and a

brown paper bag with grease-stained corners.

I winced, shoving my palm to my forehead. "Would you not talk so loud?"

"I practically whispered." He walked to the bed, holding the bag out to one side.

I slid a finger over his lips. The feel of his beard brushing over my skin shot another memory of performing the same action last night, making my stomach clench.

These fractals of remembrance were going to happen at the most inopportune moments. I was sure of it.

I grabbed one of the coffees and rested my arms on my knees, removing the lid to let the steam moisten my nose. "Um. Thank you. For the coffee mostly, but uh—thanks for letting me not die in a gutter or something last night."

"If you would've died in a gutter, gatáki, I wouldn't get paid." He half-smiled. "But you're uh—you're welcome."

Glad that was over.

I sipped the warm liquid, relishing in the heat traveling down my throat, warming my belly.

He tossed the bag on the nightstand. "You should eat."

"I'll pass." Even looking at the bag made my stomach turn.

He shook his head and uncrumpled the brown paper. "I know this isn't your first hangover. Stop being stubborn."

"You are *so* not one to lecture me on that particular subject."

He removed a bagel—an "Everything" bagel, my favorite. When he took out a small container of strawberry cream cheese, I whimpered.

He watched me as he spread the cheese on one half with perfectly proportionate schmear. "Are you sure you don't want some?"

I bit my lower lip. My stomach wanted to eat it as much as it wanted to vomit. I wish it'd make up its mind.

He tossed the plastic knife into the bag and held the bagel out to me. The smell of strawberries and grain made me pine for it even more. When I didn't budge, his shoulders slumped with a sigh.

He sat on the edge of the bed and held the bagel to my lips. "Eat, gatáki."

Our eyes fixed on each other as I took a bite. A tingle coursed down my neck, settling in my chest. His expression softened before the skin above his nose creased as if he were confused. I chewed on the bit of bagel in my mouth with the speed of a sloth, staring at him. His fingertip dragged over the corner of my mouth, ridding it of cream cheese. A glint flashed in his gaze as he brought the finger to his lips, licking it away.

"It. Good," I managed to say, sounding like a cavewoman.

"What's the last thing you remember from last night?"

I swallowed my bite of bagel, trying not to choke on it. After sipping coffee to wash it down, I pinched my eyes shut—a view of his ass from upside down. That was the last thing I remembered. "Were you…fireman carrying me?"

"You were dancing on the bar and about to start a striptease. It called for drastic measures."

Groaning, I dragged a hand over my face.

He brought the bagel to my lips, urging me to take another bite. The act of him feeding me, not caring I refused to take the food in my own hand, enthralled me as much as it scared me. Still, I bit.

"You don't remember walking back to the room? And—after?" He pierced me with his stare.

My throat tightened. After? What happened after? I rubbed my lips together, concentrating on the sweet residue from the cream cheese, and shook my head.

His gaze dropped, and so did his hand with the bagel. He grunted as he stood and turned away. "Well, we better get a move on...*Harmony*."

My neck went numb. "How the hell do you know that?"

He bent forward, pushing his palms against his knees with a wry grin. "You told me. Last night." His finger flicked a crumb from the corner of my mouth.

"I was drunk. It didn't count, so forget I ever said it."

"Not a chance."

Heat prickled my cheeks, and I clambered off the bed in a huff. As I whirled around the room like a sandstorm, he leaned on the wall, folding his arms and grinning.

"I told you my real name," he said.

I froze mid-way to shoving underwear in a side pocket. "What?"

"You heard me."

With the underwear still in my hand, I strode over. "Tell me again. You know mine."

"One little problem." He held up a finger. "A woman once said to me, if it's said while drunk, it doesn't count." His lips took a villainous curl.

My eyes narrowed into slits. He pushed off the wall and stood next to me, pressing his hip against my ribs. The proximity made my head race.

"Cute undies." He slid on his sunglasses.

The ball was completely and utterly in his court. The worst part was…he knew it.

"Let's go, Amazon. We've got training to do." He bumped his back into the door.

I forced the rest of my clothes into my bag and slung it over my shoulder. "Training?"

"Uh-huh. You agreed to it last night." He held the door open for me with his booted foot. "Not letting you waddle your way out this one, though, gatáki. You would've agreed to it eventually anyway."

Good Lord. What else did I agree to last night? Selling my soul?

The sun burned my eyes. "Ugh. I'm never drinking again."

"You people always say it, but never mean it." He twirled the fob key in his palm.

"You people?"

He tensed. "People. Humans. Us."

If it weren't for the car's pristine cleanliness catching my attention, I might have pried further into that remark.

"Did you wash the rental car? Who does that?"

He opened the door and peered at me over the rim of his Aviators. "I figured you'd appreciate not having dried vomit on your door."

I blinked. And here I thought I remembered making it to the room successfully, *not* puking. "But how—the bar was across the parking lot." My mouth formed a tiny "o" as I tried to piece it together.

"You somehow managed to stumble over it when we were

walking. At least it was ours, and not someone else's, right?" His bright smile shined in contrast to his dark beard.

It took a lot to embarrass me, but my cheeks burned nonetheless. I whipped open the door and flopped into the passenger seat, curling a hand over my eyes.

He crawled in with a chuckle. "Happens to the best of us."

Something in my gut told me it never happened to *him*.

I focused out the window. "Just drive, Spartan." My neck stiffened.

"Spartan?"

My mind became one big mess of flutters, and I pointed at the steering wheel. "It's the right pedal. Drive."

He didn't move for a beat, and then the car pulled away.

Tapping my hands on my knees, I shifted my eyes, hesitant to ask the burning question. "So…last night."

"Yes?" A hint of a smirk tugged at his lips.

This bastard was going to make me flat out ask.

"Did we—I mean, I woke up, and it looked like you had been—"

"We slept together." He kept his focus in front of him and sniffed once.

My heart fell to my feet, and my stomach did several swirls. "We did?"

He rubbed his chin. "Too bad you don't remember, huh? Didn't seem to have any complaints, though."

On the one hand, mortification twisted my insides like a sponge. On the other, I really did hate I couldn't remember it.

He pulled his sunglasses to the tip of his nose. "Calm down, gatáki. All we did was exactly that. Sleep."

"You spooned with me?"

He used his forefinger to push the Aviators back up. "Mmhm."

I think I preferred us to have had sex—far less intimate in the grand scheme of things. "Why?"

"You asked me."

My mouth opened, but no words followed. A vibration went off in my back pocket, and I grabbed my phone.

"Good God. Ten missed calls and fourteen texts from Chelsea," I mumbled, pressing on her face to dial her number.

"Harm! What the actual fuck?" Her voice screamed through the earpiece.

I held it away from my face, grimacing. "Didn't realize I had a curfew, Chels."

"You were supposed to get drunk, not fall off the face of the planet."

"Usually, those two coincide for me."

I peeked at Mars, who half grinned.

"Did you at least get back to the hotel alright?"

I leaned my head back. "You hired the bodyguard. What do you think? I even managed to keep my shirt on. You should be proud."

Mars turned to look at me, and I shrugged.

"Are you in the car?" Chelsea asked.

"Yeah, we're—" I lowered the phone and focused on Mars. "Where the hell are we going?"

"My gym."

"*Your* gym? You own a gym? Who *are* you?" I scrunched my nose at him before getting back with Chelsea. "We're going to

Mars's gym. To train."

"Well, that's development. I'll meet you there in a few hours. Got some news."

Her tone didn't sound as chipper as I would've liked. "Bad news?"

"See ya in a bit, Harm." She hung up.

I sighed. It was definitely bad news.

"You're doing it again," Mars said with extra gruff.

"What now?"

"Focusing on the negative."

I pulled the seatbelt away from my chest and turned fully in my seat. "And you don't? I can tell you're always one wrong move or one misinterpreted sentence away from exploding."

He scratched his chin like a wolf. "You're not wrong, but there's a big difference between you and me."

I raised my brow, waiting for an answer.

"I *am* negativity," he growled, fishtailing the car into the gym parking lot.

The turn jolted my body backward, slamming it against the seat. Without missing a beat, he cut the engine, opened the door, shut it, and walked across the empty lot.

Ticking. Bomb.

The sign read in big, bold lettering: The Bulldog. A snarling black bulldog's face glared down over the entrance.

"How'd you come up with the name?" I held back a gasp once he flipped the lights on.

It was a gym fit for The Karate Kid. Every inch had a mat except for the areas with bench presses or other weight machines.

"I like dogs." He tore his jacket off, tossing it in a corner.

Back to four words or fewer sentences. Lovely.

He'd disappeared into the back and returned with a folded set of sweats, handing them to me.

"So, you live in Santa Fe?" I ran a finger over the bulldog logo on the front of the sweat pants.

"Vlákas, no. My manager does. I'm hardly ever here." He pointed to the back. "You can change back there. Meet me on the center mat."

He'd taken on a more commanding personality—one which demanded respect and knew its authority. I wasn't sure whether to be annoyed or strangely turned on by it. After slipping into the sweats, I met him on the mat. He tossed me a padded sparring helmet.

I furrowed my brow. "Seriously?"

"No gloves. I'm actually going to clip you. What good will it do you to practice choreography? You need the real deal—a consequence for missing a block."

There was no "try" in his statements. A tad unnerving.

"Alright. I'll play it your way." I slipped the helmet on, rolled my shoulders, and lifted my fists.

He circled me with the glazed stare of a predator with its prey. I remembered the same intensity in his eyes during the MMA fight, but I hadn't been as close to experiencing it. He launched his right fist. I blocked it with my forearm and countered with a left jab.

He dodged it. "Good."

The padded helmet pressed into my forehead, reminding me to avoid getting hit. He lunged, faking a right hook. I almost fell for it but pulled back, focusing on his left. He kicked me in the ass instead.

I grunted, ignoring the sting. Leaping forward, I gritted my teeth and threw a barrage of punches. One left hook. A right one. Jabs. Uppercuts. We looked like a Bruce Lee movie. Mars's brow pinched, eyes not moving from mine. He grabbed my arm mid-swing, spun us around, and grazed the side of my head with his elbow.

Even with padding, it hurt like a motherfucker.

"Half of that was damn sloppy, Makos. You started solid and got desperate. Focus." He pointed down, making his tattooed forearm bulge.

His words annoyed me, but I let it slide. Flashes of the battlefield pulsed in my mind. Unlike before, they didn't make me stagger or fall to my knees—they propelled me. I threw swings I'd never thrown, moving across the mat with the grace of sliding over a frozen lake. He couldn't hide the expression of shock with his slightly parted lips.

I jumped with my fist held back. His chin shot up, and as I came down, his arms enveloped my waist, and he pulled me to the ground. I waited for the harsh impact of the mat on my back, but instead, his hands gripped mine, holding me inches from falling. He stared at me with narrowed eyes before yanking me back to standing.

"New moves?" He cocked an eyebrow.

I wiped my clammy palms over my thighs. "Trying something new, yeah."

"Do it again." He backpedaled. "Only this time, I'm not going to go so easy on you."

My stomach clenched. The flashes didn't come this time. The same drive I'd felt moments ago flourished into an urge to win. I fought with the same intensity I always did, even managed to tag Mars's ear, which incited a growl.

"Lucky shot. Be careful, though. You're getting sloppy again," he said, lifting his knee at my chest.

Throwing my forearms in a cross pattern, I deflected his knee down. He spun on his heel, sending a roundhouse kick. I blocked it, but it knocked me off balance. Kick. Punch. Kick. Kick.

"Get off the defense, Makos. Hit. Me," he roared.

I cried out as I threw all I had at his chest. His hands caught my foot with lightning speed.

"Why are you taking this so seriously?" I yanked myself from his grasp.

He kept hold. "War is nothing *but* serious."

"I'm not going to war, Mars. It's a goddamned cage fight."

"And that's why you're not the best." He let go of my foot, lifting both hands.

I scoffed, letting my foot land on the mat with a *thwack*. "What the hell does that mean?"

"It takes passion fighting in a war—a passion for winning. You spend every day fighting an internal battle with yourself when the resolution is in that ring. *That* is your battle to win the war."

I tore the helmet off.

How could such a brute be so poetic?

"Let's try something else," he said, walking away.

He came back with two wooden swords, swinging one

around with a flick of his wrist. He tossed the other to me, and I caught it in one swift motion, throwing it from palm to palm.

"Swords? I've never fought with one. I think the only sword I've ever held was a fake replica of the *Braveheart* sword."

"That's a claymore, which is a tad larger. These are Greek. Xiphos, to be exact."

The way he said the word "xiphos" made my stomach flip over itself.

"Normally, you'd use this as a secondary to your javelin, but since you fight in close-quarters at all times, these will work."

I looked at the blade. "How is this going to translate to MMA?"

"The same rules apply. And you have a lot more to lose as much as to gain when fighting with a sword. A punch could equal a slash to a pertinent artery or cutting off a limb." He slashed the blade back and forth, making a figure-eight pattern in the air between us.

My heart thudded against my ribs. It looked so natural to him—effortless.

"I don't know the first thing about sword fighting."

"Go with your gut instinct, gatáki. It's why you're training with me." He didn't let me stew on it any longer, stepping forward with a downward strike.

I flung my arms up like an orangutan and somehow managed to block his blade with mine. A new-found spring formed in my step, and I pushed his sword away. He cocked his head to the side and swung at my neck. I ducked, countering with a slash to his leg, hitting it.

He looked down and then lifted his eyes with a mix of anger and intrigue. Every slice of my sword, he'd duck, dodge, or parry. I went for his leg again, but he flicked his foot up, turning away on his opposite heel. He swung his blade to my left side. I dodged, and he quickly countered to the right. I grabbed his forearm, forcing it out of the way, and brought my sword down, stopping at his neck.

My chest heaved, gazing down at my wooden blade pressing into Mars's skin.

"I thought you said you've never fought with swords before?" His gaze was like a lion circling his mate.

I expected him to be pissed I'd gotten the better of him. But the way his pupils dilated, his breathing matching the heaviness of my own, I ventured to say he wanted to kiss me or…more. "I haven't."

"Am I interrupting something?" Chelsea stood at the entrance.

The corner of Mars's jaw bobbed, and he cracked his neck before turning away. I kept the sword in the air for a moment, still stunned over my performance.

"We were sparring," I answered.

"I can see that. With swords, no less. Interesting choice."

Mars rubbed his bicep. "I feel more at home with a blade in my hand. Apparently—" He looked at me over his shoulder. "So does she."

"Maybe you're in the wrong profession, Harm." Chelsea whipped out her tablet, not bothering to take her purse off.

"Hit me with it already." I twirled the sword in my hand.

Mars watched me, combing his fingers through his beard.

"There's no pulling the wool over your eyes. I have bad news and good news. Bad news first?"

"Whatever." I posed with the sword above my head before pointing the tip down and slicing the air with it.

Mars's stare turned feral, and he widened his stance.

"Three people have pulled out of their matches with you. They only want to go for the title." Her bright eyes stared at me, unblinking.

I made a tsk sound. "Saw that coming. What could possibly be good news?"

"The owner of the MMA league is holding a Halloween party tomorrow night." She bounced.

I rested the blade of the sword on my shoulder, trying to ignore Mars's sultry gaze. "Your point?"

Chelsea rolled her eyes. "His mansion is in Santa Fe. And *everyone* will be there. It's the perfect opportunity for you to rub elbows and get yourself back on top."

Looking up at the ceiling, I let out a heavy sigh. There'd be no arguing with her. "When's the last time you've seen me do anything for Halloween?"

"Great time to start." She yanked an orange bag from her purse, holding it out to me by the handles, and shaking it. "Your costume."

I cocked an eyebrow. "My entire costume is in there? What is it, a bikini?"

Mars leaned to one side, scoping the bag.

"Nope, but guaranteed to turn some heads. I've gotta run." She squished my cheeks together, making my lips look like a fish. "Make me proud tomorrow."

I fake smiled. "Always."

She turned away with a flick of fiery hair, pausing near Mars as she passed. Playing with her necklace, she chewed on her bottom lip. "Have a nice day, Mars."

He half-waved. "Bye, Chelsea."

As soon as the door shut, I tossed the bag on a table and spun my sword. "Ready for round two?"

Mars used his foot to hoist the blade back in his hand with a gleam in his eye. "I've created a monster."

He had no idea.

TWELVE

I LINGERED ON MY reflection in the bathroom mirror. Chelsea had gone too far this time. Not only was she forcing me to go to a Halloween party, but she made me dress as an Amazon—an ancient, scantily clad, estrogen-raging Amazon warrior. A sports-bra-shaped top with a wide beaded strap wrapped around the back of my neck and secured in a crisscross pattern right above my cleavage—beads, leather straps, and fur scattered all over it. Running a hand over my bared midriff, I played with the loincloth design complete with belt and dozens of beaded strings that hung down the front and over my ass. I secured the fur and leather gauntlets on my forearms, tightened the rope armband, and finished with the thin strip of braided leather around my forehead.

"I guess I should be thankful we're in Santa Fe in October," I mumbled to myself, fumbling into a pair of knee-high boots.

Taking a deep breath, which further accentuated my already

bursting bosom, I walked out to the room. Mars sat at the table with his right ankle resting on his left knee, flipping through a magazine. He glanced up and did a double-take, his eyes widening.

"That bad, huh?" I played with a string of beads hanging from my top.

"Uh." He threw the magazine on the table and dragged one hand over his beard, then the other, eyes roaming up and down my body.

I blinked, putting my hands on my bare hips. "Uh? Mars throw me a bone here."

He scratched the back of his head and stood up. "You look…" He lingered over my body before panning up to my face. "Good."

"I'll take it." I crossed my arms. "Where's your costume?"

He'd been staring at my chest and shot his eyes up. "My costume?"

"It's a Halloween party. You can't go dressed as a bodyguard."

"Why not?"

"Mars."

"I'm kidding. I'm kidding. It's uh—in the bathroom." He paused beside me. His eyelids grew heavy as he took in the sight of me up close.

Our gazes met as he chewed on his bottom lip.

My breathing quickened, and I hugged my folded arms tighter against my chest. "You better hurry. We're going to be late."

He traced his fingers around the beard surrounding his

mouth before disappearing into the bathroom.

I let out a shaky breath and bit my fingernail, waiting for him. After only a few seconds, the bathroom door creaked open. I'm not sure what I expected to see, but I certainly didn't expect Mars in full Spartan armor when I turned around.

My hand clenched around the beads of my top, scanning him from head to toe. Sandaled feet, with metal greaves covering his shins and knees. Leather pteruges flaps hung over the tunic—a bronze chest-plate with carved abdominal muscles and pecs that did no justice to his natural physique. A cape extended to the floor, secured at his shoulders. The helmet shadowed his face in the darkness, the red plume standing out in bright contrast.

I ran my fingers over the armor on his chest. "Holy shit. This isn't plastic." I knocked my knuckles against it—cold, hardened steel.

He slipped the helmet off, and I fought the urge to pounce on him at the sight of his hair down. A braid hung on the right side, laced with a brown strip of leather, and a silver bead with Greek designs.

"You're observant." Sarcasm laced his tone.

My eyes couldn't decide between staring at the armor or his face framed by that gorgeous hair. "Where did you get this? Was Medieval Times having a consignment sale or something?"

His gaze dropped to my fingers, tracing the grooves of armor over his pecs. "I had it laying around."

"Wait. You're not a—" I leaned in to whisper. "You're not a LARPer, are you?"

He scowled. "A *what?*"

"Never mind. You can't go in there with this."

"You're making this very difficult, gatáki," he grumbled, walking back into the bathroom.

I rubbed my hand over the back of my neck and almost choked myself when he returned. Gone was the metal armor. He stood bare-chested, bronzed, and glorious with only the leather shoulder pieces and tunic remaining.

He held his arms out at his sides. "Does this please you?"

"Almost," I whispered, my eyes lingering on his tattoo.

"Almost?"

I shot my eyes to his face and forced my hand to rest at my side. "I meant, yes. Yes. That'll work. We now look like a pair of ancient strippers. I'm sure it's exactly what Chelsea was going for."

He moved for the front door, adjusting the gauntlets on his forearms. The lamplight glinted off the xiphos sword slung on his hip.

"Mars, they're not going to let you bring a sword into the party."

He narrowed his eyes at me over his shoulder. "I'd like to see them try and take it."

I held my palms up and shook my head. It wasn't worth the argument. I'd simply wait for the moment where I got to say, "Told ya."

Per our usual, we were silent during the car drive to the mansion. I had to keep my hand under my chin to keep my face forward and avoid ogling him. Throughout my life, I never saw myself as someone with particular tastes or preferences in men. Each passing day around Mars, I began to realize it was because I'd never met *him*. We were like passing ships in the night. Each knew the other was there, but given the darkness, it was easier to pretend we didn't exist.

We pulled through the circular drive, and Mars reluctantly handed the fob to the valet. As we walked to the attendants at the front door, every pair of eyes fell on us.

"Name?" The attendant asked, tapping a pen against his clipboard, his gaze roaming my body.

"Makos. Should be for two."

Mars's arm snaked around my waist, and he pulled me to his side. I raised a brow at him, but he remained laser-focused on the attendant staring at me.

The attendant cleared his throat and jotted something on the clipboard. "Here we are." He stepped aside, removing the red velvet rope from its stand.

"Oh, sir. You can't bring that inside," the other attendant said, reaching for the hilt of his sword.

Mars turned away, bringing me with him. "You touch it, maláka, and I'll cut off your hand."

The attendant's eyes widened, and he gulped, shifting his eyes to the other guy with the clipboard.

I laughed and curled my hand over the one Mars had clenched on his sword, making his shoulders relaxed.

"It's a replica. Is it still not allowed?"

A lie.

The attendant pulled at the collar of his jacket. "No, ma'am. No weapons allowed. Even fake ones."

I pressed my lips to Mars's ear. "I've seen what you can do

with your bare hands. If we get in trouble, I highly doubt you need the sword. Just leave it. We can't cause a scene."

A growl vibrated at the back of his throat, and he slipped his arm away from me long enough to remove the sword and belt. He wrapped the belt around the blade and held it out to the attendant with one hand.

"I hope you cut yourself on it," Mars said through gritted teeth.

I chuckled and tugged at his bicep to follow. "Being on edge is normal for you, but you seem extra moody. What gives?"

He glanced down at my bare stomach with a tightened jaw before curling me against him again. "This is going to be a long night, is all."

When we'd first met, I probably would've pushed myself away from him. But something about his arm around me struck a primal nerve in my gut.

Spiderwebs stretched across chandeliers and lamps, adding to the Gothic decorations in the atrium while fog floated over the floor. Colored lights of gray and purple added to the eerie atmosphere. A techno version of the song *Monster Mash* blasted through the room.

"Makos?" A voice called out.

The MMA owner walked over, dressed as a baby—pacifier, diaper, and beer bottle in hand.

"Anderson," I greeted with a weak smile.

Mars may as well have been invisible as Anderson scanned my attire. Mars's grip tightened on my hip.

"Wow, you look like a smoke show. Amazon, right? Chelsea's idea, I take it?"

I nodded—the less of a conversation I held with this guy, the better.

Anderson jumped when his gaze fell on Mars. "Holy shit. Mars. I didn't even recognize you." He threw out his hand for Mars to shake.

Mars stared at it with a scowl. I bumped him with my shoulder, and he shook it. The poor man winced as Mars squeezed so hard his fingers turned purple. Once he let go, Anderson laughed and rubbed his hand.

"Hell of a shake you got there. Damn shame you had to retire so early. You were the best the MMA's ever seen."

"I had other battles to fight," Mars responded monotone.

Anderson looked back at me. "Heard about your loss. You'll get it back, sweetheart." He winked.

I tensed and took a step forward. Mars idly pulled me back, caressing his callused fingertips over the skin on my hip bone. It damn near made me shiver, forgetting all about Anderson's insult.

"Are you two together?" Anderson between us.

Mars and I spoke at the same time.

"No," I said.

"Yes," Mars said.

Anderson chuckled and shook his head. "It's none of my business. You two enjoy the party. Makos, tell Chelsea to give me a call. I guarantee I can get you back in the ring again."

I gave a single nod, surprised over his quickness to vouch for me.

"Amazon," a woman's voice beckoned.

Jesus. Could we get three feet into the place before someone else called my name?

Kelly Fitz. The woman who stole my title. Fury shot up my spine, and if it weren't for Mars's hold on me, I might have head-butted her right on the spot. She wore a cheetah costume—whiskers, tail, face paint, and all.

"No hard feelings, right?" A sinister smile pulled at her lips. "The best woman won."

Mars turned me away, the red glint flashing in his gaze as he focused on her. "A tinge of humility is in order. Warriors shouldn't fight for hatred of what they're fighting. They should fight for the passion they have for themselves."

Her smug expression melted away, and tears filled her eyes as she ran away.

"You made her cry."

He rolled his shoulders. "I tend to have that effect on women."

I cocked an eyebrow.

"Except for you." He searched my face before his gaze lifted to the open space in the center of the room—the dance floor. "Would you—"

I turned to face him and backpedaled toward the center. He followed me with a curious squint.

"Were you going to ask me to dance?" I looked up at him with heavy lids.

He traced his fingers over my lower back, his pinky finger snuggling into the top part of my skirt. "Yes." It came out husky.

"I'd have never suspected a brute like you had moves." I ran my hand up the ink on his arm.

He moved closer until the bare skin of his chest pressed against my shoulders. "I've taught some of the best warriors war dances."

"You mean soldiers?"

He sucked on his bottom lip, running his fingers over the hanging beads of my top. "Same thing."

He tapped his hand against the middle of my back in time with the pulsing bass from the techno song playing.

How was one supposed to dance to this music?

He lowered his face, pressing his cheek against mine and hovering his lips over my ear. "Do you hear my heartbeat, gatáki?"

I closed my eyes. His heart's steady pace started to overpower the music until it was the only sound in the room. "Yes."

"Concentrate on it," he whispered.

We started to sway back and forth as I did what he asked. Slowly a different song played—ancient, harmonious, and sultry. It began as drums followed by the introduction of plucking strings and pipes—byzantine. The melody transported me audibly to ancient Greece.

"Open your eyes," he commanded.

My lashes fluttered, and I stared up at him with ethereal tunnel vision. Other people were undoubtedly around us, but all I could see, all I cared to see…was him. He spun me around, pulling me to him. My back slammed into his chest. He skirted a hand around me, pressing his palm against my bare stomach. I wrapped my arms around his neck, swaying my hips to music only the two of us could hear.

He brushed the hair away from my nape, dragging his lips

across my skin. Pushing a palm against my hip, he spun me around to face him, holding my hands above my head with one of his. Our chests heaved in unison, pressed together. Keeping my hands in the air, he used his other hand to trace a finger over my lips, down my neck, and just as he neared the valley between my breasts, he slipped the hand around my waist.

He waltzed us around the dance floor, burning me with his gaze. I couldn't take my eyes off him. Every moment longer, with his skin pressed against mine, I became his. We were fighters both internally and outwardly—warriors with mutual respect.

He dipped me and splayed his hand over my abdomen, gazing at it as if he wanted to devour me. And then his focus moved lower. He blinked and shook his head, lifting me with a growl. The ancient music disappeared. The pulse of techno music flooded into my ears, disorienting me. When I managed to regain my composure, he was gone.

"Mars?" I called out, doing several circles.

I could barely make sense of left or right. He'd pulled me into his world, scorched me with his touch, his darkened gaze—only to abandon me in the middle of a sea of people? Part of me wanted to be pissed, but the other fought for a reason. There had to be a reason. There'd *better* be a damn reason.

After searching all corners of the room, I moved to the first hallway. He sat on a chair, hunched over with his forearms on his knees. He glared at the ground like it was his worst enemy staring back at him.

I folded my arms as I walked. "What kind of a bodyguard lets their client out of their sight?"

The glare disappeared, and his eyes brightened as he lifted them to me. "I could hear if you were in trouble."

"From out here? How?"

His jaw clenched. "I just can. Alright?"

No. It wasn't alright. Half-assed answers and hiding so many secrets—too many secrets—I was done with it. I'd gone beyond the point of irritation, and yet my blood burned for him—pined for him. No more denying it. He'd held the reins on the dance floor—and I let him. Now I needed the sense of control back, to take what I wanted. Moving to stand in front of him, I shoved his shoulders back against the seat. He canted his head to one side, watching me as I slipped onto his lap, straddling him.

I'd half expected him to ask me what I was doing, or was I sure I wanted to do this, but as he had from the first day we met, he surprised me by asking none of it. His hands trailed up my thighs until they reached my hips, pulling me tighter against him. I ran my fingers over the braid in his hair before slipping my mouth over his.

He moaned against my lips, moving his hands to my backside, squeezing it. I slid my arms around his neck, tangling my fingers in his dark hair. There was a brief moment when I wasn't sure who I was anymore. I played with fire, taking things to another level with Mars, but didn't think twice about the scars it could leave. He wound his burly arm around my waist and started to hoist me up.

"Wow, why don't you two get a room?" A stranger walking through the hallway said, laughing.

Mars flopped back down to the chair with a heavy sigh,

breaking the connection of our lips. I tapped my forehead to his and slid from his lap. He cleared his throat as he adjusted himself through his tunic.

"I uh—forgot where we were for a minute. It's the atmosphere, the dancing, I—" I sounded like a stuttering idiot.

Mars stood with a wide stance. "Harmony."

A name I once loathed sounded like a breath of fresh air when it rolled off his tongue. "Yes?"

"I need to tell you something, but I'm not sure how."

I didn't like where this was going.

Suddenly feeling exposed, I curled my arms around myself. "Is there someone else?"

He frowned. "No. Of course not, but—this could be worse." He dragged a hand through his beard.

Worse? What could possibly be worse? He had some secret family on a discreet island? Did he like to dress up as animals during sex? I wasn't even sure if either of *those* would be a deal-breaker.

"Do you want to go back to the room?" My question sent a tingle over the back of my skull—the implications of it.

The skin between his eyes creased. "Yes. Is that alright with you?"

After that heated lap session, I wanted to be anywhere else but here. "Yeah."

The entire car ride, Mars's knee bounced uncontrollably. I didn't dare say anything or even try to soothe him. Something told me he had to get through this one on his own. When we walked back into the hotel, he let out an exasperated snarl and paced the room. It wasn't exactly the *action* I'd hoped for, but

I could tell he needed someone, and not just anyone, to listen to him.

"Mars. Calm. Down."

He clenched his fists and threw his arms out at his sides like Wolverine. "It's what you don't understand. I'm the epitome of *not* calm. I was born, *made* for the exact opposite."

I pressed my back to the door, letting him take out his temper tantrum. "What the hell are you talking about?"

"I've got so much festering inside me, and I can't *do* anything about it." He kicked the desk, causing the lamp to shatter on the ground.

I froze. I'd been here at a certain time in my life. Unable to control the rage, taking it out on inanimate objects. To watch the destruction of something made dealing with myself breaking easier.

"I can't help who I am. The reason they bred me. And now with the way of the world, what is the point of my existence?" He let out a monstrous roar, slamming his fists into the bed in front of him, snapping the frame.

"Jesus Christ, Mars. Someone's going to call the cops."

His nostrils flared, and he gazed at me with frantic eyes. "Do you know the worst part? I've had to hide it from you. Lie to you."

My sinuses stung. "Lie to me about what?" It came out louder than intended.

He dragged the back of his hand over his nose. "Vlákas." He gripped my shoulders. "I'm Ares. God of War." His eyes flashed red.

THIRTEEN

HIS LIPS DIDN'T QUIVER into a smile. The corners of his jaw tightened, and one eyebrow ticked. He wasn't kidding. A vague memory surfaced from the other night—him whispering the same words to me as I fell asleep.

"You've told me this before," I squeaked.

His eyes searched my face almost frantically. "Yes. You said it made a lot of sense."

"In a world where myths and legends exist, sure. But Mars—" I cocked my head, staring up at him, waiting for him to lose it and laugh so hard he bent forward. It didn't happen. "You can't be serious? You think you're the God of War?"

His grip tightened on my shoulders before dropping his hands to ball into fists. "I don't *think*—" he yelled, pausing and shutting his eyes. "I don't *think* I'm the God of War. I *am*," he finished in a more calm tone. "Do you remember the way you felt in your dream? The visions? How it all seemed real?"

I blinked so rapidly it blurred my vision as I backed up until my calves hit against the nearest surface to brace myself.

"Morpheus. The reason I tried to avoid him touching you? He's the god of dreams. What he incites in you are your deepest desires or what could've come to pass in a different life path."

I rubbed the skin between my eyes. "Are you trying to say what I dreamt, us on the battlefield together, and—" I gulped. "After, were mirages of what could've been if—" The words escaped me, the stale air in the room devouring them.

"If you would've been alive in those times, yes." He kept his distance, even though his constant shifting stance and tense posture suggested he wanted to come closer.

There was no denying how real the visions felt—the smells, the feel of smoke tendrils curling around my fingers, his skin pulsing against mine as we—

I shot to my feet, my heart racing, remembering how alive I'd felt in that tent—with him—with…war.

That red glint in his eyes, the strength, my crazy dreams. It couldn't be possible. It just couldn't. "Why now? And if you are real, why are you, a Greek god, roaming earth?"

He sucked on his teeth. "You said it yourself, gatáki. It sounds crazy claiming yourself a god, especially in the modern age where we're merely a footnote in history—reduced to myth. We still exist, and we're anything but figments of stories created by mortals. We blend in and still use our powers. Only now, we do it without fear or worship. We do it because it's what we were born to do."

Focusing my gaze, I shifted between his eyes and lips as he

spoke. He carried himself with a fierce and masculine grace that pulled at a primal part of me. A heathen side buried deep, yearning for remembrance. I wrapped my arms around myself as if the world were falling to pieces around me. With each step closer to him, the earth shattered a little bit more.

He stood still, his brow cinched, distorting his features. When I stood at arm's length, I touched his cheek—a radiating heat vapored from him. He was every bit as real as I was—flesh and bone, anguish, and lust.

"I don't know how to believe you." My voice—small and fluttery—didn't sound like me. It belonged to a woman seeking hope again—finding a calling. That hadn't been me for as long as I could remember.

Lifting his chin, he sniffed the air like a bloodhound. "I can show you." His hand slid over mine, the rough calluses on his palm scraping over my knuckles—hardened skin forged by war itself, by weapons built for destruction. "Right now. I can show you, Harm."

The way he looked at me had every nerve sizzling under my skin. "Show me."

I let him lead me out the door, down the hallway, and outside to the parking lot. The cold air whipped over my bare skin, reminding me we both still looked like we'd come from a Renaissance Faire. But I didn't care. Right now, it was him and me, and the rest of the world could fuck right off.

Street lights flickered, buzzed, and popped as we neared an alleyway. Clouds covered most of the moon and stars, leaving a faulty light as the only sliver of illumination. It flashed on and off in spurts like an erratic strobe light.

His nostrils quivered, his grip tightening on my hand before he growled and turned, stalking toward the alley. He let go before we rounded the corner, squeezing my biceps.

"Stay here." His voice was a general giving his soldier a command.

I nodded, nerves scratching at the inside of my belly. He said he'd show me. I agreed to it before knowing what it meant. Was he going to kill someone? Invoke a horse and chariot from thin air? My nails dug into the brick wall beside me, two of them cracking.

A man's voice muttered, "Here. Take it. Just let me go."

It was enough to make me peer around the corner. Five men with dark hoodies, half their faces covered with cloth, surrounded a businessman in a suit holding his wallet. The speed and intensity of Mars's steps increased with every inch he gained. Their heads whipped in his direction, two of them aiming pistols.

My eyes widened as I reached out. "Mars!"

A shot rang out. I sank to my knees, the asphalt bruising them as I covered my head. Peering over my forearm, I saw Mars's hand launch out and curl into a fist. He threw the same hand at the ground and the subtle sound of metal clanking against stone pounded in my ears.

Did he…catch the bullet with his bare hand?

I shifted across the alleyway, securing myself behind a wall. The would-be victim in the suit clutched his briefcase and crouched behind a dumpster.

"What the hell?" An armed man said, raising the gun to shoot again. "Who are you, Freak Show?"

Mars shoved his palm against the barrel right as it fired. He grabbed the man's forearm and launched the gun into his face. The man cried out, holding his bleeding nose. Another man charged, and Mars lifted his arm and splayed his hand. The man flew backward as if catapulted by a random gust of wind.

My neck went numb—the bathroom door that one night. I'd blamed a blast of air conditioning, but what if—no. *No, Makos.* I beat my palm against my forehead.

The man launched into the wall while another ran up to Mars. He spun around, shoved his hand into the man's chest, and lifted him from the ground like a stuffed bear.

"Tell me, what sort of vlákas satisfaction does it give you to rob a single defenseless man, hm? There is no conquest here. Only petty means to temporarily fill your own pockets." He roared his words, holding the man up with one hand. The man clawed at Mars's arms, gasping for breath.

Conquest. It meant pillaging and looting a village as a means of intimidation—conquering lands, not stealing from a hard-working man at gunpoint.

And there I went again, as if the warrior life, the mentality of it, had always been a part of me. And now, as I caught sight of the menacing yet intoxicating form that was Mars—the tigress in me beckoned.

The man with the broken nose ran past me, holding the gun up, ready to fire at Mars's back. The man shot, but I slammed my elbow into his shooting arm, breaking it. The man cried out in agony, and I caught the firearm as it fell to the ground, landing on my side with a grunt.

The man he'd thrown into the wall had regained

consciousness, and he ran at Mars with a knife he pulled from his jacket. I lifted the gun, ready to shoot to kill. Mars opened his hand at me, and the gun flew from my hands, exploding into a hundred pieces once it landed on the ground. I stared wide-eyed, remaining on the ground, digging my nails into the hardened surface beneath me. Mars dropped the man he'd been holding and caught the other man's knife-wielding arm as he struck.

He turned him around to face the other one as he got to his feet, touching both men on their shoulders. Mars's eyes glowed blood red as they turned on each other, punching, kicking, and grabbing. Police sirens bounced off the walls of surrounding buildings. Mars's gaze turned on me, the fiery intensity diminishing to a smolder. For a moment, I forgot how to breathe—forgot how to rationalize. Should I be scared of him?

Was all of this real, or was I just as insane as he was?

I jumped to my feet, sprinting away. The destination was unclear, but I needed to escape. To think, to process, to maybe even…cry. My sinuses stung, and I ran until my legs and lungs burned, begging me to stop. Passersby stared at the Amazon flailing through downtown Santa Fe, and I let them. I flopped onto a set of stairs in front of a closed bank, dropping my head between my knees. Tears threatened, but I forced them back with every bit of strength I had left.

"Have I completely screwed things up?"

His deep voice laced with that accent sent a delicious chill over my chest. I slowly lifted my head, looking up at him through strands falling over his eyes. I'd never seen a man so fierce yet surprisingly beautiful. His eyes fell to his feet, and he flicked the corner of his mouth with his thumb.

"Tell me. What am I supposed to say right now? What am I supposed to think? How am I supposed to react?"

He licked his bottom lip with a squint. "I don't have those answers for you, gatáki." He did a quick twist on his heel, turning to sit on the steps near me.

"You're still going with this? The whole Greek god thing?"

He rubbed the back of his neck. "It's been over a thousand years since I presented myself to a mortal as what I am." He hung his hands between his legs. "But back then, people believed in us." His brow furrowed. "I knew convincing a modern mortal would be difficult, catastrophic even, but I didn't predict the pang of guilt I'd feel seeing your anguished face." He lifted his gaze to mine.

Tears rolled down my cheeks, and there was nothing I could do to stop them.

His face fell, and he turned to me, canting his head to one side. He lifted his hands, dropped them, and then lifted a single finger, brushing it across my cheek. "Why are you crying?"

I wanted to feel his skin against mine, wanted him to wrap his arms around me, but I knew it'd only make it worse. Pinching my eyes shut, I shrugged away from him. "This changes everything, Mars."

He curled his hand and rested it on his knee like he wasn't sure what to do with it. "It's the price I pay, but what should I have done? Strung you along?"

My vision blurred. "You really are him," I whispered, staring into those midnight eyes. The same eyes that beamed at me as we fought side by side against opposing forces. The same eyes that kept my gaze as he drove into me in the tent afterward.

"Yes." He turned his back to me.

I clapped my hands over my mouth. Two bullet-sized holes were in his costume. No blood. No wounds. Not even welts that would've been there if they'd used fake rubber ammo.

"I'll call Chelsea in the morning. Ask her to transfer in a new bodyguard," he said in a low, solemn voice as he brushed a fingertip down my cheek—a touch so quick and fleeting. Defeated. He pushed to his feet.

I grabbed his forearm, the smell of leather and musk tantalizing my insides. He stared down at me with hooded eyes, his arm tensing under my touch. "Don't. Let me think my way through this."

He traced the tip of his thumb over my bottom lip. "Fair enough."

"I need to talk to Chels. Alone." I stared up at him. "Please."

He leaned forward like he wanted to kiss me but rubbed the back of his neck instead. "I'll be down the hall."

"Because you can still hear if anything goes wrong. I thought you were talking out of your ass." I stood up, dragging my hands over my face.

"Yes. I'll know."

I walked toward the hotel, Mars trailing behind me. Snapping my fingers, I turned on my heel.

"Are you going to be able to hear our entire conversation?"

Mars's eyes shifted. "I'll—tune it out as much as I can."

I blinked once, waiting for him to smile, throw his hands out to his sides, and tell me I was being Punk'd. He didn't.

Turning back around, I called Chelsea.

"What's up?" She answered.

"Hey, could you meet me at my room? I need to talk to you."

Silence. "You're not pregnant, are you?"

I pulled the phone away from my ear, checking to make sure I'd called Chelsea. "What? Hell no. Meet me. Okay?"

More silence. "Okay. Leaving right now."

Mars appeared beside me. "I can assume what you wish to talk to her about, but you can't tell her the whole truth, Harm."

"Are you kidding? I can barely repeat the truth to myself." I blew out a harsh breath. "She wouldn't believe me anyway."

Once we reached our hotel room door, I watched him sulk down the hallway as I hovered the room key over the lock. It clicked, and the light turned green, but my eyes stayed on Mars. He reached the bench nestled underneath a window at the end of the hall. When he turned, spotting me still standing in front of the door, he cocked his head to one side. His dark eyes called to me, making me remember how his lips felt against my neck when we danced.

He kept his gaze locked with mine as he slowly sat down. The ancient song we danced to trickled over my brain like dripping wax. With every drop, it hardened, making a permanent impression in my mind, the way his callused fingers touched my bare stomach. I dragged my hand over the skin there.

"When you said to meet at your room, I thought you meant inside." Chelsea's voice jarred me back to reality. "And why are you still in your costume?" She scanned me from head to toe.

I ran the card over the reader, grabbing the handle as soon as the light turned green.

"Long story."

With her purse hanging from one forearm, she turned to look down the hallway with a squint.

"Shouldn't he be in here? Why is he glowering in the hallway?"

I grabbed the crook of her elbow and pulled her. "He's got it handled."

As soon as I turned the light on, my heart dropped to my feet. I'd forgotten about the destruction Mars left in his wake.

"Jesus, Harmony. What the hell happened? He didn't—" Her brow cinched, and her cheeks flushed.

"No. No, he didn't. Mars has a lot of…pent up anger. Not sure if you knew that before hiring him."

"I could've assumed given his type, but—" She hugged her purse to her chest. "I didn't think it was at this level. Is this what you wanted to talk to me about? Do you want a new bodyguard?" She grabbed her phone.

I yanked it from her grasp and guided her over to the couch. "Sit down."

"You're scaring me," she said, sinking to the green cushion.

I sat on the armrest, holding Chelsea's phone hostage in my palms. "I need you to tell me how crazy I am. On a scale of one to ten, with one being, I'm worried for nothing and ten being, I find Charles Manson to have been misunderstood."

"Eight."

"You didn't let me say anything yet." I narrowed my eyes. "You think I'm a crazy level eight?"

She scratched the back of her ear. "Impulse. Please continue."

"Mars doesn't just have this…simmering anger. He's—different." I tossed her phone from one hand to the other.

"Different how?"

Did I imagine this conversation being easy?

"He's got these special skills that he can't put into full practice, or else someone could get hurt."

Chelsea cocked an eyebrow at the broken lamp inches from her foot on the floor. "Skills, huh? Looks like a t-rex raged through here."

My shoulders tensed. "He's had…special training. Like, beyond Neo training."

A Matrix reference? I really was grasping at straws.

"And you're concerned about these skills because of what effect they could have on you?" She scooted forward, squinting one eye.

The effect they *could* have? Oh, we were much past that.

"Before I knew about these skills, I—" Standing up, I clutched the phone against my side and turned my back on her.

"Liked him? You can say the words."

I whipped around, fear burning down my spine. "He—we—it's like we were born from the same mold."

"You two have things in common? I wouldn't have ever guessed, given the stubborn loner mentalities you both exude. Not to mention, you know, the whole fighting thing." She jabbed the air with her fist.

I sighed, slapping my hands against my thighs. "Chelsea, this is serious."

"Sorry." She stood, tossing her purse on the couch. "You're right. I'm not used to having these conversations with you. Well, we've never had this conversation."

"The craziest part is, those skills he has? They don't bother me at all. And they should. They really, really should." Biting my thumbnail. I stared at the swirling vine patterns in the carpet.

"Why? It sounds like these 'skills' you're so mum about may take a particular type of person to understand them. To maybe even appreciate them?"

I let my lower lip roll past my teeth and managed to find the courage to look at her.

"Am I on the right track?"

"Basically."

She half-smiled, plucking her phone from my death grip. "Sounds like you have your mind made up, Harm. You don't need my approval."

"Don't I? You're my publicist."

"Since when did you think that meant I have any control over your sex life?"

I grimaced.

"We're all adults here. And to be honest, if I step back and stop talking to you as a friend and *only* your publicist…it wouldn't be a bad thing for your image. It shows you have actual feelings inside that steel shell."

"Chelsea."

She shrugged, flicking her thumb over her phone screen. "Just being honest. Are you good?"

There's no way she could ever understand the depths of

his differences, but her words still somehow settled in. It was enough.

"Yeah. I'm good."

"Oh!" She slapped her hand on my shoulder. "Anderson got in touch with me. We got a fight set up for you with a fighter who calls herself The Trojan. It's not a title fight, but it's some gimmicky Greek deal. Okay with you?"

"It's going to have to be."

"That's my girl." She tapped her knuckle under my chin. "I have to catch my flight back to Denver. But if anything happens, that you don't *want* to happen…" She gave a devious smile.

I rolled my eyes.

"Call me. Pronto. Got it?"

"Got it."

She nodded once and backed out into the hallway. "Hey, Mars." She grinned. A different type of smile than I'd ever seen on her.

His large arm pushed against the door, keeping it ajar. His exposed abs tightened, and my breathing went out of control. Once Chelsea walked away, he slipped inside and slowly let it shut.

Click.

"Show me what you look like," I blurted.

His brow creased. "What?"

"You can't tell me this is how the God of War normally looks."

He interlaced his fingers behind his back. "What am I supposed to look like?"

I focused my gaze on his boots sliding against the carpet as he moved forward. "I don't know. Half-bull, half-man, or something?"

"That would be the Minotauros. And the last I checked, he's dead." He half-smiled.

A breath caught in my throat. "Give me a break. I haven't studied Greek mythology since middle school."

"We'll have to rectify that." Another step forward. "That is…if you'll still have me."

Have me.

My stomach did somersaults. I scraped my fingernails over my throat.

"Are you going to show me?"

"Very well."

He held his hands to the ground. Red smoke swirled around him, and when it cleared, he stood in the same armor I'd seen him in earlier—menacing, deadly, and intense. His red cape flapped as if there were a constant wind current in the room, and his skin glowed like bronze. The Spartan-styled helmet cast a dark shadow over his face with flickering flames for eyes. A shield clung to his back—javelin in one hand, a xiphos in the other.

As if he couldn't get any more attractive.

I slid forward, hesitantly reaching for the shadow over his face. Grasping my wrist, he brought my hand to his face, his beard prickling my fingers.

"The shadow is just a mirage," he said, his voice deeper and gravelly.

"And your eyes?"

"Those are mine. But the flames won't hurt you, gatáki."

I traced my fingers over the contours of his helmet. The same helmet he wore in my dream. How could it possibly be all coincidence? Unlikely. That's how. "I need to see more, Mars. As much as you can show me."

He slipped the helmet off, revealing his human face, and the tip of his tongue peeked from the corner of his mouth. "Fair enough. I have an idea. Would you mind if I skipped the car drive?" He closed the space between us and curled an arm around me.

"How else would we get—"

My words were cut short. We appeared outside in a flash of white light and red smoke beneath the moon and stars. The dew cast a sheen over the bricks of surrounding buildings.

"—there," I finished with a shaky voice. Jeans, jacket, and shirt had replaced my Amazon costume.

His nose ever so slightly grazed my cheek as he turned away. It was unnerving how much I missed seeing him in his armor. So many feelings clicked into place with Mars. Everything felt answered, yet my mind whirled with neverending questions. Why me? How did I fit into all this? I worked up the courage to flat out ask him for a fraction of a second but swallowed it back down.

"After I retired, I fought a couple of matches here. I still can't fight to my full potential, but it's the best I'm going to get for the time being."

We walked through a quiet alley to a rusted metal slab door. A slit peeled back, revealing a pair of sunken brown eyes.

"Burro," Mars said.

The slit slammed shut, and the large door creaked open. Cheers, whistles, and yells reverberated off the walls. Overhead lights flickered on and off, with the main one centered on the make-shift cage comprised of nothing but a chain-link fence in the middle of the room.

"Underground fights?"

His brow pinched. "Are you still in?"

A familiar face beamed from the crowd, her beady eyes and resting bitch face too recognizable. The woman who threatened my life and tried to have me killed. My blood heated, making my neck clammy.

"I'm in," I growled.

FOURTEEN

"WHY DO YOU HAVE that look on your face?" Mars asked.

Not tearing my eyes from Fiona, I pointed.

He followed my gaze, and his once neutral expression turned deadly. I slipped a hand over his forearm, knowing his first instinct might be to rip the spine from Fiona's body.

"I'll handle it. Sign me up for a fight with her," I said, trying to control my breathing.

"Anything goes here, Harm."

"Even better. A rare chance to cut loose."

There was a twinkle in his eye before he brushed past me to flag down the bookie.

I circled toward the back of the crowds surrounding the cage. She leaned against the metal grating with such smugness—as if her shit smelled like lilacs. It only infuriated me more.

"Is there no one to challenge her?" The announcer yelled.

Fiona pushed off the cage, waving her arms, exciting the

hordes of people into hysteria.

As he brushed his lips over my ear, Mars pressed a hand between my shoulder blades. "You're up, Amazon."

"Is there anything you can do? A way to make me not hesitate?"

I had no idea what power he possessed, but it was the first of a string of questions I had.

He cocked his head to one side. "What I can give, you already have so much inside you. It's like fire. If it gets out of control, it can consume you. But if used correctly, it has the capability of transforming you."

My gaze fell to the plumpness of his lips.

"What I *can* give you, Harmony is a bit of your spirit back." He drew a line with his finger from the center of my forehead to the tip of my nose.

A sensation trickled over every inch of my skin like static raindrops. I thought I'd felt courage before—conviction. But a new sense of fearlessness swirled through my chest like a hurricane. His gruff touch slid over my hands as he wound tape over my knuckles.

A crimson glow pulsed in his eyes. "Go get your victory. And make sure she, nor anyone else she knows, threatens you ever again."

I gave a curt nod before shoving my way through the sea of bodies.

"Looks like we have our challenger. And what a treat! Harm 'The Amazon' Makos," the announcer boomed.

Fiona's confidant swagger flittered away. Her eyes frantically searched the crowd as I slipped into the ring behind her. The roars of applause were but crickets on a calm night to me. My focus played on her—beating her, getting justice but not revenge.

"You've got a lot of balls coming here," she muttered.

I clenched my hands, making the tape creak. "A lot has happened since we last fought. Did your goon need reconstructive surgery?"

She ground her teeth, glaring at me from across the cage.

"Alright, ladies. You know the rules. There are none. Fight!" The announcer threw his hand down between us.

I slid forward and slammed my elbow into her nose. She shrieked and clamped a hand over her face, blood already staining the top of her sports bra.

"You bitch," she screamed.

"Your words are as empty as your threats."

She screeched like a banshee and stormed at me. My vision delved into slow motion, watching her act on impulse. A simple sidestep was all it took to avoid her desperate swings. I swiveled on my heel and threw my forearm at the back of her head, sending her stumbling. I slid in front of her, kneeing her in the face.

She groaned, gurgled, and collapsed on her side. Dozens of fists flew in the air from the audience.

I crouched beside her and grabbed the back of her neck, pulling her face toward mine. "If you ever threaten me again, I will *burn* you. If I catch your face anywhere near the MMA, I will *destroy* you. Do you understand me?"

She whimpered in defeat, batting my hands away with frightened eyes. I let her slump back to the floor and stood, spotting Mars in the crowd. Despite hundreds of people, I zeroed in on him like a circling falcon.

He stood still, a predatory grin playing over his lips—the God of War, standing amidst a pool of mortals. The announcer grabbed my hand and hoisted it in the air, but I didn't dare take my eyes off Mars. Ares.

"As if this night couldn't get any better, folks. Our next fighter needs no introduction. Put it together for Mars!"

Our gazes fixed on each other as I left the cage, and he moved toward it. I paused at the bottom of the stairs, waiting for him to walk past me, yearning to feel his touch. He didn't disappoint. As he passed, he gripped my hip, grazed my cheek with his, and gave a quick nip at my earlobe.

I took a sharp breath as his hand slipped away, and he walked into the ring. My cheeks flushed, and I kneaded one hand against the palm of the other. Backing up, I situated myself behind the lines drawn on the floor with duct tape.

Mars peeled off his shirt, tossing it to me. I caught it and as his scent filled the air in front of me, my insides clenched. His poor opponent did not know the man he agreed to fight—the man who was a *god*. Mars cracked his neck as he swung his arms back and forth, tensing his muscles and giving the full-sleeve tattoo shadows and depth.

Mars's opponent launched forward with both fists. Mars caught them, glaring down at him. The man panicked and head-butted him in the chest. It sounded like bone hitting against metal. Mars twisted the man's arms, making him cry out in pain. Mars kneed him in the side, reached an arm over the man's shoulder, and whipped him over his head. Both men landed on their backs, with Mars leaping to his feet in one jump. The fiery intensity built in his eyes, gaze darkening.

Mars open-hand punched the man across the face, followed by a left hook, sending his opponent's face flying into the cage. The ancient horns blasted in my head. *Familiar.* I welcomed them—let them resonate in my chest. His opponent crawled like a coward to the opposite side of the ring. The sight made Mars sneer.

"Get up," Mars bellowed, taking calculated movements around the cage. Each step felt like an earthquake beneath my feet.

The man scrambled, striking his palm at Mars's ear. He caught his arm and twisted it with a snarl. His opponent shrieked, holding his shoulder with the free hand. Mars threw his arms out at his sides, letting his opponent go. Staggered whispers, swords clanging, and dozens of hooves galloping over dirt whooshed past me.

Mars grabbed his opponent by the back of the shirt and threw him against the cage, holding him there. He let out a ferocious growl and ran the perimeter, dragging the man along with him like a sack of flour. When he threw him to the ground, plumes of red smoke and black sand shot up from the ground. Mars stepped over him, his menacing form slipping through the smoke like a mirage.

My heart thudded against my chest like a Warhammer. Every cell in my body screamed for him. Us coming here was never about the victories. It was to prove ourselves to the other. That we were worthy of each other. Mars slammed his boot into the cage door, stalking down the stairs and standing in front of me with such a feverish intensity it could've singed my eyelashes.

"Ares," I whispered.

His eyes closed, and he winced as if I'd slapped him. "Say it again."

Touching his chest, I rose, and with a feathered touch, pressed my lips to his ear. "Ares."

With a growl, he took my hand, pulling me through the crowd. When we reached a back area devoid of people, he shoved me against the wall and pressed his hand on it above my head.

"I never thought I'd ever call something sweet, but my name, my *real* name on your lips…is one of the sweetest damn things I've ever heard." His bare chest heaved.

"Ares, the God of War," I purred, knowing I was only playing with fire, but I wanted to burn.

He squinted and pressed his lips to mine, his tongue darting in, not bothering for an invitation. He moaned against my mouth, pushing his hardness against my stomach. The wall disappeared, and my hair flew over my shoulders as he warped us to the hotel room.

I blinked and pushed him away, dragging a fingertip over my self-inflicted abandoned lips.

He stood across from me, his arms at his sides, hands opened. Both of us panted, and my insides clenched so tightly I thought I'd burst.

"I know you want this as much as me, Harm. Why don't you take it?"

I wanted nothing more than to pounce on him like a lioness

in heat. He'd diminished my armor until only the piece over my chest remained. It was the most crucial piece of all—the shield over my heart.

"Because it would mean something."

He licked his lower lip. "You're always so guarded when you don't have to be."

"You're one to talk. When's the last time you let someone get close to you? Truly get close to you and not want to kick their ass?"

He snarled and closed the gap between us with two strides. He curled his hand around the back of my neck, our faces close enough to feel his breath over my cheeks. "You, Harmony. *You.*"

Our lips crashed together before my heart had a chance to catch up to my brain. The armor melted away like it was in a vat of molten lava. His grip on my neck traveled to the back of my head, tangling my hair with his fingers. I grabbed the rubber band holding the bun in place at the base of his neck and tugged it free, greedily running my hand over his abs, teasing the brim of his pants with a single finger. The feel of his treasure trail of hair brushing against my knuckles made me shiver.

He slid his hands under my shirt while still kissing, licking, and nipping at my lips. His fingertips brushed my ribs. As they dragged over the side of my breasts, I ground my hips against him, relishing the feel of his grin against my mouth. I raised my arms for him, and he lifted the shirt, bunching it at my wrists and holding my hands hostage above my head.

He peeled away from the kiss, gazing down at me, captive in his grasp. He cupped my chin before starting a tantalizing trail down my body. He paused at my cleavage, dipping his finger from one breast to the other before caressing my stomach.

I moaned, relishing the tease but craving him inside me. He undid the button of my jeans with a flick, playing a gaze both sultry and demanding over my body. Loosening his grip on my shirt, he freed my hands and undid the zipper on my pants. He chewed on his bottom lip and curled his fingers into each side of the hem. With one swift motion, they were in a pile around my ankles, and I stepped out of them, one foot at a time.

He dragged a hand through his hair as he watched me, consuming me with his stare. I reached behind me and undid the clasp of my bra, tossing it to the side once the straps dropped from my shoulders. My nipples puckered from the cold in the air mixed with the sight of him peering at me like I, too, was a god—a goddess.

I pressed my lips to his, gripping his long hair between my fingers, tugging it. He backed me toward the bed, but with a jerk of his hair, I whipped us around. We opened our eyes long enough to challenge each other. A flash of red pulsed in his gaze, and he took a grip on *my* hair, deepening the kiss to the point of devouring me.

"Se thélo," he whispered, biting the air in front of me.

The impulse to take control, to not *lose* control, had me fighting for it with every breath. We neared the bed, and he grabbed my hip, spinning me so my back was to it again. I bit my lip, pretending to succumb to his power, skirting my knee up his thigh until his clothed girth brushed against me. He groaned, and I gripped his shoulders, turning him and pushing him against the bedframe.

His pants disappeared from my grasp, and he stood in front

of me naked and glorious. I explored the manly hair scattering on his chest, his stomach, trailing to his girth that already lived up to my every expectation and dirty thought. I wrapped my hand around him, stroking as I coaxed him onto the bed.

"You win. For now, gatáki." He gave a knowing grin, obliging my command and laying on his back.

The God of War *let* me take control of him—became willingly vulnerable within my grasp. It was a sense of trust that had me beaming.

I straddled him, lowering my lips near his cheek, caressing the side of my face with his beard. He snarled against my neck, stiffening further within my grasp. Pressing my knees against his hips, I focused for a moment on the feel of the man beneath me—hardened muscle, a body built for war and chaos, yet still so capable of softness. Whether it'd been by words or actions, with the right person, the right woman, he could show gentleness. He plucked two fingers against my lace underwear, snapping them away without so much as a sting, holding up the tattered remains with a wicked smile before tossing them to the floor.

I bent forward, allowing my breasts to dip against his stomach. Lowering my lips, I kissed his ribs and dragged my tongue up to his chest, giving his right nipple a scrape with my teeth. His eyes flashed red, and he hissed, gripping my waist. I sat back, positioning over him, and ever so slowly lowered myself. Inch by inch, he filled me, and I bent backward once our hips met. He groaned and grabbed my hips, arching his head back into the pillows.

Pressing my palms against his chest, I rocked back and forth, gasping with every other thrust. His fingers moved to my ass, guiding me as we fell into a perfect rhythm. I clenched as the euphoric build-up swirled in my abdomen. Closing my eyes, I slid one hand into my hair, gripping the back of my neck with the other. As the climax overtook me, I sighed out in pleasure, sweat beading across my forehead and chest.

When I opened my eyes, Ares sat up, gliding a hand to my back. He claimed my mouth with his as he thrust into me. Pulling his lips away, he kept a steady roll of his hips and pressed our foreheads together.

"Have you ever given a man control?" His voice was husky and deep.

"No."

His girth throbbed within me. "Let me. Who knows, you might even enjoy it." His beard scraped against my cheek as he moved his lips to the corner of my brow.

Dragging my nails over his shoulders, I sucked on his earlobe. "Conquer me."

A masculine, guttural growl vibrated in the back of his throat. He grabbed my ass and hoisted me forward, making me flop onto my back. His hands gripped the backs of my knees, pushing them back, forcing me to open further for him. Sitting on his haunches, he plunged into me over and over again.

I'd given him the reins, and now my body longed for resolution. To feel *owned* by him, knowing he was equally mine—an answer to the anger, the frustration, and the constant need to take on the world by myself. No one could ever own me like one would possess a motorcycle, but on the sheets, behind closed doors, we'd give ourselves to each other in much the same manner.

He hoisted me up with my legs locked around his waist, and I wrapped my arms around his neck. My back hit the wall, his ferocious thrusts following. He held me up with his hands cupping my ass, plunging into me with the ferocity of a seasoned warrior.

My head bumped against the wall behind me as I arched backward. He kissed my neck, swirling his tongue in circles over my skin—flashes of my dream on the battlefield coursed through my mind, bleeding into my veins. We may not have fought side-by-side in the ring, but the same admiration for the other arose—two warriors united by a cosmic force to fight together. Ascend together. *Fuck* together.

He peeled me away from the wall, carrying me over to the desk. Pulling out, he rested me on the ground, his bronzed chest heaving. His eyes burst with the flames of his godly form as he stared at me.

"Are you mine, Amazon?"

His voice had gone so deep I could feel the vibration in my toes.

I *was* his. He'd owned me from the time our gazes locked for the first time in the arena. Claimed me from the moment he'd stormed into that bathroom, ready to raise hell. Consumed me since the act of him feeding me that damn bagel told us both what we were to each other.

"Yes," I whispered.

The flames snuffed out, and he grabbed my hair, yanking my head back to claim me first with his mouth. Every inch became his with several laps of his tongue. His hand trailed over my stomach, and a finger dipped between my folds. I moaned into his mouth, spreading my legs for him.

He pulled away, sucking on my bottom lip and letting it slide between his teeth. His eyes turned blood red, and he grabbed my hips, turning me around. His hand pressed to the middle of my back, bending me over the desk. As he drove into me from behind, I gasped, gripping the edges of the desk as my head flew back. He dug his fingers into my hips, plunging into me over and over. A tingle started at the base of my neck, shot down my spine, and burst through my core.

Ares paused for a split second as if he'd felt it too, his grip tightening on my hips. He bent over me, kissing up my spine until he reached my shoulder. Snarling, he bit me. A sweet pain that didn't break the skin. The tingling sensation swirled in my brain, flashing images I'd never seen before—battles throughout the ages, explosions, swords, axes, raids, and through it all, us fighting side-by-side.

I pushed onto my elbows, arching my back and presenting myself further for him. I'd never given up control—never like this. But he was mine as much as I was his, and I wanted all of it. All of him.

His fists slammed on the desk, and he wrapped a hand over one of my shoulders, grasping my waist with the other. Reaching a hand back, I explored his corded thigh muscle with my fingers. My insides clenched with every flex he made. I flipped myself around, spreading for him with my back on the table. He moved forward, ready to retake me, but I stopped him with my foot.

"Are you mine, God of War?"

His eyelids grew heavy, and he bent over me, easily pushing my foot to the side and dragging his hand up my inner thigh. His face lowered over mine, the wavy tendrils of his dark hair tickling my cheeks. "Say it."

"Are you mine, Ares?"

Red smoke mixed with flashes of light formed around us. The faint sounds of ancient battle overlapped with the music of Greece fluttered across my ears. He touched the tip of my nose with his.

"I'd start a *war* for you," he declared, driving into me.

My breasts pressed into his chest, his arms flexing on either side of my head as he triumphed over me. He was my surrender. No one or nothing else could vanquish me. We didn't look away from one another as our bodies cemented the unspoken bond. I'd said the same mold formed us. Now we melded together.

His thrusts increased, and his beard skimmed my chin as he kissed my lips. A passion pulsed through me, starting at the base of my skull and traveling over my shoulders—a passion driving from him into me—the spirit of battle itself. My back arched off the desk, hips bucking against him as I cried out. My nails dug into his back, and he grunted. As my body shivered, coming down from its volcanic release, Ares groaned into my hair, thrusting through his own release.

The smoke, lights, and sounds faded away. I pulsed around him, unsure of where the ground was anymore, not to mention the ceiling. It felt like I could float straight into the clouds.

He secured his hair over one ear and rested a hand on my thigh.

"I'm not complaining in the slightest, but what was that?"

His dark gaze wavered as if in relief. "You felt it too?"

I nodded.

He closed his eyes and rubbed my cheek with his. "I've heard of it before but never thought there was someone out there for me."

"What are you saying?"

He leaned back and cupped my chin. "A fated bond."

My heart hummed at the words whispering from his lips like a caress.

I sat up, scooting to the edge of the table and pushing the bridge of my nose between his pecs. "Did you mean what you said?"

He rested his hands on my back, kissing the top of my head. "Which part, gatáki?"

"About starting a war for me." I lifted my head, resting my chin against him.

He dragged the back of his finger over my cheek and then traced his fingertip down my nose. "Yes."

"Keep talking like that, and I'm going to pounce on you again." His scent had me writhing inside before, but now it twisted and pulled, urging me to be with him and never look back.

He slipped his fingers through my hair and rested his palms against both of my cheeks. "I don't know how, but you're a warrior at heart, Harmony. And *that* screams to me as the God of War."

A grin pulled at my lips as I walked my fingers up his legs, landing on his ass and grabbing it. "And as a war god, you should finish what you started."

"Oh?" He curled his hands behind my knees and pulled me toward him until I teetered on the edge of the desk. "Is there still more land to plunder?"

I wrapped my hand in his hair, tugging it. "And don't stop until it's ash."

Cupping the back of my head, he growled before thrusting his tongue into my mouth. "You were *made* for me."

He lived up to his title and pillaged every valley and peak I owned.

FIFTEEN

MY EYES FLUTTERED OPEN, gaze dropping to a thick arm resting over mine. I nuzzled the dark sprouts of hair, and he moaned against the back of my head. Our legs curled together, and the white sheet spread over my chest. I rolled to face him, slipping my hand into his with a smile.

"Kaliméra," he purred, brushing hair away from my eyes.

"Does that mean good morning?"

"Mm, yes, or good day in general. Once it's the evening, you say 'kalispéra.'"

I bit down on my lip. "Kal-i…mera?"

A deep chuckle flowed from his chest. "Now say it without sounding like a question."

I playfully kicked him in the shin. "Kaliméra,"

"Téleio." He brushed his lips over my cheek. "Perfect."

"I'd love to learn more Greek if you'd teach me."

He grinned and bopped the tip of my nose with his knuckle.

"Of course." He sat up and slid until his back pressed to the headboard, motioning for me to follow.

I wiggled between his legs and rested my back against his chest. He hiked one knee, and I ran my finger down the top of his thigh. A silver dagger appeared in his outstretched hand.

"What the hell?" I stared at the dagger as he twirled it in his palm.

"This?" He gave it one toss and held the handle out to me. "Have I not shown you that power?"

I ran my fingers over the smooth marble. "Um, no. Pretty sure I'd remember."

"I can conjure any weapon Hephaistos has forged for me." *Hephaestus. God of the forge? Had to be.*

He touched my tattoo, tracing over its markings. "These symbols suit you."

"Would it alarm you if I said I didn't know what they were?"

He chuckled and craned his neck to look at me. "You got permanent ink in your skin without knowing what it meant?"

"I was at the parlor, and it…came to me."

He kissed my temple with a low "mm." "Every passing day makes more and more sense."

"Are you going to tell me what they mean?"

He trailed his finger over a symbol with a half-circle on top, flowing into a line which resembled raised arms and another line ending in a check with a horizontal line across it. "Warrior." Moving his touch, he paused on the one drawn like a fancy backward "S" with two diagonal lines in the center. "Immortality."

I stiffened. How did I pick a symbol meaning immortality

all those years ago?

He smiled against the side of my head as he landed on the final mark. A straight line with opposite-facing triangles on each end and a swirly "S" shape through the center. "Harmony."

"Do you think a god or goddess influenced me to get this design? These symbols?"

He continued to draw lazy circles over the tattoo. "Perhaps. Or you dug it up from a place deeply seated."

"Tell me more about you, Ares." I nestled against him like I was a child waiting for storytime.

"What do you wish to know?" He made the dagger disappear and reappear from his palm several times.

"Everything."

He smiled against the top of my head. "Not sure we have time for thousands of years of my life, but I'll tell you the highlights."

"I'm all ears, Spartan."

"How much of Greek mythology do you know?"

I puckered my lips, dipping into my ten-year-old brain. "Zeus. Titans. Underworld. Apollo. Aphrodite." My shoulders tensed. "Wait. You banged Aphrodite. Your *sister.*"

He sighed. "Vlákas. Thousands of stories, and you had to remember that one."

Keeping silent, I waited, pleading for him to tell me it wasn't true.

"I have a rare opportunity here to clear the air on a few things. One being an affair with Aphrodite. I swear you tell your sister she looks beautiful *one* time, and mortals run away with it like olive branches in the wind."

"So…you didn't sleep with her?"

He curled his arm over my chest, resting his hand on my opposite shoulder. "No. I've never even thought of her that way. Let me tell you something. Homer—you know who that is, correct?"

I tilted my head up to throw him a look of exasperation.

"Right. I had to ask. Homer hated me—hated what I represented. He preferred Athena's version of war. Less violent. More strategic. At least that's the spin they put on it." He traced circles on my shoulder with his fingertip. "Despite what most may think, war is often necessary to progress. It isn't always diplomatic. Humans were inherently created to fight for what they believe in, and then you add free will into the mix…well."

I rested the back of my head against his nape. "You represent Sparta, and Athena represented Athens then."

"Insightful. Yes."

"It's one thing for Homer to hate you, but the story with Aphrodite is pure humiliation." I frowned.

"More people feared me than reveled in what I could provide. There were few temples in my honor. Those who worshipped me were often called cults." He trailed his hand down the side of my face. "Who was I to blame them? They misinterpreted me as a symbol of catastrophe. When in reality, I was the representation of regeneration."

"Not everyone is as open to change," I whispered.

If we genuinely shared this—fated bond, as he called it… why me?

"Exactly. When I was younger, the ridicule drove me crazy. Zeus exiled me from Olympus because I couldn't control my anger. My rage." His hand resting on my shoulder balled into a fist. "My own father threw me from our home rather than try to help—to teach me how to use the powers bestowed on me."

He was abandoned by a father he had, but who was unwilling to be one. The words hit home and made my chest tighten. "What did you do?"

"My uncle, Hades, was more of a father to me than Zeus ever was." He made a tsking sound. "Probably because he too was dealt a poor hand from the King of the Gods."

"And once you were in control, you didn't try to go back to Olympus?"

"No," he snarled. "The last thing I was going to do was come crawling back to dear old dad. I've done fine. Besides, war isn't even the same anymore."

"Battles are fought every day all over the world."

He scraped his beard against my forehead. "Wars of today are far less poetic. Now you can kill a man from miles away with a well-aimed shot without them ever seeing your face."

"Unlike a sword?"

"Yes. It also took far more cunning to survive. Spraying bullets is one thing, but knowing how to swing a sword, another matter entirely. The world has lost its intimacy—with war, each other, all of it."

Somehow in a deep-rooted place within my soul, I *felt* his words. "The heroes of Ancient Greece—Achilles, Theseus, Perseus. Did any of it have to do with you?"

"I pushed them all through the frenzy of war. Gave them

the extra passion and energy to succeed because I knew only in their successes would Greece progress."

"And you received no credit because to give you credit would've glorified you," I muttered, my frown deepening.

"To put it mildly," he replied, his voice trailing off. "But at the end of the day, the name Ares will always be synonymous with the God of War. Homer, on the other hand, gets tossed in with a chubby yellow oaf obsessed with donuts."

I let the words sink in with widened eyes before bursting with laughter.

He gave a wry grin.

I needed to feel it again—feel the passion driving through me with a sword against my palm. Now that I knew who he was.

I turned to face him. "Why don't we continue this storytelling session elsewhere?"

He cocked an eyebrow. "Where do you suggest?"

"Your gym," I replied with a grin, sliding off the bed. "Now that I know who you are, I want to spar again."

He rubbed his chin, squinting at me like I was the world's most complicated chess move. "I don't want to hurt you, Harm."

"You know you never would, but I want a chance to show you what I'm truly made of. Give me a challenge. In between jabs, you keep telling me about your life."

He stood in front of me, trailing his fingertips down my cheeks. "For a mortal, you're taking this all incredibly well. I can't say I saw this coming."

You and me both, buddy.

"In the back of my head, I think I've known since the moment I met you. I can't explain it. I just…knew. Like the symbols in my tattoo."

A fated bond…

His eyes twinkled, and he bent his head to kiss me.

"Care to make this trip a little faster? There are no witnesses here. None at the gym." I rolled my bottom lip between my teeth with a smile.

He chuckled. "Genuinely, did *not* see this coming." With a simple touch from him to my shoulder, we appeared in the middle of the gym through a flash of light and smoke, fully clothed.

"I'd never get tired of that." I beamed up at him.

His smile faded, and he rubbed the back of his neck before turning away.

Was it something I said?

"You say you want to show me your full potential." A xiphos appeared in his hand, its blade glinting from the overhead lights. "Is there a reason you held back before?"

I paced the borders of the mat. "Before, I felt caged."

"And now?" He tossed the xiphos to me and produced a javelin.

I caught the sword and locked gazes with him. "I'm invigorated with a newfound valor." Taking position, I raised the sword and slid one foot forward. "Is that your doing?"

"Partly, perhaps." He flipped the javelin across his back and to the opposite hand. "Each god influences mortals in different ways. But whereas Apollo inspires creativity, I inspire destruction…"

He launched his javelin, and I swung my sword down, deflecting the blow.

"Victory," he continued, standing upright before twirling the javelin in his hands above my head.

I ducked and slid across the mat on one knee.

"Justice." He did a quick spin to avoid my thrust at his right shoulder.

I dropped to my knees and slashed at the back of his leg, nicking it with my blade. He cocked an eyebrow, tripped me onto my back, and pointed the javelin at my face. I smiled as he sunk, his hair falling over my face, framing it.

"Protection," he whispered, his lips brushing mine.

"Are you saying I need protection?" I pushed the javelin aside and sat up on my elbows.

"Everyone does at some time or another. It doesn't make you weak."

"Even the God of War?"

"Even me," he said with a deep huskiness.

I raised my forearm, holding it out as if a shield were strapped to it. "My shield is yours."

His eyes blazed. "The blood we would've shed."

His words. His gaze. Everything about him sent my heart racing.

"Tell me more," I whispered.

He hoisted me up. A shield appeared in my hand, followed by a matching one in his.

"The Trojan War," he started, beating the hilt of his sword against the shield.

"I'm familiar."

He slashed at me, and I blocked it with the shield—the sound of metal crashing into metal bounced off the gym walls.

"Our beloved Homer wrote me as a coward—weaker than the other gods." He slashed, turned on his heel, jumped, and stabbed downward.

I blocked one blow with the shield, deflected the other with my blade, and slammed my shield into his.

"More lies?"

"An endless string. He stated Aphrodite was the one who convinced me to fight alongside the Trojans." His javelin poked from the top of his shield.

I sidestepped away, bringing my shield up, snapping the weapon.

He lowered his shield with a twinkle in his eye—an expression bordering on shocked and impressed.

"You were extremely loyal to the Greeks. How could she have possibly convinced you otherwise?"

"She didn't. Zeus commanded me. I think it was because he knew they'd lose and didn't want me on the victor's side."

"I'm guessing all the stories about Zeus aren't fabricated?" I darted forward, planting blow after blow into his shield, moving him backward.

He grunted when he neared the wall, throwing his shield and xiphos to the ground. "Our stories have all been fabricated to a point. How would a mortal know the affairs that happened in the Underworld? On Mount Olympus?"

"Fair point."

He threw his fists at his sides, making billowy red flames waft over them.

"That, however—" I stared at the power coursing through his veins. "Isn't fair."

"Is war ever?"

My stomach flipped and twisted. Resting the blade of my sword on top of my shield, I eyed his hands, ready for the first strike.

"You're going to shoot fire in here?"

A challenging grin quirked his lips. "Better get to blocking."

He threw one arm out, palm up. A fireball launched at me, and I blocked myself with the shield. The metal sizzled and popped.

"Homer described me as 'hateful Ares,' 'the war-glutton,' the 'curse of men,' to name a few. How could I be anything but gluttonous for battle? And the only men I would curse are those too weak to fight for honor."

Another fireball. This one left a fist-sized hole in my shield, the edges glowing neon red before leaving behind blackened remains.

"Did Athena really hit you over the head with a rock?" I winced.

The fire blazed brighter, swirling up his arms. "A rock hit me, yes. But not from Athena. A javelin hit a nearby cliff, but I'm a *god*. It felt like nothing more than a mild tickle."

"And the pitiful Ares scream that sounded like ten thousand men?"

He shook his head, the red flames leading up to his shoulders. "A chorus of men screaming from my repeated javelin throws."

He slammed his hands together, sending a shockwave of fire. I lifted my shield over my head as the flame burst into it, sliding me across the mat. When I opened my eyes, only half of the shield remained, and I stared at Ares through the smoking hole left behind.

"How did you know I'd be able to block that?"

He wiggled his fingers, making the fire on his hand hiss. "Because I wouldn't be fated to you if you couldn't."

My heart raced, goosebumps littered my skin, and every neuron in my body shouted for him.

I tossed the damaged shield aside as he threw another ball. Front somersaulting forward, I hurled my sword at him. He leaned to one side, catching it by the blade with a quirked brow.

"You tell these stories like you need to convince me of who and what you represent." I sauntered toward him, crossing one foot over the other. "If men feared you, *good*. We didn't need that kind on the battlefield. Their purpose was elsewhere. A fairly good-looking guy told me once, battles aren't won by doing something half-assed."

The flames disappeared as he lifted a hand to brush his thumb over my chin. "Are you sure that's what he said?"

"Something like that." I shrugged, offering a wry grin.

He held my xiphos in one hand and materialized a gold spear with four prongs. The two in the middle were longer and thinner, while the other two were thicker.

"Try fighting with this."

"Is this—a trident?" I flicked the pointy end.

"Tridents are for sea gods. I had Hephaistos add an extra prong."

"How mature of you."

"And everyone thinks I'm *so* serious." He winked.

"So, what do I call this then? A quadrident?"

He let out a deep, masculine chuckle. "Whatever you want to call it, the blades still work the same."

"Not entirely sure I know what to do with this." I twirled the handle in my palm, watching the reflections bounce off the golden prongs.

"You said that about the xiphos too." He dragged a hand over the top of his head, securing the dark tendrils briefly before they fell again. "Are you going to keep underestimating yourself or give it a swing?"

His fiery gaze pierced me, sending a mixture of lust and fury.

I thrust the spear forward. He deflected. In a circular motion, I swung the weapon around my head, attempting to clip him. He slid backward with a grin. I spun around, hurling the spear with me, and it crashed into the side of Ares's sword.

"You're a natural," he cooed. "I dare say it's in your blood."

I cinched my brow. "You keep saying that. What does it *mean*, Ares? What does this say about the entire life I've led?"

"I don't have an answer for you. I wish we'd have met sooner. Maybe I could've kept you from going through all that—" His throat bobbed as he gulped, staring at me across the room with a heated gaze. "Pain."

Sinuses stinging, I stared at the conviction on his face as he shared his truth. I thrust forward, slid back, and jumped, striking down. His blade caught between the prongs, and I yanked the hilt from his grasp.

The intensity in his stare suggested he was moments away from repeating last night's hotel room desk act. Heart pounding, I ran forward, dipped the prongs, and swung up, aiming for his chest. He grabbed the spear right below the prongs and yanked it from me, throwing it into the wall like a javelin.

He wrapped a hand around my wrist and pulled me forward. I collapsed against him, welcoming the kiss, opening my mouth wider to let more of him in.

He slipped away, nibbling on my lower lip. "The dream you had of us on the battlefield…"

The darkness of his eyes was like looking into a well—bending over to peer into its mystery, trying to make out where the blackness stopped, and the water began—bending, bending, bending…until you fell in.

I nodded.

"Were we in an ancient battle?"

"Spartans."

He cocked his head to the side, trailing a fingertip between my shoulder blades. "And after we were victorious?"

The fact he didn't need to ask *if* we were victorious made my stomach clench.

"We raced to our tent."

"Our tent?"

"Uh-huh."

He brushed his beard against my cheek, skirting his lips over my earlobe. "And what did we do in *our* tent?"

"Celebrated. Multiple times," I whispered against his neck.

"Mm," he growled, his nose dipping to my collarbone.

"I'm game for reenacting it if you are." I raised a brow.

"And what would we be celebrating?"

"I'm sure we can think of something."

"You should probably save your strength for the fight

tomorrow. Sex is like a battle to me. I *never* go 'half-assed' as you so eloquently put it." He bumped his knuckle under my chin.

"That wasn't very nice." I pouted.

He grinned. "I'm not nice. Or haven't you heard?"

I rolled my eyes and sighed, turning away to let my raging hormones settle or die trying. "So, fireballs, huh? Any other powers I should know about? Especially ones that can singe my hair?"

He yanked me back to him, wrapping his arms around me. "There's plenty you don't know. But I prefer to keep an air of mystery. I wouldn't want to bore you."

"I don't think that's possible."

He canted his head to one side before diving to my neck, kissing it.

"Although, if you're hiding the fact you can summon a chariot with fire-breathing horses from me at will or something, I may never forgive you." I snickered.

His lips fell away, and his grip tightened against my back.

"Ares?"

"About this fated bond…" He gave several pecks to my neck.

I pushed him back. "You can summon a chariot with fire-breathing horses?"

"Yes." He slow-blinked. "But I haven't had a reason in a very long time."

I stayed silent for a moment, contemplating.

"Can I see it?"

"I'm not exactly sure the gym could contain it."

Silence fell over me again.

He trailed a hand between my shoulder blades, leading to the base of my spine. "I promise I'll show you when the time is right."

And just like that, he turned my insides to goo and sent my nerves igniting into explosions.

SIXTEEN

I WENT TO BED that night with a tornado of feelings that refused to make sense battling each other—confusion, lust, inspiration, anger. Even with Ares's body snuggled behind me, his scent sending a wave of calm over my skin, I lay awake for what seemed hours.

"Finally. I thought you'd *never* fall asleep. Mortals and their puny brains in constant use." A woman's deep, raspy voice spoke from somewhere in the darkness of the room.

I tensed and sat up, staring down at myself very much asleep.

"Yes, you're still sleeping." The mysterious woman's outline barely stood out from the blackness spilling over the room, sitting on the corner of the desk with her legs crossed, the top one bouncing.

Storming from the bed, I clenched my fists at my side. "Who the hell are you?"

She slunk from the shadows, stepping into the sliver of

light from the moon peeking through the curtains. "Eris. Goddess of Discord." Her black hair fell in waves down to her knees, streaks of vibrant red scattered throughout. "I'd say the pleasure is all mine, but this anything but a courtesy call." Her eyes were midnight pools. No iris. No pupil. Only pure sin forged into a visual orb within her skull.

Every fiber of my being screamed this chick was bad news, but try as I might catapult at her, it was as if an invisible shield rose between us. "How are you in my dreams?"

She traced black pointy fingernails twice the length of her finger down the leather corset hugging her thin torso. "Morpheus owed me a favor. Besides, it's the only way I could talk to you without my lug of a brother butting in." She flicked her hand at Ares's slumbering body, making the nails click together.

"You have thirty seconds before I'm entirely bored of this conversation."

She made a *clicking* sound with her teeth. "Down, tigress. I'm simply here to make you think about your next move."

I fake yawned.

Her high-heeled boots made holey impressions in the carpet as she sauntered to the side of the bed, leaning over Ares. My blood boiled, going on the defense. Sleep made him vulnerable.

"By Olympus—" She took a whiff of the air over the two of us sleeping before she canted her head at me. "A fated bond. I didn't think such a thing existed for our kind anymore."

"How could you possibly know that? Ares even barely knows what it is."

She made her way back to me, crossing one foot over the

other. The black skin-tight leggings shifted with every step. Lowering her nose to my neck, she took a deep inhale. "Because you reek of it—of him."

My knuckles groaned as I clenched them harder at my sides. I wanted to tackle her to the ground and beat the red highlights from her skull. "Is there a point to this?"

"There's only one way the two of you could be together." Her thin dark brows rose. "He is immortal after all."

My throat constricted and dried at the same time. I'd been so wrapped up in his declaration there'd hardly been time to come to grips with what he *truly* was.

"Didn't think about that one, did you?" She scraped a nail over my cheek with a sigh, her hand slipping through the invisible shield she put up. "And how selfish would it be for the God of War to ask you to become something you're not? That you were never meant to be?"

My lip twitched, attempting to mask the indecision she caused.

She trailed her claws down my arm, puckering her wine-stained lips before continuing. "You were born a mortal. You've made a life for yourself as a mortal. And you're expected to give it *all* up for what? A guy?"

I tightened my jaw, making it quiver.

"Live your life, Harmony." She tilted her head over my shoulder, her breath chilling against my skin. "Grow old with your family and friends, so you don't have to watch *them* die."

Family. It goes to show how much she knew about me.

I shifted my eyes to Ares, watching the steady rise and fall of his chest as he slept so soundlessly—peacefully. The God of

War. *My* war god.

She slid a sleek fingernail under my chin, turning my gaze back to her. "Do you want to be the woman born to be Ares's plaything? Or do you want to make a name for *yourself*?"

Her words stung. My lip twitched as I tried to hide my expression. The moonlight gave Eris's pale skin an iridescent sheen, and I focused on it.

"Why don't you cut through the bullshit and tell me why you're *really* here?" I stepped forward, bouncing off thin air with a grimace. "You're the goddess of causing trouble, so why are you so keen on warning me? Out of the goodness of your cold black heart?"

Her face scrunched, and she wriggled her long nails. "Ooo, such sass." She shot her arm out, snatching my face and tightening her grip. "You're not strong enough to be one of *us*, girl."

"You don't know a damn thing about me." I tried to pull away, but she held firm.

"Don't I?" She arched a thin brow. "You are a fragile flower dangerously close to withering in the wind. Such brittleness has no place amongst the war gods."

"And the truth comes out."

She hissed as she brought our faces inches apart.

"Were you like this as a kid too? Horrible with sharing?" I clenched my jaw to keep it from shaking.

She scratched a nail down my cheek as she yanked her hand away with a snarl. "We do not need another war god and you least of all. Go back to your mortal life. Forget him. Don't let Ares cloud your judgment just because he can give you a good fuck."

I threw my fist back, ready to strike, but let out an angry growl remembering the shield that'd stop me. "Are you done?" I shot my eyes to hers, nostrils flaring.

Laughter fluttered from her belly, husky and downright criminal. "I've said all I needed to say. Remember it in the days to come." She half-grinned, revealing pointy canine teeth.

In a flash of embers and lightning, she was gone, and I jolted awake with a gasp. Surveying the room, I reassured myself she wasn't there. But every moment spent with her embedded itself under my skin like a parasite.

"Bad dream?" Ares murmured beside me, his large hand slipping over my thigh.

"You know how it is."

He grunted. "That I do. Come here." He opened his arms wide and inviting.

I settled against him, curling my hands over my chest.

He dragged a finger over the fresh scrape on my cheek. "What happened there?"

"It's just a scratch, must've done it myself in my sleep." I offered a weak smile.

Eris's visit played like an old-time film reel in the back of my mind, but I'd sift through it another time. For now, I'd nuzzle into the warmth of the war god sprawled out on the sheets, waiting to wrap himself around me. His beard grazed the back of my neck as he molded himself to my backside, and I fell asleep intoxicated by the scents of leather and chaos.

I was up before the sun, sitting on the edge of the bed, tracing every spot on the carpet Eris's heels had touched. The more I thought about her words, the more confused and pissed off I became.

Ares grumbled behind me. "You're up early. What happened to rest for the fight?"

"I've got a lot on my mind."

"This fight is in the bag, gatáki. You have nothing to worry about." He brushed my arm.

I batted his hand away and stood. "You can't expect me to give up my life. You know that, right?"

Ares's eyes widened for a fraction of a second. "What? Who said anything about—"

"How am I supposed to know if any piece of my life has ever been my own?" I slapped a hand over my forehead. "I mean, was I meant to be yours from the moment I was conceived? Born? Turned eighteen?"

His once softened expression turned to stone. "Vlákas, Harm. Where is this coming from?" He stood, rolling his shoulders back.

I tried to ignore the sight of him standing there in only a pair of black boxers—the wide frame, chiseled muscle…

Turning my back on him, I folded my arms, clamping my hands at my sides. "I'm so confused. For the first time in my life, something felt right. Felt…in place. But how can something feel so complete and so disjointed all at the same time?"

"It's not how it works."

"What?" I regretted the scowl I gave him over my shoulder as soon as I'd done it.

"A fated bond? If you truly were born for me, Harmony, it'd be the same of me, for you."

My eyes darted in every direction as if they tried to piece together the jigsaw puzzle floating in my brain. "Then why wasn't I born an immortal to begin with?"

He beat his knuckles against the opposite palm. "You'd be a different person. And I'm a lot to handle."

"I'm no walk in the park, Ares."

His eyes fell shut with a masculine purr when I said his name. "Let me take you somewhere."

"Where?"

"Greece."

"Greece? That's halfway across the world we'd have to f— "

He appeared in front of me, wrapping his arms around my waist. "We won't have to fly."

"You can teleport that far?"

A silent nod. His eyes pierced me, trying to dig through the confusion I exuded.

"Okay," I whispered.

The word no sooner left my lips, and we were in the middle of an open-air marketplace. Pillars surrounded us on every side, scents of freshly baked bread and olives floated through the air. The sun beamed from the cloudless blue sky. We stood in our regular clothes, our appearance blending in with the rest of the Greek crowd.

Ares draped his arm over my shoulders, his leather jacket accentuating his scent. "I brought you here to relax. No one is asking you to do something or anything. But every Greek should experience the country. Open yourself to her."

I'd expected Ares to be rigid under my touch in public—for a permanent scowl to overtake his features. He had a reputation to uphold, didn't he? But now and again, he'd soften for me. *Me*. The fact I knew he could kill dozens of men, monsters, or anything else that crossed his path, drove me wild. But knowing at the end of the day, his harsh overtone could transform into a feather-like touch pushed me over the edge.

"Somehow, this feels right. It feels like—home."

Ares gave my neck a quick kiss before holding his finger up at a nearby vendor.

"Kaliméra," they both exchanged.

"Póso kostízei?" He asked the clerk and dropped his lips to my ear. "How much does it cost?"

I smiled and mouthed the words back to myself. The vendor had rows of brown circular dough with a glaze.

"Dío," the vendor answered, holding up two fingers.

Dio meant two. That one was easy enough to understand.

Ares slipped a colorful bill from his back pocket. He pointed at the dough and swished his finger back and forth. "Záchari. Záchari."

The vendor flashed a bright smile. "Nái." He grabbed a metal container and sprinkled powdered sugar over the dough, wrapping them in wax paper.

Ares handed me one, and I blanched at the sight of him acting so…normal.

"Loukoumades. Greek donuts."

I took a bite and all but salivated. Cinnamon. Honey. And the perfect amount of fried crunch.

"Ares has a sweet tooth. Who knew?" I covered my mouth

with a hand, still chewing on the delicious dough. "Oh shit. I shouldn't be saying that name."

He waved his hand. "As páne sto diáblo."

I arched a brow.

"They can go to hell," he snorted.

We strolled the brick-lined walkways of the marketplace. The sun continued to blaze, and I tried to imagine what an ancient agora would've looked like in comparison. "Do the other gods go by aliases?"

"Most of them, yes." He shoved the rest of the donut in his mouth and licked the remaining sugar from his thumb.

My stomach clenched, spying his tongue lapping over his fingertip. "Do they uh—do they all use the Greek accent?"

"No." He balled his wax paper into his hand. "It's the most obvious, but they all do their own thing. I do mine."

I stared at the scattering of powdered sugar in his beard at the corner of his mouth. Biting my lip, I pointed and tried not to laugh. "It looks like it's snowing. On your face."

He tilted his eyes down like he could see it and then lurched forward, wiping his face against my mouth.

I laughed and pushed at his chest. He pulled me against him and licked the corner of my mouth, ridding it of sugar. I beamed up at him, still somehow laughing. I'd never smiled so much in my life.

It was almost enough to make me forget about Eris. Almost.

"How are you like this? With so much fury inside you and barely able to use your powers to unleash it? You're here in a marketplace acting like a mortal." I bit my lip. "I can barely manage to act like a mortal on any given day."

He sighed, brushing his lips across my forehead before resting his chin on the top of my head. "It's hard to explain. I feel a sort of—peace with you at times."

A man brushed past us, slamming into my shoulder from behind.

Ares's gaze turned feral, eyes glowing red. He slammed his forehead into the unknowing man's face.

Fuck.

I jumped forward, clamping my hand on the man's nose to stop the bleeding. "You're fine. You'll be fine. Not even broken, just—" Grabbing the man's hand, I switched mine for his. "Keep pressure."

The man was far too terrified of the towering war god standing next to me growling to complain. He shrieked and ran off. Several patrons stared at us, whispering and pointing. I grabbed his bicep and led him to a quieter area, away from the hustle and bustle of people haggling and shoving money in every direction.

"Peace, huh?" A goofy grin spread across my lips.

His eyebrow bounced. "I did say, 'at times.' It's different when someone tries to hurt you."

"He bumped into me."

"Semantics."

"Come on, you raging inferno, let's sit down." I pointed at a white bench nestled under a shaded tree.

Ares sat rigid with his hands curled over his knees. At any other moment, the sight may have been amusing. But now, I'd begun to understand. There was this constant rage in him. An urge to protect, serve, and never lose. It must've been exhausting being at two-hundred percent, one-hundred percent of the time.

A kitten scurried past our feet, a little girl shrieking, following its trail. Her small hands were outstretched, tripping over the occasional cobblestone that stuck out from the rest. "Gatáki," the girl cried as she passed us.

I slowly turned my head to Ares with narrowed eyes. "Kitten? That's what you've been calling me this entire time?"

"Is *that* what the word means? I thought it meant pool sludge." He eyed me sidelong, a hint of a smile hidden within the scattering of hair around his mouth.

"You're lucky. If it'd been coming out of anyone else's mouth, I'd—"

"You'd what?" He swooped in, wrapping his arms around my upper and lower back, pressing his nose against mine.

"I'd—I'd."

No one else. No one had ever rendered me speechless.

"Tell me about your life, Harm," he spoke against my cheek.

"And why would someone like you care anything about my shit show of a life?"

He leaned back, interlacing our fingers on his lap. "Someone like me?"

"Someone who represents destruction, battling, war?"

"And victory. And courage. And protection." The rage within his eyes settled, a serenity shadowing his gaze. "There's no way you could know how it feels to have a mortal woman look at you with anything but hatred. I couldn't even say the same thing for most of my family."

Telling him about my life was a dark hole I wasn't sure I

wanted to crawl into. These past few days with him made me forget my past existed. *Days*. How was it possible to feel this way about someone in a matter of days when I barely had love from a parent.

"Alright." I lifted one foot onto the bench.

He brushed a thumb over my knuckles.

"With how long you've been around, I'm sure you've heard this story thousands of times."

"Impossible," he responded, dropping his voice an octave.

I quirked a brow.

"None of them were you."

Heart. Squeezed.

"My mom was single. Got around a lot. Mostly because she didn't make much money as a waitress and needed a way to get her fix."

A falcon flew overhead, cawing before it swooped up to the roof of a nearby building.

"Cocaine was her drug of choice, even did it while pregnant with me. It's a wonder I'm still alive."

Ares squeezed my hand, remaining silent but reminding me he was still there.

"She told me giving birth to me was one of the most painful experiences of her life. Is it horrible that I'm *glad* I gave her that much pain?"

"No," he gruffed.

I tilted my head back, letting the sun warm my cheeks. "She swore up and down that a muse appeared. They sang to her for inspiration—to soothe her. I didn't believe her at the time. But now I wonder if it was true."

"It's possible. If I had to guess, it wasn't for your mother so much as it was for you."

My head snapped back down. "What do you mean?"

"To make sure you existed." His eyelids grew heavy.

"She did say it's the reason she named me Harmony." My voice disappeared into the distance.

He brushed a finger across one side of my jaw, then the other. "Keep going, gatáki."

"From what I can remember, my mom was rarely home. And when she was, she was too high to function half the time. Imagine a four-year-old taking care of themselves. A human one that is."

He stayed silent.

"I remember the look on my uncle's face when I opened the door, and he realized I was home alone." I stared at our hands locked together. "He was the reason I didn't turn out even more fucked up than I already am."

"You? Vlaménos? Far from it." He waved a hand down his body, referencing himself with a cocked brow.

I shook my head with a small grin. "When my uncle died is when the anger issues started. Without my mom to care about it, I got into a lot of trouble at school. One of my teachers, Ms. Hestia, for whatever reason, took me under her wing."

"In what way?"

"In more ways than a teacher should. She made sure I had enough food, bought me school supplies, shoes. She even signed me up for my first martial arts class." Suddenly the cracks in the cobblestones interested me.

"What's the matter?"

"I honestly hadn't remembered her until right now. A woman who went above and beyond for me." My grip tightened around his hand.

"Harmony," he said, keeping his voice soft.

I looked up at him like a doe caught in headlights.

"If I were human, you'd have broken a finger by now." He jutted his chin at our hands.

I let go with a gasp, clapping my hands over my mouth.

"Harm, what's the matter?" He rested a hand on my bicep, idly kneading it.

"Hestia. Isn't she a goddess?" I asked through the muffling of my hands.

He curled a single finger over mine and dragged them away from my face. "Yes."

"Do you think it was her?"

He canted his head to the side. "We've already established there's some kind of connection with you and our world."

A man bumped into my foot as he squeezed past us to the courtyard.

Ares played his seething gaze on the clumsy mortal. Before I could mutter the word 'baklava', Ares stood up.

"Ares," I murmured, touching his forearm with my fingertips.

His eyes, ablaze with red, snapped down to me.

"I think your tolerance for the public is done for the day. Let's get back." I stood up, keeping my tone cool and even.

The longer he looked at me, and the more pronounced my grip on his arm became, the more the tension and fury in him thawed. He pressed a hand against my upper back, ushering us to a deserted alleyway. With one hand on my shoulder and the other on my hip, he transported us back to America.

Later that evening, I stared at a black smudge on the tiled floor of the locker room, lost in my thoughts. My fingers subconsciously did and undid the Velcro strap of my glove.

"We'll figure it out." Ares leaned against one of the lockers with his arms folded over his chest.

My eyes lifted to meet his. "That's not what I'm worried about."

He frowned and took a step forward. "I'd never ask you to do it, Harm."

"Why?" A pit formed in my stomach.

He froze. "What do you mean?"

"You say we have this fated bond. That you never thought it'd happen to you. You know the only way we can be together, so why wouldn't you ask me?"

He rubbed the back of his neck, idly chewing on the hair near his lower lip. "Because I'd feel like a vlákas."

"It'd be my decision. So, why wouldn't you ask me?"

We stared at each other, dissecting, yearning, fleeting.

"Well, I have several pieces of interesting news," Chelsea's voice chimed.

She whisked into the locker room, swinging her purse onto the bench beside me. As usual, her phone had her attention. Ares retreated to the lockers, leaning back and propping one booted foot against the metal.

"You two can stop pretending," Chelsea said with a smirk.

I raised a brow. "Pretending what?"

"As if your relationship is platonic anymore." Her gaze lifted. "I applaud it. I really do. But I'd be lying if I said I'm not slightly hurt that as your friend, you didn't bother mentioning it."

"Chels, it's new. We—"

"Well, the whole world knows now. Hope you're prepared." She displayed the phone screen.

A shot of Ares and me in the marketplace with his arms around me, kissing my temple, us grinning from ear-to-ear. I should've been annoyed, but all I could do was stare at how happy we looked. How normal we seemed.

Ares shifted behind me, reaching a hand over my shoulder and scrolling through the other photos. Him kissing the sugar away from my mouth. Our hands interlocked, talking in mid-sentence—a shot of him seething at the man who'd bumped into me.

"Is this going to be a problem?" Ares's voice rumbled in my ear.

I shook my head.

Chelsea snatched her phone back. "Good. Because the other news bothered me more."

Ares drummed his fingers on my shoulder.

"Priscila and the man who tried to *kill* you miraculously turned themselves in yesterday. Both had broken noses." She arched a thin auburn brow.

"Good," I snapped.

Her eyes blinked with the speed of a jackhammer. "Good?

That's all you have to say, Harmony? Good? You never told me someone tried to kill you. Don't you think that's something your publicist, your *friend*, would've liked to know?"

"Because you would've freaked out about it just as you're doing now. Probably even cancel the tour. We took care of it. Threat detained."

Ares's body pressed against my back. Heat radiated off him like a furnace, and I fought the compulsion to melt into him.

Chelsea's bottom lip quivered as it always did when she got angry. She pointed at Ares. "Is this your doing?"

"It was a team effort." He walked his fingers up my spine.

She thinned her lips. "I had half a mind to quit."

"Chelsea." I reached out.

She held up her palm. "But I'm not quitting because I care about you more than just as a client. Pull shit like this again, though, Harm, and I'm seriously out the door."

My throat tightened, knowing another lie, a bigger lie, loomed right behind me. "Understood."

She nodded and then pulled me in for a hug. "I can handle more than you think."

"I know. And I won't forget that again, Chels." I gave her a quick squeeze.

She stepped back, tossing her red hair over one shoulder. "Right, then. Announcements are in five minutes. Mars, with Priscila in jail, there's no more need for your services. I'll have a check for you in the morning." After giving a firm nod, she left. The sound of her heels rhythmically clicking across the tiled hallway faded away.

"Let's get this joke of a fight over with."

He massaged my shoulders. "It's not a joke."

"The fight doesn't count, Ares."

He pressed his lips to my ear. "Every fight counts. Not every battle will win you a title."

"Are you sure those photos aren't going to bother you?" I turned to face him. "What if word got back to Olympus that the God of War is a big softy?"

"First off, I'm anything but soft." He pressed himself against me, his acute hardness grazing my stomach. "And having a passion for your woman is anything but weak. Why would I be ashamed to show it?"

You were made for me.

If I genuinely had some cosmic connection with him, with the gods and goddesses of Greece, why were he and I just meeting now? So many questions.

"Time for a Greek to beat a Trojan. Again."

They had both fighters enter at the same time, given there was no champion. I tried my hardest to maintain a neutral face. One which suggested I was there, but maybe not entirely happy about it. My usual *Wonder Woman* music played, and I bounced on the balls of my feet, throwing jabs as I made my way down the path. Despite Ares no longer being my bodyguard, he still followed my trail—the protective side of him in full swing.

My opponent, Talia the Trojan, came out on a horse. A real live horse. The need to eye roll was strong, but I managed to hold back. I'd hoped the horse would take a shit as it walked, but no such luck.

Ares took a spot outside the cage, catching my gaze with

a knowing glint in his eyes. I'd win within ten seconds. He knew it. I knew it. And the sooner it happened, the sooner he and I could...celebrate my victory.

Talia worked the crowd, sashaying a full circle around the ring, throwing her arms up in the air with a battle cry which sounded like a dying cat. I rolled my shoulders and beat my fists against each other, waiting for her show to subside.

The announcer walked to the center as some epic song by *Two Steps From Hell* boomed over the loudspeakers. I couldn't contain that eye roll. This was borderline humiliating. I was Ares, and this entire situation was Homer himself.

"The Trojan War. A battle of epic proportions that fueled the future. And now we re-live it tonight, with a fight for the century between The Trojan and The Amazon," the announcer said.

Epic proportions? Hardly.

He didn't have us touch gloves, and as soon as his hand came down for us to begin, I strode forward.

Dodge left. Dip right.

The ancient horns blazed in my ears, making my chest swell. I squatted down and brought my fist forward in an uppercut, planting it straight into her chin. Her feet flew off the ground, going airborne, and she collapsed on her back.

Knock out.

The crowd went silent, clearly hoping for a show. If I had more of an ego, I might have been insulted they arranged for me to fight a woman with such little skill. It took several moments for them to cheer, but I was already on the other side of the cage.

Ares latched onto me before my feet stepped from the stairs, wrapping his arms around my waist and hoisting me up.

"That was the work of a warrior queen," he said, his voice husky.

I scratched my nails against the back of his head, grinning down at him. "Let's get out of here."

"If there weren't so many people around, I'd have had us out of here already."

I waved at Chelsea over his shoulder. She rolled her eyes and flicked her wrist as if to say, "Go on, get outta here."

Not bothering to change my clothes, we pushed past the crowds. Ares was like a linebacker protecting his running back. Our insatiable lust was the football I clung to my chest. Once we reached outside, he led me away from prying eyes.

An owl flew overhead, landing on a maple tree branch with a single "who." Its bright yellow eyes reflected the full moon above, and its head swiveled back and forth.

"An owl? In downtown Denver? That's odd," I said, mesmerized by the bird.

Ares snarled. "That's because it isn't an owl. It's my sister." A sword appeared in his hand.

SEVENTEEN

~~~~~~~~~~~~~~~~~~~~~~~~

"HARM," ARES YELLED, THROWING me a twin xiphos.

I caught it with ease as the world blurred around me. Like paint in water, the sky swirled, followed by the ground until we stood in an open field. Stars scattered half the cloudless blue sky, with the full moon shining bright. The owl flapped its wings, flying from the tree, and in mid-air, transformed into a woman with deeply tanned skin.

A white hood hung over her face, shadowing her features. The hood came to a point like a beak toward the front; ornate golden patterns represented the owl's large eyes and feathers. Armor plating covered her shoulders in golden glimmer, traveling down to a breastplate. The white cloth continued over her hips, forming a tunic with golden flaps. She threw her arm out to one side, producing a sword and swinging it once.

"Ares, my brother. It's been too long." Her voice was smooth, sultry, and breathy.

Glancing between the two gods, I tightened my grip on the sword.

Just what I needed. Another unwanted godly visit.

"Athena. What are you doing?" He asked through a snarl, shifting his feet across the dirt.

Her hooded head turned from him to me. My heart fell to my feet.

"There's been much talk on Olympus of your newfound interest in this mortal." She raised the sword above her head.

She splayed her hand, and a circular golden shield appeared on my arm. She charged at me, and I lifted the shield, resting the blade of my sword on top.

Out of the corner of my eye, Ares appeared at my side. Athena aimed her hand at him, and he slid across the dirt. He dug his heels in, creating a crater once he stopped.

"For once in your life, big brother, *don't* interfere," Athena yelled. "I'm not here to fight you. I'm here to fight—" She pointed the point of her blade at me. "—her."

Her sword slashed in front of me, rattling against my shield. I spun around, swirling the sword with me. Our blades collided with such force, it sent sparks flying in every direction.

"Good," Athena said, a flash of a thin-lipped smile peeking from the confines of her hood.

Was she trying to kill me or just toying with me?

Ares appeared behind her. She whirled around to block his blow, and the two of them engaged in a sword-clashing of divine proportions. I backed away, partially hiding behind my shield in case something exploded.

There was no telling what her appearance meant. Eris's

intent was clear—a conversation to make me question everything that had happened recently. Athena's goal may have been similar. No more room for another war goddess, and they wanted to make damn sure of it.

Despite their different styles, they both fought with equal skill. Aggression fueled Ares's moves with force and harsh lines. While Athena moved smoother, more lucid, like dancing a ballet routine with a sword.

They fought as if I were a specter—an on-looker. I could've tried to get away, but I didn't want to leave.

"Why are you doing this?" Ares growled, producing another xiphos.

He did a barrel roll in the air toward her, bringing each sword down on hers in rapid succession. Athena threw her fists out to each side. A yellow pulse resonating from her chest flashed the surrounding area, making Ares backpedal. When it reached my shield, it almost knocked me on my ass.

"Don't tell me you haven't given it any thought, Ares." She morphed behind him.

Ares gritted his teeth, turned on his heel, and swung both swords at her. The blades bounced against her crisscrossed gauntlets with an echoing crackle.

"Why don't you just come out and say it, Athena," Ares roared.

She flicked off her hood, revealing long dark brown hair flowing in waves down her back—a braid on one side with gold beads and ribbon intertwined. She appeared in front of me again, striking her sword against my shield. It sent a vibration down my arm and into my chest. I batted her arm away with the blunt edge of the shield before leaping into the air and striking downward with one knee bent. Her dark eyes brightened, watching me suspended in the air before blocking my blow.

"Are you familiar with your female ancestors, Harmony?" Her hands rested at her sides as she circled me.

I kept still but followed her with my eyes. "You're the goddess of wisdom. You tell me."

The wind rustled leaves around us, sending our hair in floating wisps.

She laughed. "Wit as well. It's no wonder my brother, and you were made for each other."

Ares walked up behind me with a growl vibrating in the back of his throat. His scowl distorted the skin between his eyes and forehead.

"Did you know your mortal is the descendant of Amazons, Ares?" Athena gave a wry grin, twirling her sword as she continued to circle us.

"What?" We asked at the same time.

Ares's glare softened into confusion.

"Did you not question your visions? Why they felt so real?" Athena traced a line in the dirt.

"How did you—" I snapped my mouth shut, somehow forgetting who she was.

Athena slashed at my side, jolting me from my trance. I deflected her blade with the shield, putting extra fervor in my swing.

This game was getting old.

Ares prowled past me, slicing his blades in opposite directions at Athena's head. She dropped to her knee and slid between Ares's legs.

"What do you *know*, Athena?" Ares puffed his chest.

She spun to her feet with a flick of her dark hair. "All action. No talk. Such is the God of War. Does the name Otrera mean anything to you, brother?"

Ares blinked rapidly, his face neutralizing.

I tightened my grip on the sword. "Who's Otrera?"

"An ancient Amazonian Queen, Harmony. Her second in command, the princess, had a passionate affair with a Spartan soldier, thus producing your bloodline. And if you didn't know, my brother has always had such a weak spot for Amazons. He married Otrera. But alas, mortality can be so… final." She shook her head.

Ares growled and splayed his hand. A blast of red lightning and smoke slammed into Athena's abdomen, throwing her to the ground.

Athena chuckled as she hopped to her feet. "Inherited some of father's power, have you? That's new."

"Have you come here just to remind me of my past, or did you have a *point*?" His powers bubbled in his palm, ready to lash out again.

"While Otrera was a renowned warrior, she wasn't worthy of it, Ares. *She* is." Athena pointed at me with the tip of her blade. "Did you not think he'd get word of this? Our father sent me to—test her."

"Worthy?" The sword felt limp in my hand. "Worthy of what?"

Half of Ares's upper lip lifted. "I would never ask her. And he has *no* business with any of this."

"Oh, but he does. To be a war goddess, especially one tied to you, can't be bestowed upon just anyone. She should at least have the choice. The Fates put you in each other's paths because you were meant to *be*." Athena made the sword in her hand disappear, followed by my shield.

"You all are expecting me to give up my life for one I never knew I was meant to live." My voice cracked as I spoke.

Athena turned on her heel, canting her head from one side to the other.

"Those don't sound like your words, Amazon." She squinted, moving closer, scanning me. "Eris. She got to you before me, didn't she?"

Ares's face snapped to me, and I tried not to look at him.

No, I didn't tell him. What good would it have done? It was something I needed to work out on my own.

"Why should that matter?" I lifted my chin.

"Oh, it matters a great deal. All Eris ever does is cause calamity and chaos. It's her purpose." Athena flicked something from her well-manicured fingernail. "Not to mention how petty she can be. Do you think she wants competition? Let alone another woman?"

A breath escaped my lungs. I'd let Eris get into my head. She spent five minutes with me and made me question every instinct, and I wanted to beat her senseless for it.

Ares wouldn't look at me, his gaze focused on the glint of his sword.

"What a goddess you would make." Athena curled a long finger under my chin, lifting it to meet her eyes.

My neck felt numb. "A goddess? But I—" I stumbled

backward, and Ares's arm launched out to catch me.

Goddess. Not just immortal, but a Greek goddess.

"No one's saying anything, gatáki. Athena's sticking her nose in where it doesn't belong."

"You know what I speak is true, Ares. And you say you sneer at cowards."

My blood boiled, so it didn't surprise me when Ares lurched forward with his blade drawn. He raised it, pulled the hilt back to his ear, and pointed the tip at Athena's throat.

"It isn't cowardice not wishing to burden her with even the thought of immortality, war goddess." He snarled his last words, glaring at her.

"You've never been given enough credit, Ares." She pressed the back of her hand to his blade, slowly pushing it away. "War. Chaos. It's all needed to maintain balance. But even war itself. You, brother…" She placed a single finger on his chest. "Need balance." She turned her chin at me. "Or… harmony."

Ares's eyes widened, and he dropped one of his swords. A sight to behold, the God of War letting a weapon fall from his grasp.

I was the cure for his fury.

"You two complement one another. Your passion pushes her to strive for more, and her humility levels you. Together you are the perfect representation for the zeal of battle without the distraction of the unquenchable fury." She poked Ares in the chest with the same finger already there. "You most of all."

"We've been at each other's throats for eons, sister. Why help me now?" He batted her finger away.

"This isn't only about you. Whether I like it or not, this responsibility falls on you. But it doesn't have to be on your shoulders alone." She pursed her lips, peering at me with sad eyes. "You've both had such burdens thrust upon you." She looked back to Ares, resting a hand on his forearm. "Lift them for each other. Talk to her."

Ares snarled and turned away, dragging a hand over his beard.

Athena slipped her hood back on. "Hear him out, Harmony. And listen with an open heart." She swirled her hands, kicking up dirt and leaves. "She's the best of both your worlds, brother. Another like her won't come along for centuries. If ever."

She thrust her arms skyward, morphing into the brown feathered owl.

We stood in downtown Denver without the ancient weapons previously laced in our grasps.

I didn't know how to bring up the subject. Instead, I deflected. "Does it hurt when you port?"

We stood feet away from each other, the crisp mountain wind tossing our dark hair over our faces.

"No." His jaw tightened.

"Does it exhaust you?"

"Not after my teenage years, no."

Time to rip off the band-aid.

I stared at my boots. "Was all she said true?"

"We shouldn't talk about this here." He sniffed once, striding forward and wrapping his limbs around me.

I gripped his arm to keep him from porting. "But we *are* going to talk about it?"

"Yes," he whispered in a gruff voice.

I glanced around at our public surroundings and tensed. "Shouldn't we go somewhere more—"

Poof.

"—private."

Whatever was going on had him so rattled he didn't care who saw his godly abilities. This couldn't be good.

Judging from the water surrounding us, the mountains, and ruins in the distance, I guessed we were in Greece again.

"Where are we, Ares?"

He took my hand and led me into town. "Sparta."

The way the "r" rolled off his tongue made my chest tighten. "Why here?"

"Most of what Athena said made sense. About your ancestry—the visions. The dreams. How do you feel here?"

I closed my eyes and let the smells and sounds work with my senses. Birds chirped, people murmured in a nearby crowd, and children laughed. There were scents of freshly baked bread, olives, cheese, and the salt of the sea hanging in the air. Swords clanked, rhythmic beats of sandaled feet marched against the dirt, and fists beat against the metal armor on their chests, saluting a commander.

My eyes flew open, seeing no sign of the latter noises. I bit the inside of my cheek as I ran my thumb over Ares's knuckles.

"I feel…home. Even more than when we were in Athens."

He nodded and led me over to a vendor's stand. My eyes brightened as I watched him flick his hands about, ordering two cones of ice cream.

He remembered.

Pressing a hand to my lower back, he guided me over to a bench facing the water and far enough away from prying ears.

He handed me a cone, making my heart swell when I saw the tiny bits of cookie dough resting on top. "Are you buttering me up?"

"Creamy desserts seem to make you happy." Ares rubbed the back of his neck before lowering to the bench. He didn't lean back, staying rigid.

"So, about Otrera…" I kept my gaze on my knees.

Ares held up a hand. "I'm going to stop you right there, Harm." He turned to face me, taking my hand in his. "Yes, I was married before you. To her. Only her. She was fierce, loyal, and a great leader to her people, but Harmony, she wasn't you." His eyes searched my face.

Jealousy. Possessiveness. New feelings for me that made my mind ache.

"And after she died…" His throat bobbed. "I never had the heart to put myself there again."

All these years. All this time of being immortal and watching mortals die—consequences of falling in love with a human woman. I bit the inside of my mouth.

"It should've been you, gatáki."

I met his gaze, stomach fluttering.

He squeezed my hand. "It was always meant to be you."

I stared at him, taking several bites and licks of my ice cream before turning my gaze to the blue waters of the Mediterranean Sea in the distance. "Is it possible?"

He paused mid-lick of his chocolate ice- cream, arching a brow.

"I'm going to guess it is. Otherwise, Athena *and* Eris wouldn't have brought it up." Ice cream melted down my hand as I looked at him. "I could become a goddess?"

"Yes." He plucked the dripping liquid from my hand with a single finger. "But why didn't you tell me Eris came to see you?" He slipped the finger in his mouth.

"What good would it have done? There was truth in what she said, though she spun it in the most venomous way."

"Eris only cares about herself."

"She made me think about whether or not I wanted to give up my mortal life." My eyes dropped to his lips, briefly remembering the way they felt on my neck before lifting my gaze.

"And?"

"I realized aside from Chelsea, I haven't had much of a mortal life. Sure, I became an MMA champion, but I have five more years tops before my body gives up on me." I swirled my tongue around the sweet cream. "And then what?"

His right knee bounced once. "Does the idea of becoming a goddess frighten you?"

"How could it not? Having powers? Responsibilities over something controlling the universe?" I gleamed at the cerulean water, focusing on the ripples the wind caused. "Immortality."

"Athena's right." He lapped his ice cream, leaning on his knees.

"About which part? She talked a lot."

Ares chuckled deep and husky. "She does that. But I'm referring to her saying you're worthy of it."

"Oh, please. I've come from nothing and have done little to prove anything in my life, Ares." I bit halfway into my ice cream, wincing from the brain freeze.

"You can become anything regardless of coming from nothing." He turned to face me, slipping his free hand over my thigh. "Harmony, a true goddess of war, *my* version of war, has the strength to be a leader, trained to fight—to obliterate. But can choose *not* to."

I peered at him, unblinking, licking my ice cream as I let his words sink in.

But Chelsea. What about Chelsea? Would I just up and leave her as a friend? A client?

"Discretion isn't my forte, as you've witnessed." A weakened smile played over his lips.

Silence fell over us. I spent my entire life never knowing where I fit in with the universe. I'd always felt estranged from everyone around me. And now it all came crashing over me in so few moments, sputtering from Greek gods' lips. I wasn't ready to admit out loud how much sense Athena made—not to mention Eris too. The opportunity to live forever after thinking I had a human expiration date.

I couldn't tell if my tongue went numb from the ice cream or the daunting thoughts of living for eternity.

Ares popped the tip of his cone in his mouth with a light crunch. After licking the remnants from his thumb, he leaned back, stretching his arms over the length of the bench.

"My father created Athena."

I straightened. "Created?"

"She wasn't born. He created her." He flicked his tongue against his teeth and shook his head. "There was a prophecy that a son would overthrow Zeus. Being that I was born with the power of war, I honestly think he feared me."

"The King of the Gods fearful of his own son?"

"Crazier things have happened. But I believe that's why he created a daughter, bestowed the same power on her. It made her far more likable. Never underestimate the power 'Loyalty of the People' holds."

"And would you ever try to overthrow him?"

He turned his chin, gazing at me with softened eyes. "I haven't nor will I ever have a desire to be King of the Gods."

That wasn't a no.

"Hades? Poseidon? No one else has bothered to try?"

"My uncles possess far greater power than me, but they have honor. If it weren't for Zeus—" His eyebrow twitched. "They'd be dead."

"What if I said I was considering this?" My throat tightened, and my eyes darted back and forth, searching his face for the expression I hoped to see.

"I'd say you were crazy, but it doesn't surprise me." He canted his head to one side. "You must have questions."

"This fated bond. What would that mean if I became a goddess?"

He ran his hand over his beard, moving his gaze to the sky. "It means a division of power—a balance. Not to mention the connection we already feel. It'd be tenfold."

My stomach twisted, and I clenched my knees together. "I'd be taking part of your power?"

He cupped my chin with his hand. "No, gatáki. I'd be *giving* it to you. With two people to balance the fury of war, it'd equalize."

I dove into his eyes like they were melted chocolate. "I don't know what to say or how to say it."

"I can show you how it feels—to have this power."

"How?"

He slid his hand to the back of my neck. "Normally, a simple touch would do, but—"

His lips slid over mine, coaxing them apart. As the kiss deepened, an overwhelming surge coursed through my body, settling in my chest. Hairs on my arms stood on end, and a passion punched at my ribcage, yearning to be set free.

I gasped and pulled away from the kiss, but Ares kept a hand on my neck, continuing the cosmic connection. Gasping, I gripped his forearm.

"This is so intense. How do you deal with it every day?"

"I've had eons to learn. It wouldn't be like this for you. As I said, we'd be sharing it."

Fighting past the impatience every cell in my body shivered with, I concentrated on the immense power. With a flick of my wrist, I could move mountains—shape seas. Carve my name in the clouds. My soul formed insurmountable holes through the years, but the power mended a few of them.

His hand slid away, and so did all the power. Dizziness swept over my brain, and I slapped a hand on my forehead.

Ares grabbed my shoulders. "Are you alright?"

"Can you take me back? I need time alone. I need to think. This is all too much."

"Harmony, no one is asking you to do this."

"I know. I know. And please do *not* say anything about my having a choice again, or I may burst."

He clucked his tongue against his teeth. "I know by now when to back off." With a frown, he slipped a hand over my shoulder and ported us back to my apartment.

"Thank you." I shifted my gaze to the coffee stain on the carpet. "I really do need to be alone, Ares. The threat is gone, you heard Chelsea."

His jaw tightened, and he beat his knuckles against his thigh. "I've got a goddess of chaos to deal with anyway." Words wrapped in a bitter snarl. "See you soon." He disappeared in a flash of light and smoke.

It wasn't a matter of anyone asking me. It was the overwhelming sense that I might *want* this. This could be my missing link. Maybe I really was crazy.

EIGHTEEN

𝌆𝌆𝌆𝌆𝌆𝌆𝌆𝌆𝌆𝌆𝌆𝌆𝌆

I'D BARRICADED MYSELF IN my apartment for the past two days, ignoring every phone call and text Chelsea sent me. If she weren't out of town, she'd have beaten my door down by now. A normal woman would've immediately confided in her best friend—sought their approval for the crazy decision they were about to make. I don't think anyone would describe me as a normal woman. Whether I gave Chelsea the chance to believe me was my choice. In life, there wasn't always time to stew on the outcomes. Decide now. Organize the potential crumbling pieces later, but *make* a choice.

I sat on my couch with my head between my knees, groaning.

A mysterious *whoosh* filled the room, sending my hair flying. With narrowed eyes, I flipped my head up and threw a punch. My fist collided with flesh and bone.

"It's me!"

I blinked several times. "Dino?"

"Yeah." He rubbed his chin with a grimace. "You sure pack a hell of a right hook. Now I get it."

"Dino. You're a—you're…" I stared at him wide-eyed.

He closed his eyes and sighed. "Shit. I forgot you didn't know who I am yet."

Holding my hands in front of me, ready to defend if necessary, I backpedaled.

"No need to be on guard with me." He held out a large terra cotta hand. "My real name is Dionysos."

Shifting my gaze from his face to his outstretched hand, I shook it. "Dionysos. God of wine?"

"And festivity, wild frenzy—" He paused, a wicked grin sliding over his lips. "Pleasure."

Growling, I turned away. "I've had it up to here with Greek gods lately. What are you even doing here?"

"I've heard all about these visits and can see why you're pissed."

I let my hand flop at my side and arched a brow.

"Word gets around fast with us." He tousled his long hair as he scanned my mediocre apartment. "Homey."

"You still haven't answered my question."

Dino walked to my coffee table, picking up an empty take out carton. "You haven't gone outside in two days. Don't you think this is a bit overkill?"

I pushed past him and picked up the cartons, pizza box, and paper cup. "I've got a lot on my mind."

"Does his name rhyme with 'cherries'?" He snickered.

I'd yet to take the garbage out, and the added trash made it overflow. Using my foot, I forced it down.

"Look, I thought you could use a friendly face to talk to that wasn't a meddling goddess or someone you're screwing." He held his arms out to his sides.

"Talk about what?"

"Oh, come on, Harm." He spun on his heel and sat on an armrest of the couch. "The way I see it, it's only a matter of time before I'm your big bro-in-law, so here's me starting things off on a good foot."

I crossed my arms in a huff. "You're acting differently."

"How am I supposed to be acting?"

"Like a party-hardy frat boy?" I raised my brows.

He pressed a hand over his stomach like he experienced acid reflux. "Partying twenty-four seven? Sounds exhausting." Shifting his weight, he crossed his scuffed boots at the ankle. "Don't get me wrong, I *am* a party-hardy frat boy, but I can be serious when needed."

Biting back a smile, I moved into the living room to stand across from him. "And how long do I have before said seriousness starts to drive you crazy?"

A snarky grin pulled at his lips. "Fifteen minutes tops, so you better start yappin'."

"Why is this such a difficult decision?"

"To become a goddess? Are you kidding? I'm not going to pretend like I have any idea what it feels like to go from mortal to immortal, but even that sounds insane."

Groaning, I dropped to the floor and sat with my legs crossed. "Not helping."

"Alright." He squatted in front of me, steepling his deeply

tanned fingers. "What's stopping you?"

I pinched my eyes shut, mulling it over. "I'm not entirely sure if I'm ready to give up being a mortal."

"Is it really all that great?"

I shot him a one-eyed glare.

He lifted his palms. "Sorry. Man, you're a spitfire." His fist playfully nudged my shoulder. "If that's what you're worried about, then it's simple."

"Simple? Seriously?"

"Uh, yeah." He snorted. "I thought you were going to say being tied to that brooding oaf for eternity."

Ares and me—together. Forever. The thought should've frightened me or at least made me nervous. Instead, an excitement bubbled in my stomach.

"He's so much more than what's on the surface, Dino."

"I know. I'm joking around. I give the guy a hard time, but that one night we got drunk on ambrosia wine—" His eyes widened, and his cheeks puffed out. "Let's just say we both said a lot of things."

I'd have to pry that story out of Ares at some point.

"You say it's simple. What do I do?"

"Your life hasn't been normal since the day you met Ares. Do things you'd normally do. Alone. See how you feel." He quirked a thin brow and bounced in his still squatted position.

"You think it'd help?"

He shrugged. "I'm no god of wisdom, but I *have* been around for a damn long time."

"Thanks."

"None of that. What is family for, hm?"

Family. I hadn't given it much thought, but with Ares, with all of this, I'd also be gaining what I never had. Albeit a fucked-up family, but I'd have one.

"You good?" He cocked his head to one side.

Staring at my hands, following the lines and grooves, I nodded. "I will be."

He clapped once. "Perfect." Rising to his feet, he snapped his fingers. "By the way, don't be surprised if you get more annoying visitors. And not near as cool as me."

Like a beached manatee, I rolled onto my side and stood up, groaning. "Why is everyone so concerned with me?"

"You've got to understand something, Harm. Being a war god isn't a small task. Cripes, I don't envy any of them. Give me partying and wine all day long. Way less responsibility."

I frowned.

He slipped a hand over my shoulder. "But I know you could do it. You have to believe that yourself too."

"Zeus doesn't seem to think so. He sent Athena to—"

"Fuck Zeus. If you want the job, take it. Don't let any of the other assholes in this family tell you otherwise."

Pride swelled in my chest.

"Are we uh—supposed to hug now or something?" Dino squinted.

"I'm not much of a hugger."

His eyes formed slits as he gave a lop-sided grin. "Well, now we have to." He pulled me in, wrapping his burly arms around me and patting my back several times.

I grunted and slapped him between the shoulder blades once.

He pulled away and, after squeezing my shoulder, backed up. "I'm sure I'll be seeing you real soon." With a wink, he disappeared in a swirl of fog and ivy.

Normal. He said to do something normal. What would I be doing today if I'd never met Ares?

I winced, hating to even think about it.

The gym? Too many people. The movies? Please. When was the last time I'd been to one?

My neon orange running shoes called to me from a nearby corner. I could use a nice long run. It was an everyday activity and also a way to clear my head. Perfect.

With every pound of the asphalt against my feet, I'd nick another thought—another concern. Exercise was a given part of my life. Surely, a Greek god didn't need it. Yet, these gods also didn't need to walk amongst us. They provided power to mortals while blending in with them, and we were none the wiser.

As I passed people on the path winding through a forest preserve, irritation shot down my spine. Annoyance over a kid licking an ice cream cone and getting it nearly everywhere else but, in his mouth, a posh couple running in tandem with their AirPods protruding from their ears, an older man sitting on a bench people watching.

All so ordinary, so mundane, so…mortal. I stopped. Who was I trying to kid? I'd gotten a taste of what life I *could* have with a person—a partner that *got* me. So why was it so hard to shove my mortal life away?

I let out a tormented snarl, scaring a cyclist as he passed. My mind spun, and I clutched my head as people walking their dogs, more cyclists, and a woman with a stroller whisked past. I quickly lost control of my breathing, and the ground wouldn't stop moving.

"Harmony," Ares's deep voice spoke, soft as suede.

I opened my eyes, and no sooner had our gazes met, the world slowed. "Ares?"

He pulled me against him, swaddling his arms around me and burying his face against my nape.

"How did you know I needed you? I didn't even know I did."

"I think you know the answer to that question," he whispered.

A fated bond.

Pushing back, I searched his face. "Did you talk to Eris?"

"There wasn't a whole lot of talking. She won't be bothering you again, gatáki." Those dark eyes gave a hint of a red flash.

I missed him. In only a matter of days, I missed his company, his scent, his passion.

A man fiddling with his smartwatch as he ran bumped into me. Being already so on edge, I glared at his back, fuming inside. He didn't even apologize. I took one step forward, and Ares caught me by the elbow.

"Let's get out of here, hm?" His cheek twitched.

The relaxation started at my shoulders and eased its way down until it reached my toes. He pulled me to him again and ported us away.

Instead of appearing in my apartment with the God of War

in my arms, I stood in a darkened cave. Red smoke floated over the moist ground, and a faint shrill cackle bounced off the stone walls, chilling me to the bone.

Not this again.

NINETEEN

⌐⌐⌐⌐⌐⌐⌐⌐⌐⌐⌐⌐⌐⌐⌐⌐⌐

"OH, BUT SHE'S SO pretty, though," a woman's voice said.

"We do what we're told, Megaera," another woman's voice hissed.

A floating flame coiled around my chest, illuminating the vast cave. Three women stood in front of me—all with black hair, pale white faces, and black gowns covered in cobwebs.

With a guttural growl, I stepped forward. The flame held me captive, secluding me in its circle.

The woman on the right made a tsking sound. "Calm now, Harmony. We've only come to speak with you."

"If you're here to talk me out of becoming a war goddess, you can crawl back into whatever sewer you crawled out of."

"Oo such fire," the middle woman cooed.

"We're here to do a job, Alecto," Megaera hissed.

They floated forward, surrounding me and tracing their fingers through my hair, over my shoulders, and across my cheeks. I winced when their pointy black fingernails neared my eyes, finding I couldn't lift my arms over the fiery circle.

"Who said anything about dissuading you? We simply have questions. Concerns." The woman who remained unnamed cocked her head inhumanly to the side.

"Tisiphone speaks the truth. Who are we to deny you if you are up for the task?" Megaera trailed a slender finger through my hair.

I ground my teeth, turning my head away. "And why would I bother answering? This has nothing to do with you."

"You are wrong." Alecto dashed in front of me, clicking her nails together. "Your ascension could affect us *all*, just like any other new goddess."

Megaera rested her chin on Alecto's shoulder from behind her. "War happens to be a tad more—" She wound her hand in a circle. "—sensitive."

"Besides, you have no choice but to answer us," Tisiphone said through a bout of cackles.

"You are unable to move. Unable to *fight* us in your current state. Tell us, Harmony, how does it feel to be so—" Alecto brought our faces closer. "—powerless?" Her black as midnight eyes blinked, sending a membrane flashing over them like a damn lizard.

"And do not lie to us. We will know," Megaera hissed, brushing my hair over my collarbone.

I glared at them and said nothing.

"Oh, I like her." Tisiphone shrieked, clapping her hands together.

"Is that why you seek to be a goddess of war. For the power?"

Alecto traced a fingernail down my chest.

A mental hook pulled at my brain, coaxing the answer out of me. I pinched my eyes shut. "…No."

"Lie," Megaera snapped.

The hook plunged deeper, causing a sting at the back of my skull. "Not entirely, no."

Alecto cocked her head to and fro like a curious dog, bringing our faces so close our noses brushed.

Like snapping it with a pair of pliers, I pushed whatever hold they had on my mind away. "Explain this. I'm getting sick and tired of you gods interfering with *my* life." I opened my eyes, seething at them.

All three women's eyes went as large as bowling balls, shifting glances at each other.

Tisiphone leaned to Alecto and whispered, "How did she break your control?"

Alecto pushed her away with a snarl.

"This is between Ares and me, so butt the *fuck* out." Not being able to move made my blood boil.

Megaera's eyes narrowed, and she flicked me in the nose.

I lurched forward, making the magical binding holding me hiss in defiance.

"You're in no position to make commands, dearie." Alecto grabbed my shoulder. "Answer the question."

The hook turned into a harpoon, plunging so far into my mind, I lost it. It pulled the answer from me, carrying it to my lips. "I've lived my life not knowing where I belonged. What road I should be taking. It'd give me purpose again." The words rattled from my tongue without inflection or pause.

"A…calling…perhaps?" Tisiphone bit the air in front of me.

As I tried to fight the mental intrusion again, my jaw trembled. "Yes."

"And what about him?" Megaera picked at her nails as she swiveled her hips back and forth with a grin.

Closing my eyes, I bit my lips shut, drawing blood.

"You know exactly who she speaks of," Alecto whispered, scraping her nail over my cheek, making my eyes pop open.

The three of them moved in front of me, standing shoulder to shoulder. In a blink, they morphed from beautiful women with Morticia likenesses to hideous hags. Snakes slithered in droves where their hair used to be, some wrapping around their arms. Bat wings sprouted from their backs, and blood oozed down their cheeks from the cavities of their eyes. They took every step like a time glitch, limbs appearing higher or lower than where they placed them.

"Ares," they all wailed in unison.

"Oh…my…*god*." My gaze froze on their horrific existence, beads of sweat rolling down the back of my neck.

They zeroed in on me, the snakeheads of their hair hissing and snapping.

"That's enough," Ares's voice boomed from behind me.

Despite my current situation, my groin and heart clenched simultaneously.

Megaera gasped, floating so quickly to him my hair flew up. "Took you long enough to find us."

I couldn't see him, and it infuriated me. Looking away from the disgusting duo in front of me, I concentrated on the rock formations hanging from the cave ceiling.

"It's been so long, Air. Why haven't you called on us?" Tisiphone whined.

Air?

My cheeks burned.

"Get Harmony out of there. Now," Ares commanded.

Megaera appeared in front of me, several snakeheads brushing through my hair. "You are turning green with jealousy." She grinned maniacally, wiggling her fingers with a girly shrill.

"Let. Her. Go." His voice roared deep and throaty, causing tiny tremors in the surrounding rock walls.

"That's not your place to say, war god. We've yet to complete our interrogation." Alecto twisted her wrist in circles.

Ares moved past me, and my body relaxed at the sight of him.

"Did Hades send you?" The corded muscles of his forearms tensed.

Tisiphone grinned, biting on her fingernail as she shook her head. "No. The other one."

"Zeus." Ares brushed a hand over his beard. "Of course."

"One final question," Alecto taunted.

"This is done." Ares charged forward.

Megaera threw her palms up, freezing Ares in place.

His left nostril bounced. "That was a mistake."

"Promise you'll punish me later for it?" Megaera flashed a sultry grin.

I thinned my lips, my fists shaking at my sides.

"One. Final. Question. Harmony Makos, what would you

miss most of your past life?" Alecto claimed my attention by touching her finger to my forehead, clamping my mind with a vice.

I blinked, casting my gaze downward. "The bittersweetness of mortality."

All three women canted their heads back and forth.

"Even with your warrior by your side?" Megaera asked, still holding a bewildered Ares in her magical grasp.

"Yes. He doesn't know how it feels." The words cracked as I said them, and I couldn't look at his face.

The three women exchanged glances and gave a single nod.

Alecto released her hold on my brain, and my shoulders slumped. She whipped around, floating to Ares. "You should know the mortal's made up her mind, God of War. But Zeus will be none too pleased if you bypass his approval."

Veins bulged from Ares's neck. "I don't give a maláka about his approval. And you can tell him I said it. Now release us and *leave*."

Tisiphone giggled as she waved at me. Once the flame around me disappeared, I charged for Alecto. The snakeheads in her hair reared, baring their fangs and hissing. I hissed back, and all three goddesses vanished in a plume of smoke and wicked laughter.

My limbs went numb at my sides. "What the *shit* was that all about, Ares?"

"The Furies. They were testing you at the behest of dear Dad. It makes him feel 'involved,' I'm sure." He held his hands in front of him, kneading one of his palms. "Was it true?"

"True?" A small part of me hoped he wouldn't ask.

"You don't think I'd understand you missing your mortality?" He frowned, but the way his forehead creased bordered on a scowl.

"Mortality makes life precious. It makes you wake up determined to make the most of every day because you don't know if it will be your last."

"And you think I don't make the most of my days in the universe because I'm immortal?" His throat bobbed.

"That's not what I meant."

He cupped my face with one hand. "There's a reason mortals have described me as being the most human-like of all the gods."

I slipped my hand over his.

"My actions—the choices I've made through the ages. I've lived as if Olympus itself could take away my immortality at any given moment. I wanted to know with the utmost certainty I've left a lasting impression on the world. That my time here *meant* something."

His words struck a chord, like flicking on a light switch.

"There's something I need to do," I mumbled, fishing in my pocket for my phone.

"Harm?" He arched a brow.

I dialed Chelsea and bit my cuticles, waiting for her to answer. It rang and rang. One more ring, and it'd go to voicemail.

"You know, I shouldn't have answered. Give you a taste of your own medicine," Chelsea spat.

"I deserved that, but I have a favor to ask, and I'm pretty sure you'll dig it."

Silence.

"Fine. I'm listening," she finally responded.

"Get me a match with Kelly Fitz. I'm taking it back."

Kelly was so ready to "wipe the floor with me again" as she put it during weigh-ins, it only took Chelsea twenty-four hours to orchestrate the rematch. Sometime between our trip to Greece and the Furies pulling my thoughts from me, I'd decided the life of a goddess was an intended path. A war goddess alongside the God of War himself.

So why hadn't I told Ares yet?

Let him squirm—just a little.

We'd done our walk-ins, and the crowd roared their applause. With my title at arm's reach, I'd win it and move on to the next chapter in my life.

Slipping the mouth guard in, I beat my fists together in one corner of the ring.

"Amazon," Ares beckoned.

I lowered my head, aligning my ear with his mouth.

"Win this thing, so we have a reason to celebrate, hm?" A wicked glint flashed in his eyes.

No words of wisdom. No warnings. My insides damn near strangled themselves.

Giving a curt nod, I turned my attention to my opponent. The horns blazed through my skull. Instead of an intrusion, they were a calling. Luring me home—showing me the way.

Kelly glared at me from across the ring. I couldn't punch

the smugness off her face fast enough. The ref's hand dropped, and Kelly ran forward. My past self would've been surprised, maybe even thrown off guard with her advance. Not anymore. I leaned left, dodged right, ducked, and jumped back with every punch thrown.

Brow furrowing, she squinted at me as if I'd already become a goddess, and she could see the fiery vapors wafting around me.

No. This was for me. My last fight as a mortal to know I'd beaten her fair and square.

She jabbed with such wrath, the skin over her shoulders turned bright red. I blocked with my forearms, waiting for the sound of her labored breaths. She sashayed backward, hoping I wouldn't follow, allowing her time to rest.

Not today.

I caught up with her and threw jabs I had no intention of connecting. She dodged them all and swatted at my fists.

"What the hell are you doing, Makos?" Annoyance oozed in her tone.

I rolled my shoulders. "Giving you a chance to win."

Imagining the quadrident's hilt pressed against my palm, I leaped, raising my fist above my head. In full Superman-punch form, my knuckles collided into the side of her head. Her body stiffened, and she fell to the ground in a slump on her side.

I closed my eyes, blocking out the sounds of cheering and yelling, focusing only on the air flowing through my nose and mouth. There was no way to know for sure if the feeling of victory would be the same as a goddess. I'd bottle it up and lock it away if I could. But for now, I'd paint every tingle cascading over my skin to memory.

The ref held my fist up, ambient noise rushing in, and he wrapped the belt around my waist.

"You've just won your title back, Harm. What will you do now?" The announcer held the mic out.

Purposely avoiding Chelsea's gaze, I said, "Retire."

The cheers transformed into scattered whispers and eventual silence.

"I have to say I'm shocked. Is there a particular reason?"

I locked eyes with Ares through the cage. "I've got other battles to fight."

Shoving the belt into the announcer's chest, I clambered out of the ring. As soon as my feet landed on the stairs, I pushed off, knowing he'd catch me. His arms wrapped around my hips, resting under my ass, and I planted a kiss on him. Hundreds of flashes from surrounding paparazzi leaked through my eyelids. I slid down his chest, gripping the lapels of his jacket.

He sucked on my lower lip as he peeled away. "Did that mean what I think it meant, gatáki?" His voice was throaty, deep, and breathy.

I quirked a brow.

"Harmony," Chelsea yelled. "Locker room. Now." She pointed and stormed off, her neck flushing.

I held five fingers up to Ares and patted him on the chest before following her.

As I neared the locker room door, I could hear her foot tapping against the floor.

"Hey," I said.

She stopped pacing and stared at me. The redness had made it up to her cheeks.

"Hey? You drop a bomb like that, and all you can say is, 'hey'?"

"Chels, it was a last-minute decision. And if I would've said anything to you, I may have talked myself out of it."

She shook her head slack-jawed and put one hand on her hip. "Harm, why? For the love of God, why? It doesn't make any sense."

"I meant what I said out there. I've got other things to do with my life. A purpose beyond being a gladiator."

"What purpose?" She folded her arms.

I cracked my neck with a sigh. "I don't know how to explain it."

"Try," she said, raising her voice.

Her irritation was understandable, but she seemed extra flustered. It was unlike her.

"Are you okay?"

Her eyes blinked rapidly, and she sniffled.

"Chelsea?" I stepped forward.

"Tim broke up with me."

"What? I thought he was getting ready to propose?"

"That's what I thought. It turns out he was seeing someone else on the side, Penelope Peters."

Fury snaked over my heart. "I'll kill him."

Chelsea's eyes snapped to meet mine. "You won't do a damn thing, Harm. What's done is done. I'd like to see it as dodging a bullet. A behemoth-sized one."

"I'm sorry, Chels."

She took a deep breath, looking up at the ceiling as if it contained all the solutions. "You can imagine why hearing my number one client is retiring after discovering my boyfriend of three years has been cheating on me caused a bit of anger."

I was an ass—a hairy, pimply, smelly ass.

Cinching my brow, I let my gaze fall to a crack in the floor, wishing it'd burst open and let me jump in.

"Are you going to explain this to me or not?" Chelsea tapped her heel.

I licked my bottom lip, still unable to meet her gaze. "I've spent my entire life feeling this void—anything I did. Anywhere I went. I felt incomplete. Like I was meant for something more."

She shifted her eyes. "O-kaaay?"

"Mars has offered me an opportunity to fill the void. And not in a dirty way, so get your mind out of the gutter." I half-smiled.

A grin slowly spread over her lips.

What a relief to see.

"And you can't tell me what this opportunity is?"

I shook my head.

"I've said it before, and I'll say it again. You don't need my approval." She gripped my forearm. "You seem happy. Genuinely happy. Whatever this opportunity is, Harm, I hope it finally gives you that sense of completion."

Happy. She was right. The decision made me feel hopeful.

"I'm going to miss you like hell, though. And not just because you were my most well-earned client." She smirked.

"Shut up, Chelsea. This isn't goodbye." I laughed and

pulled her in for a hug.

"Wow. Hugging? He must have some super magical mojo," she mumbled into my shoulder.

If she only knew…

She pushed me away. "You better get out of here. The press is probably swarming by now. Use the back door."

"Are you going to be okay?"

"Not today, but there's nothing you can do to ease the sting, Harm." She squeezed my shoulder. "Now go."

"I'll call you in a few days, alright?" I neared the rear exit.

She shrugged. "A few days. A few years. Just don't be a stranger."

"You've been too good to me, Chels."

"You deserved every ounce of it, Harm. Now go get your void filled." She chuckled.

I bumped into the door. Ares leaned on the outside wall with his hands in his pockets.

"Something you want to tell me?" His eyes pierced me.

"Were you eavesdropping on my conversation?"

He pushed off the brick, slipping his hands from his pockets and towering over me. "I want to hear you say it."

I sidled up to him, pressing my hips against his. "My answer is yes."

His breath warmed my skin as he trailed his lip over my cheek. "Yes, to what?"

"To be a goddess." I tilted my head back to look at him. "Your goddess."

No sooner had the words left my mouth, I could feel his hardness pressing against my stomach.

He clenched my hip. "What made you decide?"

"Someone has to show you how to be a decent God of War. Might as well be me." I played a devious grin across my lips.

A laugh vibrated from the pit of his stomach.

"There's also something strangely enticing about being one half of a whole." I combed a finger through his beard.

"Mm, it's something I'll have to get used to myself." His lips brushed my brow. "Not that I mind. Not with you."

I bit the inside of my cheek. "How does this work?"

"You're ready?" His brow shot up. "Right now?"

"Unless we have to wait for a full moon or something?" I nibbled on his bottom lip. "I can be ravenous when I know what I want."

"Mm. So I've observed." His tongue dashed over my mouth.

"Are you going to make me wait?" It came out raspy.

He grinned against my cheek before leaning back. "Only the three brothers can do it. And I think I know which one you'd like."

"Oh?"

He one-eyed squinted. "There's only one catch."

"Which is?"

After looking around for anyone passing, he crouched and pressed his palm against the ground. A darkened staircase appeared, leading down into the mysterious depths. A chill shivered my bones.

The Underworld.

TWENTY

ARES ADVANCED TOWARD THE stairs, and I didn't move.

"Does that lead where I think it leads?"

He gave me a wry grin over his shoulder. "Afraid of a few wandering souls and floating ash?"

"It was a simple question." I glowered at him as I brushed past, suppressing a gulp once my foot landed on the first step.

His hand slid over my back, and he kissed my jawline. "I promise he doesn't bite."

"I'm about to meet the King of the Underworld. Him biting me is the last thing on my mind, Ares."

"You've met several gods. He's just another with a higher status." He led me down another two steps.

"How could I forget all the meddling goddesses the past few days?"

"Are you going to come down here so I can seal the hole or

wait for someone walking by to fall in?" A tiny smile tugged at the corner of his lips.

I shifted my eyes and flopped down two more steps. He waved his hand and the spilling of light from outside disappeared inch by inch as the hole covered. We stood in complete darkness until his hand raised between us, a bright red glowing orb floated from his palm.

The orb brightened as he lifted it near my face. "We don't have to do this right now, Harm. I've all the time in the world...literally."

I shifted closer to him, tracing my hand through the orb, and feeling its tingles over my fingertips. "Are you trying to talk me out of this?"

His face hardened. "Never."

"Then I think it's about time I met your uncle."

He curled his arm around me. In a flash of light and smoke, we appeared on a riverbank with black sand—the fiery sconces hanging above cast flickers of orange reflections in the water— The River Styx. Here I was about to become a living, breathing goddess, and everything remained surreal.

A deep snarl vibrated from behind us, the sound of claws scraping against the sand followed. Three pairs of glowing red eyes appeared in the darkness.

"Ares," I called out, reaching for him but not daring to take my eyes away.

Ares coaxed me behind him. "Stay behind me, gatáki."

Not a lot of things admittedly scared me, but as the three giant dog heads plunged at us, I shrieked without regret.

Ares caught one of the snapping jaws with both hands, and

the dog head snorted. Ares glared, and then suddenly…all three mouths started to lick him. Ares chuckled, scratching each head under the chin. All three sets of eyes closed, and its back leg bounced.

"I missed you too, boy. Been keeping up with your guard duties?" He cooed, nuzzling his cheek against the canine's fur.

I stood dumbfounded. Moments ago, I thought I'd get eaten by a dog with three heads, and now the massive creature rolled on its back so Ares could scratch its stomach.

"If you haven't guessed it yet, this is Cerberus." Ares grinned, beating his forehead against the nearest dog head.

"I may have thought of that if I wasn't preoccupied with the thought of you getting swallowed whole by a giant dog with three heads."

Cerberus bumped one head into Ares's side. Ares squinted, a slow smile crawling over his lips before he dove into Cerberus's chest. The God of War and the guard dog of the Underworld proceeded to wrestle in a bout of barrel rolls across the sand.

Embers floated overhead, and a mysterious black fog gathered at my feet.

"Cerbie, you're supposed to—" A man with long white hair and pointed ears appeared, stopping dead in his tracks when he spied Cerberus laying on his back with all three tongues hanging out.

Hades.

I clutched my shirt and backed away. It hadn't crossed my mind we'd be showing up in this guy's kingdom unannounced.

Cerberus jumped to his feet, catching Ares underneath one paw, pinning him to the ground. Ares arched his head back.

"Ares?" Hades shifted his eyes between him and me.

Ares tried to get up, but Cerberus pushed him back down. Ares waved. "Been a while, huh?"

"I see Cerberus hasn't forgotten you." Hades's voice was deep and overlaid with scattered whispers.

Screw it. How did I become the meager mouse all of a sudden?

"I'm Harm." I held out my hand.

He smiled down at me, the glowing white orbs of eyes brightening as he took my hand. "Harm. As in Harmony? The same Harmony who infiltrates most of Ares's thoughts?"

I cocked an eyebrow, and we both turned to look at Ares. He grumbled and shoved Cerberus's paw away before leaping to his feet. "It's been a long time since I've navigated this type of—" He put one hand on his hip and with the other gestured between us. "Situation."

"We're a situation?" I folded my arms.

Hades chuckled, his white floating hair shifting with every bounce of his shoulders. "I think my nephew is referring to feelings." He poked at his chest, directly over his heart.

"As if you have the best track record with emotions. It's been what? Months with the new Queen? Doesn't make you a damn expert." Ares flicked his hand.

"You're right. I should refer you to Eros." An evil grin played on Hades's lips.

Ares glowered. "I wouldn't be caught dead around that cherub."

"As if I have to ask, but what brings you two down to my humble abode?" Hades steepled his fingers.

One of Cerberus's heads sniffed my hair. I froze, staring sidelong at the face that was twice the width of my body.

"Cerberus." Hades made a clicking sound. "You're distracting her."

Cerberus's shoulders slumped before he walked away.

"You already know what I'm going to ask, don't you?" Ares crossed his arms.

Hades nodded. "I may have thought both of you crazy if this would've happened months ago, but if a mortal woman could learn to love a god who tortures the damned in Tartarus, why could one not feel the same for the God of War?" He arched a brow.

For a brief moment, Ares and I turned into shy teenagers. We caught each other's gazes but looked away. I curled my hair over an ear, and he rubbed the back of his neck.

"I assume you've talked this through? Given it some thought? It isn't exactly reversible." Hades's flame crown flickered.

Ares slid his arm around me. "I've given her every possible opportunity to bail out. She's more stubborn than I am."

I elbowed him in the ribs. He grunted but flashed a pearly grin.

"Have you talked to him about it?" Hades frowned.

"He isn't my keeper. I'll deal with him if he chooses to whine over it."

"Good to know." He held up his palm and a swirl of smoke and embers collected. "I've dealt with him enough lately to last a millennium. I could use a break."

I stared at the embers floating in Hades's hand, in my gut

knowing it held the power to turn me into a goddess.

Ares kissed my ear. "Are you ready, Amazon?"

I turned to look at him, searching in his eyes for the final and ultimate push. A story played in his gaze—a life. The warrior. The protector. The spirit we all search for within ourselves. He represented all these things and more to all of humanity, but for me…he'd be my partner. My equal. The other half of my power.

"More than ever," I whispered.

Hades half-smiled as he brought his glowing hand toward me. He cupped my cheek and my back arched. A surge pulsed through me to the tips of my toes, searching, exploring its domain. Heat coursed through my neck, sending trickles of electricity down my spine until finally, it settled. The power raged through me as if it had nowhere to go—no means to break free. My chest heaved, and I leaped on Ares, kissing him, devouring his essence with every slide of our lips.

I pulled away, realizing we were still in the Underworld—standing in front of its king, Ares's uncle. My hands wrung together as I tried to control myself, attempting to push the power into any corner it was willing to go. It wasn't like suppressing anger. It was too much. I needed to release it, and he was my solution—the only resolve I'd consider.

"You uh—should take her somewhere," Hades said with a playful smirk. "Don't forget to give her this." He tossed Ares a glowing orange crystal.

I kissed Ares's neck, waiting for him to port us somewhere—anywhere. It could be on the top of a cliff for all I cared.

"Ares. Don't be a stranger. Stephanie's going to be quite disappointed she missed meeting you."

Ares snickered as I unabashedly reached a hand into his shirt, scraping my nails over one of his pecs. "Deal. And Hades—" He kissed the top of my head. "Thank you."

Hades bowed his head, and we flashed away, appearing in the middle of my apartment living room. As soon as my feet were on solid ground, I ripped Ares's shirt in half.

I gasped. "Holy shit." Staring at the mess I'd made of his shirt, I let my fingers drag down my prize—him. Every inch of tanned carved muscle glistened, waiting for me to claim it all.

He shrugged off the tattered remains of his shirt.

I bit down on my lip, trailing my eyes down his tattoo, landing on the orange substance glowing in his palm. "What is that?"

"Ambrosia. It's what will make you immortal." His tone was deep and commanding as he held it out to me.

I reached, and he balled his fist over it.

"Nuh, uh, uh, gatáki. What's your rush?" He gave a sly grin.

I curled my fingers in his belt loops and pulled myself against him. His hardened girth pressed against my hip. "That's not very nice."

His eyes brightened, and he wrapped my hair in his free hand. "I'm not nice." He kissed me deep and rough. With every thrust of his tongue into my mouth, more and more of me became his.

He pulled away long enough to break off a crumb of the ambrosia, bringing his fingers to my lips, placing it in my mouth. A tingle surged through my jaw.

More. I needed more. More ambrosia. More him.

"Bed," he commanded with a sultry gaze.

I nibbled one of my fingers as I backed into the bedroom. With one flick of his wrist, my clothes disintegrated. In a flash of blinding red light, he appeared in front of me, reaching behind to grab my ass.

"You're a goddess now, Harm. The only place for that power to go is out. So, use it." He closed his mouth over my neck, kissing, licking, biting.

I pressed my hands against his remaining clothes. Like falling sand in an hourglass, they fell to the ground in tiny pieces, piling at our feet.

He slowly tilted his chin down, kicking through the scattered debris of his clothes with a chuckle. "Interesting."

I wrapped a hand around his length, stroking him, coaxing him toward the bed. He broke off another piece of the ambrosia and fed it to me with heavy-lidded eyes.

"Lie down," he growled.

I thought about laying on the bed, and in a swirl of autumn-colored leaves, I appeared exactly where I intended.

Ares crawled over me. He rested the ambrosia against my lips but didn't feed me any. Instead, he dragged it over my chin and the dip between my breasts. As he took one nipple into his mouth, the brush from his beard making it harden, he slipped another piece of ambrosia past my lips.

"Do you feel it, gatáki? Eternity seeping into you with every bit of ambrosia?" He dragged his tongue down my stomach, circling my belly button.

It was like an increasing pulse that fluttered away with every piece given. His tongue lapped between my folds, and I cried out, gripping the bed sheets. His beard tickled the insides of my thighs as he trailed back up to my face, feeding me half of what remained of immortality. Every muscle clenched, and a warmth traveled the length of my spine. He lifted my legs to his shoulders and plunged into me with a snarl.

His sudden intrusion mixed with the building transition within me from the ambrosia sent me into a euphoric daze. I looked up at him as he made his eyes blaze like the war god he was. He rocked in and out of me, the volcano between my hips simmering, bubbling until it erupted. He tightened his arms over my legs, pinning me to him as I writhed under his touch.

He pushed my knees apart, wrapping my legs around his waist, and dipped on top of me. With every roll of his hips, I lifted my own to meet him. Our bodies were accustomed to fighting, dodging, predicting the opponent's movements. For once, we were able to give into ourselves, let the chips fall where they would.

He kissed me, dropping the remaining ambrosia into my mouth. Starbursts exploded behind my lids, and vibrations skirted down my legs and arms. With immortality settling in, our powers balanced one another. Ares grimaced, clenching his arms on each side of my ribs. His eyes burst open, and a wide grin slowly morphed over his face. His thrusts paused, but he stared down at me as if seeing me for the first time.

"Ares? What is it?"

"Thank you." His expression softened, but a harsh crease remained near his eyes.

"For?"

Slowly, ever so torturously slow, he moved in and out of me. "I never knew war could experience a sense of peace. Or that I even wanted to."

I took a deep breath, feeling the boulder that'd been resting on my shoulders for decades melting away.

"I know exactly how you feel." I cocked a wicked brow. "But you're not getting all soft on me, now are you?"

He thrust once, harsh and deep. "Never."

I yelped, my hips bucking skyward.

He pressed his cheek to mine. "I hope you don't have any plans for a while. We've got *a lot* of celebrating to do."

TWENTY ONE

𒐫𒐫𒐫𒐫𒐫𒐫𒐫𒐫𒐫𒐫𒐫𒐫𒐫𒐫

WE'D LOCKED OURSELVES IN my apartment for the past three days, christening nearly every square inch with our newfound partnership. If ever there'd been an officially consummated relationship, it was ours. I sat on the couch wearing only a flannel blanket, mindlessly scrolling through the TV channels. Yet again, the surfer named Simon Thalassa popped up. I paused, watching him effortlessly conquer each wave his board had the pleasure of gliding across.

Ares's presence loomed behind me, the scents of leather and soap permeating the air. His hand dipped over my shoulder, running his callused fingertips across my collarbone.

"I've never had one ounce of interest in surfing, but this guy is good." I pointed at the blonde surfer.

Ares made a *pfft* sound. "He should be, considering he's the king of all the seas." He reached in front of me and hit the power button for the TV with a grunt.

"King of the—" I snapped my gaze to him. "Simon is Poseidon?"

"Uh-huh," he said monotone before planting a quick kiss on my neck. "Get dressed."

I slipped off the couch, not bothering to bring the blanket with me. Ares's eyes roamed over my naked body, his teeth biting into his bottom lip.

"Are we going somewhere?" I stretched my arms above my head.

Ares groaned as he slid forward, trailing a hand up my thigh to my hip. "What kind of war god would you be without armor and weapons?"

My heart fluttered with anticipation. "You should've led with that." Grinning, I snapped my fingers and appeared fully clothed, despite Ares's pout.

"Heph has a blacksmithing shop in London. He hasn't made a new set of armor for a god in quite some time. I'm sure he'll be ecstatic." He curled his arm around me, and within seconds, we stood in the streets of London in front of a small shop. A wooden anvil sign hung over the door with the words: "Vulcan Blacksmithing."

"And who is he in the continually confusing family tree?"

"My brother. One I get along with."

"Half-brother?"

"Yes. I mean, technically, he doesn't have a father, so maybe a full brother?" Ares scratched the back of his head.

"How can he not have a father?" I held a palm up. "You

know what? Conversation for another time."

We slipped through the front door, a bell chiming as we entered. Every countertop had several layers of dust, cobwebs clung to every corner, and rusted tools scattered over the tables.

"Are you sure he's here?" I ran my finger across the counter with a grimace.

"He's probably in the back."

I smacked my palm on a bell resting on the counter. Dust fluttered through the air, making me cough. We stood in silence, waiting for him to show. Ares beat his fingers against the counter before slamming his hand down on the bell three more times.

"Heph," Ares shouted, trekking from one side of the shop to the other. He peeled back curtains, peeked in closets, and still no sign of the God of the Forge.

A blue circular portal swirled in the air in front of us. A man with cropped dark brown hair in a black duster jacket stumbled out of it, covered in bright green sludge, and the portal disappeared.

The man slid a hand over his brow, ridding it of slime before snapping fingers at the ground, flinging the ooze at my feet.

"Every bloody time," the man said, his deep voice rich with a British accent.

"Heph," Ares said.

Heph widened his dark eyes and then furrowed his brow, shifting his glance between us. A gnarled scar traveled down the right side of his face, partly covered by a trimmed full beard.

"What's this all about then?" He pointed between us, sending more sludge flying.

"Thought I'd stop by for tea and crumpets so we could catch up," Ares gruffed. "Why do you *think* I'm here?"

Heph chuckled. "Right you are. What'll it be this time, brother, a claymore twice the size of Wallace's? A mace worthy of slaughtering a cyclops?"

"We're here for me," I chimed in.

Heph turned with a brightened grin. "Ah, yes. You are a goddess, aren't you? I know I'm hardly ever here in this time or dimension anymore, but I should still recognize you. Shouldn't I?" He arched a brow at Ares.

"A recent development. She'll need armor, a xiphos, javelin, shield. All of it."

"The whole shebang. I love it. Follow me then. The forge out front here won't do your godly self any justice." He motioned with his hand for us to follow.

"Am I supposed to ignore the fact you appeared from a portal covered in green slime?" I asked as he led us into a room with a forge the size of half a football field.

"I'm a bounty hunter, love. I go where the money is, and it's not always right around the corner." Heph waved his hand and molten metal glowing orange pooled in a nearby vat.

"Vlákas. You reek, Heph." Scrunching his nose, Ares fanned Heph.

The green sludge had dried and caked against Heph's face and clothes.

"Aren't you going to change?" I plugged my nose with two fingers.

Heph stuck his bottom lip out. "Nah. It reminds me of my mistakes." He threw an arm out, making a giant hammer appear. "You'd think with the number of times I've killed harpies, I'd have learned by now to be farther away when dealing the final blow."

Ares shook his head with a small grin. The fact I lived in a world where you could throw the idea of an interdimensional bounty hunter into a conversation so casually baffled me.

"You two don't seem to loathe each other. I'd been under the impression that was a normal custom with this family." I picked up a chrome-plated pair of tweezers.

Heph plucked it from my grasp. "Rule number one. No one touches my tools, 'cept for me. Got it?" He tossed the tweezers back to where I'd found them.

"Sure." I frowned.

Heph shrugged off his duster jacket and tossed it to a corner. His arms were tanned, muscular, and cut, but not as bulging as Ares. A tattoo wrapped around his left forearm—a crane in flight, its wings melting into the same molten lava of Heph's forge, forming an anvil near his wrist.

"You could say we have something in common, eh brother? Both cast from Olympus. Me because our dear sweet mum thought I was the ugliest thing she'd ever seen. Ares because he threw the occasional temper tantrum." Heph's lips thinned, and he stared into space before shaking his head.

"This family really puts the 'diss' in 'dysfunctional,' hm?" I flashed a smile at Ares who'd already been staring at me— beaming at me.

"Oh, it's not all bad, love. Look at it this way, there's never a dull moment, and you can simply poof yourself away." Heph rolled his wrist and flicked his hand in the air with a flourish.

"Now about this armor." Heph wrapped his hands around my ribcage, concentration straining his face.

Ares snarled and shoved Heph away from me.

Heph slow-blinked with a sigh. "Do you want it to fit or not? 'sides, if I were going to try to cop a feel of your darling girlfriend here, I wouldn't be doing it in front of you, would I?"

The corners of Ares's jaw bobbed, and he grunted. "Fine."

Heph nodded once and proceeded to squeeze my shoulders, forearms, and head. His hands lingered over my chest, and his fingers wriggled. "We'll just account for a little extra room for that…particular area."

He dipped his hands into the hot liquid without so much as a wince. "Any color preference?"

"I've always been partial to red." I caught Ares's gaze, idly licking the corner of my mouth.

"Do you drink the blood of your enemies from their skulls too?" Heph removed a xiphos with a golden blade—red leaf emblems swirled around the hilt. He held it out to me, beaming at his newly born weapon baby.

I took it with both hands, holding it as if it'd wither away. "Heph, this is gorgeous."

"It's been a long time since I've been able to forge for a god. And I *always* strive to outdo myself. Isn't that right, Ares?"

Ares shook his head, leaning past me to gaze at the wondrous sword in my palms. "Incorporate a wildcat somehow." He squeezed my hip.

"One step ahead of you." Heph removed his arms from the lava, holding them upright like a prepping surgeon.

He walked over to me and pressed his hands against my

shoulders. Black and golden armor materialized, a flap of red over my right shoulder, followed by a roaring lion's head on my left. He pressed a finger against my sternum, and the armor formed a breastplate with ornate Corinthian leaf patterns. Gripping my forearms, he made gauntlets with red trim appear. Continuing the process, he touched my body where he wanted the armor to mold until I stood fully decked in my brightened gold, black, and red armor, complete with tasseled skirt and shin guards.

The heated intensity in Ares's gaze suggested he'd sprawl me on the floor and take me, no matter if Heph were here or not. It made my chest tighten, and I hadn't even seen myself in full war goddess mode yet.

"The final touch." Heph removed a Spartanesque helmet from the vat. It matched Ares's with the added element of swirling leaves brushing up the sides. He gave a knowing smile as he slipped it over my head. "It only seemed fitting, love."

Ares stared at me with flared nostrils. "I didn't think you could get any more beautiful, gatáki. This, godhood, all of it, really was meant for you."

I walked over to a metal shield resting against a table, peering at myself in my goddess of war attire. Ares was right. I couldn't imagine myself any other way now. Dragging my fingers over the lion on my shoulder, I held back tears stinging my eyes.

"Right then. You should be all set. I'd love to stay and chat, but duty—" Heph's back pocket buzzed, and he frowned, grabbing it. His thumb scrolled over the screen with a wry grin. "Your sister. I swear she's bloody obsessed with me."

Ares squinted. "Which one?"

Grinning like a hyena, Heph's worked his thumbs feverishly across the touch screen keyboard. "Dite."

Ares laughed, hearty and deep. "Please. She'd never make it past that mug of yours."

I bit the inside of my cheek, chest warming, watching the two brothers throwing verbal jabs at each other.

My family. *My* family. Unreal.

"Never underestimate the power of personality." Heph breathed on his knuckles and rubbed them against his shirt. "But you're right. The only reason she ever texts me is to ask about sending clients her way. I often wonder why I ever bothered giving her my number in the first place, and then I remember those—" He trailed off and held his hands in front of his chest like he held two watermelons.

"Didn't you have to leave?" Ares grumbled.

"I do. I got a big score in the Yaminite district. Flesh-eating slug monsters are overrunning them. I didn't even know that was a thing." He shrugged, held out his hand, and his jacket flew into his palm. He slipped it on, finally rid himself of harpy guts, and the blue portal appeared behind him.

"Thanks for the armor." The orange sparks from the hot forge near us reflected off the sleek armor hugging my body.

Heph saluted as he backed away. "Enjoy it. And Harm—" He bowed and gave a snarky grin. "Welcome to this shite show of a family." Pushing off the balls of his feet, he leaped into the portal behind him.

Ares dragged his finger over the metal covering my breasts. "How do you feel, Harm?"

"Like I'm ready to take on the world." I peered at him

through the slits of my helmet and gave one twirl of my sword.

His attention snapped over my shoulder, brow cinching into a scowl. He stormed for the back door.

I slipped off my helmet. "Ares? What is it?" Following him, I paused at the exit, looking down at my armor. Waving a hand over myself, I changed back into street clothes.

Ares stood in the alley behind the shop, seething at a dark-haired man in a grey suit casually leaning against one wall.

The man slid one hand from his pants pockets and rubbed the light beard on his chin. "We've always been at a point of contention, son, but to not call on me to create your goddess girlfriend? That stings. First Apollo, now you? At some point, I think I should be insulted."

Son?

Which would make him…oh shit. *Zeus.*

"You think I give a maláka about how you feel?" Ares growled, widening his stance.

"Fair enough." Zeus pushed off the wall, pulling the sleeves of the white shirt underneath his jacket. "You honestly still think after all these years, I kicked you out of Olympus because you threw a few tables? Yelled and cursed at me a time or two? Hm?"

I slinked far enough away to give them privacy but still allow me to see.

"What in Tartarus are you getting at, old man?"

Zeus sighed. "You've always had my thick-headedness, so allow me to enlighten you. You were made for more than life on an ethereal mountain. Look at all you accomplished through the ages. It required you to be here." He pointed down. "On Earth. Not rubbing elbows and drinking ambrosia wine with the other gods."

Ares glared and closed the space between them. "Are you seriously trying to tell me that you did it on purpose? That you weren't a horrible father? It was for my own good?"

"It *was* for your own good." Electricity sparked over Zeus's hand.

Ares laughed as he threw his hands up, turning away from the King of the Gods.

"The power you were gifted was too much for one god," Zeus added, raising his voice.

"And so, you cast me out to let me figure it out on my own?"

"You needed that hate. It *drove* you to be the war god you are today." He dragged a hand through his hair, pausing to tug it. "Besides, you found a kindred spirit in Hades—both depressed fools despite the power given to them. And I'm sure there were plenty of conversations of your mutual hate over me." Zeus's head lowered, breaking eye contact with Ares.

"This is why you stopped by? To say you're annoyed I didn't ask you about Harm and talk about the past?"

"I had a feeling you'd bypass my approval. It's why I sent Athena and The Furies." Zeus's dark gaze landed on me. "But we still have yet to meet. You're a goddess now, Harmony. Which makes me your *king*."

I slipped out from my hiding spot.

Ares slid between us. "What are you doing?"

"Introducing myself," Zeus said with narrowed eyes. Electricity pulsed over his hand as he pushed Ares aside.

His eyes roamed over my face and body, but not in the flirtatious sense. No, he was dissecting me. He extended a hand—the same hand that'd just had lightning coursing through it. "I want to make one thing clear. You have an immense responsibility now, Harmony. I'll be watching to ensure you uphold your side of it." His jaw tightened. "If you don't—" Electricity sparked in his eyes. "I'll make sure you do.'

I stared at him wide-eyed before managing to nod my head. Words like "You can count on me, sir." Or, "You don't need to worry about me, sir," should've flung from my mouth, but instead, I became mute.

Ares stepped in front of me. "Why do you have to be such a prick about everything?"

Zeus pulled on the jacket sleeves for each arm, sliding them further over the white shirt underneath. "It's not my job to be nice, Ares. It's to make sure everyone does their *malákas* jobs." He leaned his face into Ares's, and the two masculine gods stood toe-to-toe at the same height.

"I'm glad you threw me off Olympus." Ares's cheek twitched.

"That's the spirit." Zeus plucked at the corner of his mouth with his thumb. "You'll be seeing more of me, Ares." He shot his powerful gaze to me. "Get used to it." Before Ares had a chance to retort, Zeus disappeared in a crackle of lightning.

I stared at a fracture in the concrete that traveled between my feet.

"Vlákas. This family," Ares mumbled.

Zeus's words played on a loop in my head. Not just about him threatening me if I didn't do a good job but his immense responsibility to keep all of the gods and goddesses in line.

"I need to see what I can do with my powers. Can you take me somewhere? Anywhere?"

"You don't have to prove a damn thing to him, Harm."

I locked my eyes with his. "Yes, I do."

Ares sighed and stared at me as if waiting for me to change my mind. He trailed his fingers over his beard. "I know better than to argue with you." He motioned with his hand for me to come to him.

As I walked over, I masked the fear traveling down my spine. What if I couldn't do as good a job as Zeus wanted? What would he do to make sure I did?

Ares slid his hand over my shoulder. "Where we're going, they won't be able to see us. It started as an extraction mission for a prisoner of war. The enemy launched a surprise attack, forcing them into an abandoned house. They're losing drive. Passion. We need to boost morale."

"Understood."

We appeared in a stone-carved building with entire walls missing from obvious explosions. It was absolute chaos— gunfire, shouting, grenades detonating in random places. Five men in military-grade camo uniforms were scattered throughout the room, clutching their rifles to their chests. Whenever there was a break in the gunfire, one would pop up, aiming through a window to take as many shots as they could before falling back into cover.

"They have us surrounded. We're sitting ducks in here!" One man yelled, adjusting his helmet.

"Where the fuck do you suggest we go? Sarge isn't answering

on comms either," another responded.

Ares made a beeline for a man shaking and cowering in a corner. He hadn't spoken nor tried to shoot back since we arrived—the weakest of the bunch.

I, on the other hand, was drawn to the one at the front of the room. He'd returned fire and exchanged a magazine in the few minutes since we'd arrived, but he didn't chime in with the others. Little did he know, he was a natural-born leader. In a situation like this with no outranking soldiers, someone needed to take charge.

Ares yelled like a drill sergeant at the man in the corner. The man couldn't see or hear him, but the drive exuding from Ares made the man blow out two quick breaths, prop up on the window sill and shoot two rounds.

I crouched by Mr. Leader, merely watching him for a moment. He grimaced every time he slammed back to the ground. Blood stained his jacket on the left side—a bullet graze. Despite his wound, he still led the charge. Three grenades hung from his utility belt and several more magazines—plenty of ammo.

I slid a hand over his shoulder, pushing every bit of passion within me into him. "You all can make it out of here. They'll listen to you if you tell them what *is* going to happen versus what *could* happen. Take charge. Save your people."

The man's eyes narrowed, and he looked from one soldier to the other. I slid my hand away and backed off, my chest pumping with the hope he'd do what I knew he could.

"Everyone, listen up," he ordered, demanding their attention.

Ares looked from the man back to me.

"How many grenades do we have? Magazines?"

They all answered in varied numbers.

"Good. We head out the back, use the grenades as a diversion to get to the next patch of cover. There's plenty of it between here and the extraction point." He lifted his head just enough his eyes peered over the sill. "I've counted rounds, and the main shooter will have to reload soon. When I give the go, everyone haul ass. Understood?"

Everyone responded in resounding whoops and hollers. As the firing paused, they all ran as instructed toward the back.

Ares stepped beside me, crossing his arms over his chest. "I don't think you're going to have to worry about Zeus getting on your ass, gatáki. You were born for this."

As I watched the soldiers make their way out without so much as a scratch, an unfamiliar swell spread through my chest like liquid fire—pride, not only for myself but for humans themselves. I'd damn near given up on them as a mortal myself. Even amid chaos, there's always opportunity.

EPILOGUE

SOME MONTHS LATER...

WE SAT BEHIND COVER, switching out the magazines of our weapons. I peeked around the corner, counting the number of assailants.

"I see three on the left, four on the right. Dino and Chelsea are directly across from us on the other side," I said, holding my paintball gun vertically.

Ares chuckled. "You know his name is Dionysos, and yet you still insist on calling him Dino."

"He'll always be Dino to me." I grinned and checked that the chamber had an adequate number of paintballs loaded.

As the first months went by of the two of us sharing the responsibilities of the more passionate side of war, regeneration, and progress, we never took a moment to simply be—to have fun, to let our bodies recuperate from the stress of godly intervention. We made a pact to do something "normal" once a week. Not only to take a break and let loose, but it comforted me to remember my mortal side—the human side. We'd done it all—ax throwing, bowling, laser tag. But the one we kept circling back to time and time again…was paintball.

I asked Chelsea to join, not expecting her to say yes. When she agreed, I'd drilled her on just how painful getting hit by a paintball, despite three layers of clothing, could feel. After she complained about my goddess-like nature not being affected by them, she told me it was something I liked, and she wanted to support me.

Yes, we had "the talk" about four months ago. It took three days to convince her, a week to start talking to me again, and another week to accept it. It was like she went through the stages of grief. In a way, I guess the old me really had died.

Ares grumbled when I suggested Dino tagged along. He softened at the idea when I'd told him about Dino's visit before becoming a goddess. Plus, I *knew* Ares wanted the opportunity to thwart him with paintballs. He'd loaded his gun with yellow paint, knowing Dino couldn't stand the color. Something about it reminding him of piss.

"Oh my God!" Chelsea yelped from another log across the way. "A spider was just crawling up my pant leg!"

"Can someone remind me why they teamed me up with the wet blanket?" Dino shouted to us.

Ares and I grinned at each other.

"Excuse me?" Chelsea scoffed, the sound of three paintballs exploding against armor followed.

I flipped onto my knees, peeking over the edge of the log. Dino had three blue paint spatters on his chest. He narrowed his eyes at Chelsea before dropping them to look at her handiwork.

Chelsea's mouth gaped, and she frantically shook her head. "My finger slipped. Honest."

Chelsea still managed to look pristine with her auburn hair pulled back in a low, wavy ponytail despite playing in an athletic event. She even bothered to slather on make-up. I told her it'd end up sweating off underneath thc goggles, but she insisted.

"You better run," Dino teased.

Chelsea looked from him to me and then behind her before sprinting away.

Dino chuckled and stood up, not worrying about paintballs, considering he was already out. "It's all up to you two now," he said to us with a wink before chasing after Chelsea.

"You take right, I take left?" Ares peered at me with those sultry eyes of his.

I tugged his beard. "I thought you'd never ask, my Sparkly Snicker-Doo."

"The name's growing on me."

"Careful God of War, or I *will* call you it in public."

Hc slid a hand over my inner thigh as he grazed my chin with his beard. "I'm terrified."

Even as a goddess, he still made my heart race. "Shoot now. Play later." I gave a tiny lick to his grinning lips before switching my focus to approaching players.

We jumped from our shield, aiming our paintball guns at

mortal strangers. Every shot landed home, and we continued to work the tree lines until we reached the center. My gun clicked. Empty.

"I need to reload," I said to him over my shoulder.

Ares switched directions, shooting in mine instead. I ducked down as I popped the magazine and slid in another. He placed a hand on my back, shooting over me, covering me. When I stood up, my gun loaded and cocked, we reached over each other's shoulders, firing at approaching players from behind the other. His eyes sparkled at me.

We continued this charade of fighting back-to-back or shooting over each other's shoulders, covering the other when they had to reload ammo. As the numbers dwindled, the godly adrenaline was at full force, and I planted a kiss on his lips. Our intuition didn't cease when we were kissing. It didn't dwindle when we were doing...*anything*. As we devoured each other, we shot anyone who dared tried to stop us.

I pulled away with my hand still resting behind his neck and peered up at the only man who could've ever closed the widening gap in my life. It turned out it wasn't a man at all.

He rubbed the tip of his nose against mine. "I think we got them all."

Groans and moans from several players thwarted with paintballs surrounded us. Paint splatters of yellow and red. Our colors.

"We should probably find Dino and Chelsea," I said through a lustful sigh.

We made off to the forest, looking for any signs of them. When we were a reasonable distance from the paintball battlefield, a blue portal opened in front of us. Heph toppled out, not covered in goo this time.

"How would you twats like to fight in a *real* battle?"

"Name the time and place." I bounced my brow at Ares, taking a step forward.

Ares caught the crook of my arm. "Depends on what you're up against."

"What if I told you, brother, that in another timeline, one of the captured Titans has escaped?"

"Maláka," Ares growled.

"Exactly. And you both were the second and third best choices to fight the big beasties. I'm not going to tell you which is which." Heph squinted one eye.

The skin between Ares's eyes crinkled with concern.

"I'm up for it if you are, Spartan." My confidence had soared these past months. It was as if nothing could stop me. And it was time to test the limits.

"Let's do it." Ares grabbed my hand. "It may even be time to summon the fire-breathing horses." He grinned at me.

"Aren't I invited?" Dino's voice asked from behind us.

He stood there alone with his arms out.

"Why would you be?" Heph scoffed.

Dino rolled his eyes and tossed his paintball gun into the dirt. "Are you still hung up on that whole Hera business?"

Heph's eyes shifted. "No. I just don't bloody like you."

Dino glared at him, and Heph leaped into the portal.

"You better not have upset Chelsea." I bit back a smile.

"I didn't. I didn't. One paintball clipped her in the shoulder, and some got on her Versachagucci something or another shirt. Why did she wear it to a paintball match? You got me."

I cocked my head to one side. "You should get to know her better, Dino. I think she'd surprise you."

"Her? She has a stick so far up her a—" He pointed behind him with his thumb.

I interrupted by lifting a palm. "Trust me. The best things happen unexpectedly. But they can't happen if you don't give them a chance."

Ares's sultry stare warmed my cheeks. I didn't have to look at him to know he was staring at me, probably even smiling.

Dino scratched his cheek with a squished brow before turning his attention to Chelsea batting branches in the thick of the forest.

"Ready to save the universe?" Ares snaked an arm around my waist.

"I don't think this Titan knows what it's up against." I trailed my hand over his forearm, tracing the armor tattoo.

He nipped my earlobe. "I told you, Amazon. The *blood* we could shed."

Heph's head poked out from the portal. "You two mind shagging *after* the giant monster wrecking a city is, I don't know, stopped?" His brow shot up.

"One last thing," Ares said, holding up his paintball gun.

He shot Dino twice in the chest, spattering yellow paint over his shirt.

Dino jumped back, but it was too late. "Bro."

"Now we can go." Ares tossed me a sinister grin and chucked the paintball gun.

Dino seethed at the yellow stain on his clothes. "I won't

forget this."

"You better not," Ares replied.

Grinning, I tugged Ares into the portal, and we whisked into the unknown.

Together. Always.

THE
CONTEMPORARY MYTHOS
WILL CONTINUE

COMING SOON

Catch the first book in the Contemporary Mythos series:

HADES

The King of the Underworld may have found a woman
truly capable of melting his cold, dark heart.

HADES (Contemporary Mythos, #1)
BUY IT ON AMAZON

Catch the second book in the Contemporary Mythos series:

It's not easy being a *true* rock god.

APOLLO (Contemporary Mythos, #2)
BUY IT ON AMAZON

ALSO BY
CARLY SPADE

Be sure to check out the first in Carly's paranormal romance series: *After Midnight*. Vampires, shifters, Aztec mythology, and enemies to lovers.

IRRESISTIBLE DEMISE

Available on Amazon

EROS

NEXT IN THE
CONTEMPORARY MYTHOS
SERIES:

"HI. I'M GOING TO cut straight to the chase, slick. Do you like to play matchmaker on the side?" Alex asked the bartender, folding her hands on the bar top.

The bartender's brows pinched together, and he chuckled—deep and slightly raspy. "I'm sorry?"

I shoved past Alex, forcing her down onto a stool. The bartender's gaze met mine, sending a quiver through my stomach. His eyes were like a peacock—the blue part. A wavy piece of hair hung down over his forehead like Clark Kent, and when I glanced past his lips, I had to grab the bar to keep from stumbling backward. He had it—the cleft chin.

"I uh—" I couldn't stop staring at it. Cleft chins were one of my weaknesses. And the dimple in his chin was deep enough to collect water. "She uh—was talking for me."

I could feel Alex staring at the side of my face and elbowed her. She batted my arm away.

"Oh, yeah? Care to explain?" The bartender asked as he leaned forward.

A light scattering of chest hair peeked from the two undone buttons of his plaid shirt. His firm forearm muscles flexed as he gripped the edge of the mahogany.

I thinned my lips and folded my hands in front of me. "I run this dating website. You might've heard of it, E-romantic?"

He shook his head. "Nope."

"You haven't?" I scrunched my nose.

Alex thwacked my stomach to continue.

"Anyway, two of my clients dropped from my program because they came to this bar and said *you* led them to love." I poked the bar top twice.

He rubbed his chin. "Well, that's great to hear."

"So, it's true?" I glared at him.

"Absolutely." He gave a snarky grin.

I could feel my heartbeat in my ears. "It's not great. You're stealing business from me."

Alex remained silent, resting her chin in her hand, elbow atop her knee.

"How's it stealing if I'm getting no kind of monetary compensation for it?" He raised a brow.

I opened my mouth to respond and then snapped it shut. He was right.

"Why don't you tell me more about this site of yours? The first round is on the house." He pointed between Alex and me.

"I'll have a wine spritzer." Alex's eyelids grew heavy.

I had no intention of having a civil conversation with him, and now Alex sealed us into a round of drinks.

"I'll have whatever. And no Sex on the Beach." I glared at him. He seemed the type to use that drink as a flirtation device.

He bit his lip. "I much prefer it in other places. Too much sand."

One of Alex's hands gripped my knee from under the concealment of the bar.

"Name's Eric, by the way." His brow quirked.

Alex nudged her head at me. "Elani. Alex."

"Pleasure to meet you ladies. I'll be right back." His eyes scanned my face before walking away.

"Oh. My. Zeus." Alex's grip tightened on my leg.

"What's the matter with you?"

"Are you kidding? You're a total goner. He has the chin, Lani."

I grabbed a cocktail napkin and started folding it. "I'd like to think a chin won't make me throw all scruples out the window. Besides, this guy is my competition, remember?"

"Right. Right. It makes for some of the best sex anyway."

Eric swayed a shaker in his hand—a wide masculine hand.

"Is that all you think about?"

She puckered her lips. "No. I also think about storm clouds, how many different ways to kill rodents, and muscular naked man ass."

"How in the world did we become best friends?"

She stared at me deadpan. "My electric personality."

"Here we are. One wine spritzer and—" He set a glass with a bright blue liquid in front of me, placing a lemon slice on the rim. "Sex in the Driveway."

"Ha. Ha. Clever." I slid the glass toward me, trying to ignore the way the drink made his blue eyes pop.

"I thought so." He did one quick bob with both eyebrows.

Alex slurped on her drink, glancing between the two of us.

"So, you run a dating service. How does it work exactly?" He wiped droplets from the bar with a towel.

"They answer a questionnaire, and based on the answers, I've built a database with an algorithm that'll match them to the most likely candidate." I slipped the straw into my mouth, taking the first sip—sweet, peachy, and orangey.

"Candidate for love?"

"No. Compatibility."

He squinted at me and looked at Alex, who shrugged. "Please tell me she isn't one of those types who thinks love is all scientific bullshit?"

Alex sulked as her eyes roamed everywhere but him.

Eric's gaze snapped back to me. "You are. Oh, that's rich."

"It's not bullshit." I sat straighter. "My system is guaranteed to find them a partner for *life*, not just some euphoric feeling that's bound to end in heartbreak."

He folded his arms, extenuating his already wide frame. "Wow. The world's certainly done a number on you, eh?"

"What would you know about love anyway? I don't see a ring on your finger."

Alex slid off her stool, crouching and sidestepping toward the bathrooms.

Eric brought our faces closer. "And you're presumptuous. I don't see one on you either. Have you not used your algorithm on yourself?"

I frowned. "Of course not."

He pushed back and held his arms out at his sides. "Do you not trust in your own creation to find you this supposed compatible partner?"

"I prefer to do it the old-fashioned way. The system is there for those that want to use it."

He snapped his fingers. "I'll tell you what. Let's make a deal."

My heart raced.

"You run the algorithm on yourself. You have three months to find Mr. Right. If you do, I won't play matchmaker anymore."

I eyed him suspiciously. "Intriguing, but what if I lose?"

A wicked grin tugged at his lips. "You shut down the site."

My jaw dropped. "I can't do that. That's my career. My income."

"You seem pretty confident in your system, so what are you afraid of?"

Fury shot down my spine. "Fine. But when I win, you absolutely stop with the matchmaking. Not here, not from some donut shop. It stops."

"Do we have a deal then?" His hand extended.

I stared at his palm as if scorpions crawled all over it before slipping my hand into his. As our skin touched, butterflies beat at my stomach, sending a tingle down my legs. We narrowed our eyes at each other, and I snapped my hand back, clutching it to my chest.

"Do you…want another?" He pointed at my empty glass, and I continued to stare at him, absently nodding.

He rubbed his chin as he walked off to make the drink.

Alex flopped onto the stool next to me, whisking her spritzer into her hand. "You two bone yet?"

I didn't look at her as I rubbed my neck, glaring at Eric's back. "We made a deal."

She choked and sputtered, running her sleeve across her mouth. "I go to the bathroom and come back to you playing Hades? Making deals?"

Alex's Greek roots ran deep. The random drops and references to myths and gods didn't even phase me anymore.

"If I win, he won't play matchmaker anymore." I finally tore my gaze away from him.

She chugged down the rest of her drink. "Lovely, but what do you have to do?"

"Use my algorithm on me."

"Lani."

"I know, but I should have enough confidence in my system to trust it on myself."

"If you say so." She smacked her lips together.

"I have three months to find him. I can do this." I splayed my hands on the bar, feeling short of breath. "Right?"

My breathing grew shallow. The straw fell out of Alex's mouth, and she frantically waved her hands at my face, trying to calm me down.

"What happens if you don't?" Alex thinned her lips.

I cinched my brow, biting my lip as I looked at her. She'd helped me build this business. And here I went putting it on the line over some petty form of competition. My stomach gurgled.

"Lani?" She narrowed her eyes.

I leaned away, whimpering.

"Here we are. More Sex in the Driveway." Eric set the drink in front of me.

I slurped it so fast it gave me brain-freeze. Palming my forehead, I made a *gah* sound.

"Wow. Little antsy?" Eric asked.

Alex smacked her hand on the bar. "Let's see you in action."

"I could take that request in many ways." Eric smiled at her with a hooded gaze.

"As much as I appreciate your gutter mind—" Alex pulled on the collar of her shirt. "I'm referring to your supposed matchmaking skills. Elani told me about the bet. And I don't care if you did a blood bonding shake. I want to make sure you can do what you claim."

"You have a loyal friend here," Eric said to me, tapping his knuckle against the bar.

A lump formed in my throat. I did. I really did. All the more reason, I was the scum of the Earth.

Eric's eyes scanned the room, narrowing with each inch he took in. "Alright. Observe."

He walked to the main floor, rubbing his hands together as he approached a blonde woman sitting by herself.

"Oh. He's actually going to do it. He's serious?" We both turned in our stools to watch.

Eric smiled at the woman, bending over to whisper in her ear. His fingertips grazed her arm and I could've sworn silver shimmers floated over it.

I blinked several times and rubbed my eyes. The shimmers

were no longer there. Eric pointed across the bar to a man sulking by the jukebox. The woman slipped off her chair, smoothing her dress. Eric pressed a finger to her lower back, urging her on and off she went.

He made his way back over to us, keeping his gaze on the newly found couple. The man at the jukebox perked up when the woman introduced herself. Eric folded his arms, but I caught his finger pointing at them. The jukebox kicked on, playing *These Arms of Mine* by Ottis Redding.

"This is one of my favorite songs," the woman shrieked so loudly we could hear her across the room.

Mine too.

Eric dropped his lips near my ear. "Satisfied?"

My insides folded over themselves, and I froze. "You've proven your worth. Now time to prove mine."

Alex eyed Eric as he slid behind the bar, a twinkle in his eye.

"Perfect. Have your first date here as proof you're taking part in the deal. I'll even surprise you with a different drink for each date."

"You think there's going to be that many of them?" Alex asked with a snort.

"No." He gleamed at me. "I *know* there will be."

My insides twisted all at the same time, my teeth clenched in anger. I hadn't mixed emotions like this since the finale of *Lost*.

"How much do I owe you for that second drink?" I dug out my wallet.

He shook his head. "Don't worry about it. You're metaphorically paying me back in spades. Trust me."

My chest tightened, and I grabbed Alex's arm. "Let's go, Alex."

"See you soon, Elani," Eric's voice crooned.

I risked a glance over my shoulder. He dragged a hand through his relaxed, wavy, medium-length hair, tussling it just right. A breath hitched in my throat, and I pushed Alex outside.

She forced me to face her. "Hey. Are you going to tell me what you bet?"

"The site." I pinched my eyes shut. "If I lose, I have to shut it down."

Alex's face remained blank. Her lip twitched, and she slid her hand over my shoulder, staring me down. "Then you better win."

I'd spent most of my adult life searching for my missing half and now I had only ninety days to find my eternal partner. The same length of my previous failed attempts. For the love of Zeus.

STAY TUNED!

WWW.CARLYSPADE.COM

ACKNOWLEDGEMENTS

FIRSTLY, TO MY HUSBAND, you were a direct inspiration behind Ares's personality in so many ways. A strong man who isn't afraid to show his vulnerable side to the woman he loves. Thank you.

To my beta team, you all seriously rock so much more than you know. With each passing book your continued support and love of these words keeps me going. And your honesty only helps make the stories better.

To my critique partner, AK. I had so much fun diving into the world of Ares and Harm with you and as always, your suggestions and enthusiasm were out of this world.

To Brittany G, thank you for spending countless weeks brainstorming with me and the continued GIF exchanging.

To my parents, you remain my biggest fans and I'll always appreciate your love and support. Apologies in advance for the beefed-up sex scenes in this one. Whoops. LOL.

To the readers, I know Ares isn't one of the more popular gods and I thank you for taking a chance on this book. Here's hoping if you didn't like him before, you do now, and if you did like him, here's hoping you still do! LOL.

Finally, to Molly, the wonderful talent behind the Contemporary Mythos covers. You really knocked it out of the park with this Ares cover and I give a sincere thank you for the inspiration it gave me.

ABOUT THE AUTHOR

CARLY SPADE is an adult romance writer who has been writing since she could pick up a pencil. After the insanity of obtaining a bachelor's and master's degree in cybersecurity, creating worlds to escape to still ate at her very soul. She started writing FanFiction (which can still be found if you scour the internet), and soon felt the need to get her original ideas on paper. And so the adventure began.

She lives in Colorado with her husband and two fur babies, and revels in an enemies to lovers trope with a slow burn.

Find her online:

WWW.CARLYSPADE.COM

Printed in Great Britain
by Amazon